Claire Zorn lives on the south coast of New South Wales with her husband and two sons. Her first young adult novel, *The Sky So Heavy*, was a 2014 Children's Book Council of Australia Honour Book for Older Readers, shortlisted in the 2013 Aurealis Awards – Best Young Adult Novel and shortlisted in the 2014 Inky Awards. Her second young adult novel, *The Protected*, was the winner of four awards: the 2015 Prime Minister's Literary Awards for Young Adult Fiction; the 2015 Victorian Premier's Literary Awards – Young Adult Fiction Prize; the 2015 Children's Book Council of Australia Book of the Year for Older Readers; and the 2016 Western Australian Premier's Book Awards – Young Adult. It was also shortlisted in the 2015 Inky Awards. *One Would Think the Deep* is her third book for young adults and was awarded the 2017 CBCA Book of the Year for Older Readers.

clairezorn.com
@ClaireZorn

Also by Claire Zorn

Young Adult

One Would Think the Deep

The Protected

The Sky So Heavy

Picture Books

No Place for an Octopus

WHEN WE ARE INVISIBLE

CLAIRE ZORN

UQP

First published 2021 by University of Queensland Press
PO Box 6042, St Lucia, Queensland 4067 Australia
Reprinted 2021

uqp.com.au
reception@uqp.com.au

Cover design by Jo Hunt
Cover photographs: Girl: Cyndi Monaghan/Getty Images; Mountains: Sergey Nesterchuk/Shutterstock; Horse: Creative Travel Projects/Shutterstock.
Author photograph by Lisa Grant
Typeset in Adobe Garamond 12/16pt by Post Pre-press Group, Brisbane
Printed in Australia by McPherson's Printing Group

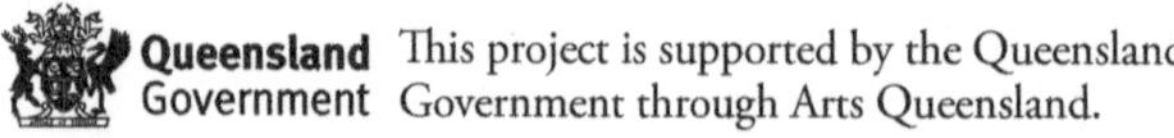

This project is supported by the Queensland Government through Arts Queensland.

The University of Queensland Press is assisted by the Australian Government through the Australia Council, its arts funding and advisory body.

A catalogue record for this book is available from the National Library of Australia.

ISBN 978 0 7022 6313 2 (pbk)
ISBN 978 0 7022 6477 1 (epdf)
ISBN 978 0 7022 6478 8 (epub)
ISBN 978 0 7022 6479 5 (kindle)

University of Queensland Press uses papers that are natural, renewable and recyclable products made from wood grown in well-managed forests and other controlled sources. The logging and manufacturing processes conform to the environmental regulations of the country of origin.

For my mother, Kaye, and my grandmothers,
Margaret and Irene

Obstinate, headstrong girl!

There is a stubbornness about me that never can bear to be frightened at the will of others. My courage always rises at every attempt to intimidate me.

—Jane Austen, *Pride and Prejudice*

ONE

It would have taken seconds to launch the missiles that started the winter. I don't know how many there were; once they detonated on the other side of the world we stopped knowing anything at all. No electricity equals no information, and no information equals chaos. I suppose we should have thought ourselves lucky. We stopped knowing anything; the people where the missiles landed just stopped. Perhaps they only saw a streak through the sky before their story ended. Perhaps it was a rolling mushroom cloud of smoke and ash that smothered them. But for me? In the moments when some powerful people over there decided to destroy three – possibly four – billion people, I was sitting in the school library pondering a history essay. To be more accurate, I was watching the tips of Fin Heath's ears turn pink when it became apparent we were probably – definitely – going to kiss. We were interrupted. Fin's mum called to tell him to go and buy as much non-perishable food as he could carry because something had gone terribly, terribly wrong. What a way to end a date.

*

The dust cloud blocked out the daylight. We went to bed in the evening, and a new day began but the sun never rose.

No power.

No communication.

No information.

No fuel.

And, finally, no food.

I don't remember the sensation of hunger. It's other things that stick. It's my sister's white knuckles as she pulled a blanket tighter around herself – her shoulder blades so sharp they could have torn the fabric. It's my father burning books for warmth. It's the taste of flour mixed with a touch of water, just enough to make a paste we could swallow. And my mother carrying our cat out into the bush in the hope he would be able to catch his own food, so we didn't have to watch him starve.

My strongest memory is of what happened in that tiny dark room. I remember the rough texture of the cricket bat handle as I gripped it and raised it above my shoulder and Fin's raspy breath as Mr Starvos kicked him in the ribs over and over again. Fin, who I hadn't seen for months, was stealing food from Mr Starvos's shop. I knew I would have to use all my strength when I swung the bat, no room for error.

And I remember Mr Starvos's words as Fin gasped for breath.

'You think you are the first to try this? You think I am not waiting for you? I need to make an example of you. I. Am. Not. Charity.'

He pulled a gun from his back pocket. A black handgun. It clicked when he loaded it. Then Mr Starvos – who used to call me Lucy Lu when I came to buy milk – pushed the muzzle into the back of Fin's head. After that I don't remember any thoughts, just the cracking thud of the bat against Mr Starvos's skull. I remember that very particular sound.

An act of violence is like a moment of punctuation between one self and another. You used to be a person who couldn't do something like that. Now you are someone who can. Who did. And who might again.

At least that's how it was for me.

TWO

Max isn't speaking. I keep watch over him in the rear-view mirror. He leans his head against the window, red-and-white Swannies beanie pulled down over his ears, cheek pressed to the glass. It's been an hour since we left the city and he's still staring straight ahead. Looking, not seeing, as if he isn't inside himself anymore – he's checked out. He hasn't slept in forty-eight hours. Beside me, Fin wears the same numb expression. Now and again he pulls his beanie off and runs his fingers through the thick stubble on his scalp before putting it back on. He rolls his head around, stretching his neck. He can't settle. The only question he asks me is if we have enough fuel to get to the camp. We do. Just.

As we drive, the wind buffets and whistles through the plastic bag covering the broken passenger-side window, a rather obvious reminder of the time a hungry guy put a brick through it. (Noll punched his face in. No-one saw that coming.)

I try to loosen my grip on the steering wheel. I'm getting better at this ice-driving business. I'm steady and careful. I don't take risks. You know the mining companies used to have most of their big trucks driven by women? Those huge, hulking yellow machines the size of houses – nearly all of them driven by women. Women are more careful. Like we have a choice.

When I take my hand off the wheel to shift gears it shakes.

It's less than twenty-four hours since Noll died; he and Matt have been added to a death count which I'm not sure anyone is keeping track of anymore. There are too many, it's incomprehensible. What I feel is not sadness. Sadness is a quiet thing – a thing that sleeps in your bones, makes them heavy. I don't feel heavy. My heart is hissing and quaking, and the anger unfurls as though through my skin. I seethe and I want to lash out. I don't want to run away from the hurt; I want to run at it and pummel it with my fists – I want to kick its face in. Is that normal? Maybe not, but it doesn't matter – normal left here a long time ago. Now my mind is packed with images of bodies lying on the icy ground. Some of them, like our precious Noll, I didn't see but can picture as clearly as if I did. Mr Starvos I saw with my own eyes; I was the one who cracked his skull. That's not a normal thing to do, is it? I did it – my own hands, my own body – me. I'm angry that I had to.

It's not long until we get to the border fence on the south side of Sydney. I didn't think there would be the same restrictions on people leaving as there are entering, but when I see the barricade up ahead my lungs tighten and the dead crowd in on me – those poor people on bikes, who were shot trying to ride through the gate as we drove in. Hardly the safest option, but then again we live in a world of ever-decreasing options. I suppose it was either ride a bike or dig a tunnel under the fence with a spoon. As we near the barricade there's a truck parked to the side of the gate. I slow to a stop when I see a soldier sitting on the ground, leaning against the rear tyre. He doesn't move.

'I think he's dead.' Fin sighs. 'Stay here.' He gets out of the car to inspect the soldier, then turns around with a grimace.

I glance at Max in the rear-view mirror and see that he has, thankfully, fallen asleep.

'Has he been shot?' I ask Fin when he returns to the car.

'Doesn't look like it. I think he maybe froze to death or something.'

My ankle hurts when I get out of the car, a reminder of being trampled in the food riots. I limp across the slushy road to the soldier. His name patch says *Bahri*. He's young, and even though I know he's been complicit in the terrible things that have been done, I'm made weak by the tragedy of it. He's like Matt, the soldier who was barely older than us, who should have turned us in when we were hiding in the shopping centre car park but came to hide with us instead. I flinch at the thought of Matt's body lying in the snow. He shot the army officer who was guarding fuel that we needed, the fuel we are using right now. Another awful act he couldn't live with, so he chose not to live.

'My shoes are wet,' Fin says. We both stare at Bahri and I know what else Fin wants to say.

I say it for him. 'His might fit.'

Fin crouches down, and rolls up the guy's trouser leg. He undoes the laces on one of the boots and pulls it off the soldier's frozen foot. He takes his own boot off and slips his foot in, nods and does the same with the other.

I gently tug the soldier's gloves off his smooth, cold hands and pull them onto my own. They're too big but I've lost mine and these are better than nothing.

When I place Bahri's bare hands in his lap his head flops to the side, like he's sleeping. I never knew him, but I start to cry.

Fin glances at me and I see he is struggling too but neither of us say anything about it. Fin walks over to check the truck's door. It's unlocked, so Fin climbs in and tries to start the ignition but it won't turn over. No fuel.

We're returning to the car when Fin hesitates, then walks back to the soldier. He hooks his hands under the soldier's skinny arms and pulls him to the side of the road. Then he kneels down and piles snow and dirt over the body with his hands.

Back at the car he pulls me into his long arms and kisses my hair.

'You're a good one,' I say. 'But you also stink.'

'So do you.'

'Thanks.'

'Can I drive for a bit?'

'Please do.'

We drive on in our tiny car through a world irrevocably altered. We have a box of food (crackers, instant noodles, Weet-Bix and lolly snakes), two bottles of boiled water and handwritten directions to a place called Wattlewood Recreation Centre – where we may or may not find a settlement of people who prepared for the apocalypse while the rest of society focused on selfies and Netflix. The directions were scrawled on a piece of notepaper by a school teacher who we knew not so long ago, when we were young and silly and had no idea the cushy rug of our sheltered lives was about to be pulled from beneath us in the most spectacular of fashions.

Nuclear winter: it's a real blast.

THREE

I'm afraid to ask the question because I'm not sure I want the answer, but after hours of driving in silence I just can't wait anymore.

'Was Noll in pain? Do you think it was quick?'

'It doesn't make any difference.' Fin keeps his eyes on the road before us.

'That's not true.'

Fin inhales deeply. I see his eyes flick to the rear-view mirror, to his little brother.

'It was quick.'

I don't believe him, but I'm hardly going to ask Max. We will be lucky if he ever says another word. We go back to travelling in silence and I feel yuck about bringing up Noll's death and taking Fin back to that place.

'Where's the letter from Mr Effrez?' I already know and Fin knows I already know but it's a good diversion.

'In the glove box.'

I take out the white business envelope. Mr Effrez has written *To those in the settlement* in neat cursive on the front.

'It's tempting to open it,' I say. 'They won't know it was in an envelope.'

Fin looks aghast. 'It's private. What sort of monster are you?'

'The curious kind.'

'The frigging dangerous kind. Don't open it.'

'I've already read the directions and this is the only other reading material I have. This place is, what – three hours away? That's a long drive.'

'Is the list there? The names Effrez knows?'

'Yes, but it's only six words long.'

Fin's blue eyes catch mine. There's almost light in them. 'And?'

'Hmm. Let's see: *Susan, Raahel, Chandy, Mary, Elliot, Tom.*'

'Well, let's hope they're happy to see us.'

I don't know how I managed to fall asleep but I suppose your brain just reaches a certain point and decides it's had enough of this monotony, which is exactly what I feel during the moments without the distraction of panic or fear. Fin, Max and I have come from the underground car park where we sheltered in Sydney after leaving our homes in the Blue Mountains in search of food. It was us and Noll – patient, kind, thoughtful Noll, who was tormented at school and took Fin and Max in when he had every reason not to. He was the best of us; we all know it. And now he's dead, shot down when we tried to steal fuel for our escape from Sydney. We had to leave his body in the snow alongside Matt's. It's not just the dead we've left behind. I left my mum and dad and sister behind in the mountains and now Fin has left his mother in Sydney – a woman with the rank and power to offer us refuge, but who let protocol dictate her choices. She couldn't save everyone apparently, only Max and Fin. Now we are unmoored from our old lives completely.

I sleep but I don't dream. It's the sounds of dogs barking and Fin screaming that wake me up.

'Lucy! The gun! Where is the gun?'

We're stopped on a driveway in front of a tall barbed-wire barricade. To our left a carved wooden sign cheerfully welcomes us to the *Wattlewood Recreation Centre*. The car lurches as someone with a cricket bat jumps onto the bonnet. Someone else stands in front of us – a man over six feet tall who's wearing a balaclava and carrying an assault rifle. I recognise those now.

'The gun, Lucy! Where is the gun?!'

I don't know what Fin thinks he's going to do with a little handgun when this guy has the equivalent of a rocket launcher by comparison. I don't know where the gun we've brought from Sydney is. Max, awake now, screams from the back seat and Fin yells at him to shut up and get down on the floor.

I grab Fin's hand and raise it. 'Put your hands up.'

Someone is at my plastic-bag window – it will only take one hit to break through it.

'Max, sit up. Put up your hands,' I say.

'MAX, STAY DOWN!' shouts Fin.

'Fin, they might not shoot us if we have a child.' I glance in the rear-view mirror and see Max sit up and raise his hands. The dogs are barking, barking, barking. One, a German shepherd, has its paws on Fin's window and I can see down its pink throat as it growls and gnashes.

'Make sure they can see you, Max.' I lock my gaze onto Mr Balaclava's and call out, 'He's a kid!'

'They're all around the car,' Fin says.

'What the frig do they want? Our rice crackers?' I say.

'Maybe.'

A Doberman joins our friend on the bonnet. It snaps and barks inches from my face.

'I want to talk to you,' I shout at Mr Balaclava.

'Lucy.'

I ignore Fin and shout at Mr Balaclava again, 'Let me get out of the car.'

He shakes his head.

Oh for frig's sake.

'Lucy.' Fin's tone is warning.

'Get rid of your stupid dogs!'

Mr Balaclava tilts his head and takes a step closer, training the rifle on me. I suck in a breath and fight not to close my eyes. Mr Balaclava gives a sharp whistle. Both dogs stop barking and run to his feet. Then he jerks his head to the side, indicating for me to get out of the car.

'Don't move, Lucy. Do not open that door.'

'If he was going to kill us he would have done it by now.'

'Don't open the door.'

'Where's the letter?'

'I can't reach down, Luce. I have to keep my hands up.'

'Then I'm going to talk to them.'

'What the hell are you going to say?'

'That they need to work on their hospitality skills.'

My legs shake as I get out of the car and I have to grip the doorframe because of my useless ankle. I square my shoulders and keep eye contact with Mr Balaclava.

'We've been sent by Mr Effrez. J Effrez – I don't know his full name.'

Balaclava doesn't move or make a sound.

'He was our teacher. We have a letter for you and your … friends. But we can't get it with our hands in the air.'

Nothing.

'Let Fin get the letter from the glove box.'

Nothing. I glance at Max in the back seat. His arms tremble as he holds them in the air.

'You see that boy? He's twelve. He just watched two of our friends get shot and die. He's covered in the blood of his dead friend. He's *twelve*.' I grit my teeth. 'He's tired and can't hold his hands up much longer. If he drops them and you shoot him I will come over there and rip your fucking face off with my fucking fingernails.'

Mr Balaclava steps forward but doesn't raise his gun. I find this reassuring; surely if he was going to attack he would use more speed. I can see his green eyes and they crinkle a little, like he's actually smiling and a bit amused. In my peripheral vision I see his henchmen dropping away, following the silent instructions of their alpha male.

'Max, drop your hands.' I hope he can hear me through the window. 'Has he put down his hands?' I ask Mr Balaclava.

Silence.

'I said, has he put down his hands?'

'Yes.' Finally a voice.

'Like I said, Mr Effrez sent us. If you can stop trying to be scary for a moment and put down your gun, Fin can get the letter he gave us.'

'Sure. I can do that. But you've got to agree not to *try* and scratch my face off.'

I detect humour in his voice. Touché, my friend.

'No problem,' I say.

I hear the car door open and Fin's feet on the gravel.

'Put your hands up,' Mr Balaclava tells Fin. 'Walk to the front of the car and put the letter on the ground.'

'Not with that guy on the bonnet.'

Mr Balaclava's chest rises and falls with a sigh. He nods to the guy on the bonnet, who jumps down, turns and slowly walks backwards to Mr Balaclava. I can see from her shape that she's not a guy at all. She's young – maybe early twenties – but she holds herself with confidence, like she's ready to kick anything that may require kicking.

Fin walks to the front of the car where I can see him. Please, don't let Max find the gun and get all heroic. A memory of my dad singing along to a corny eighties song pops into my head. I don't want to go down in a blaze of glory. I now know there is no such thing as dying in a blaze of glory – only mess.

Fin places the letter on the ground. The woman walks forward, picks it up and then traces her steps back to Mr Balaclava. She opens the letter and stands very still for a few moments. Then she drops to the ground and hangs her head between her knees.

Mr Balaclava takes the letter from her and reads. He closes his eyes and pinches the bridge of his nose between his thumb and forefinger. He gives another sharp whistle and the three other people who were surrounding us leave the car, slip through the tall gate and walk down the driveway. The leader pulls off his balaclava and stuffs it in a pocket, revealing his thick ginger hair and beard. I suppose he would be attractive if you're into action-figure types. I don't think he's much over thirty.

'Get the boy out of the car,' Mr Balaclava says.

'How do we know you're not going to hurt him?' says Fin.

'Buddy, I don't want to hurt anyone. Do you?'

'No.'

'I want to talk, but I want the boy where I can see him.'

Fin opens the back door and beckons Max out, but he doesn't move. 'Max, you have to get out of the car. No choice.'

Max shakes his head.

'Can I talk to him?' Mr Balaclava asks.

Fin thinks about it for a moment. 'Yeah. But keep back from him.'

Mr Balaclava approaches Max with his hands up. 'Hey there, buddy. I'm Jaxon. Do you want to get out so we can have a chat?'

Max shakes his head.

'Can I talk to you while you're in the car?'

Max nods.

'Sorry I gave you a scare there, bud. I was trying to protect my people – you know how it is. You're okay now, yeah? It's safe here.' He looks at me. 'You're Lucy?'

'Yes.'

'I'll open the gates. Drive in and park your car with the others,' he says. 'Then we can go inside and talk.'

Max's legs wobble as he tries to stand. Fin puts an arm around his shoulders and waits while I park the car. In the rear-view mirror I see Jaxon watching me, then he goes to Ms Strong sitting on the ground and talks to her, his hands on his hips. She gets to her feet nodding and wipes her eyes.

FOUR

I have to lean on Fin as we walk down a wide path, following a sign that reads *Reception, Rec Hall, Mess Hall.* Jaxon, leading the way, turns back and sees Max wilting with the effort of walking on his own.

'Can I help you, buddy?' he asks. Max, unsure, looks Jaxon over. 'I'm just going to help you get to the building. You don't look too crash hot.'

Max hesitates then nods, fighting back tears.

Jaxon glances to Fin. 'Okay with you?'

Fin can't help me and Max at the same time. He gives a grim smile, nodding his consent for Jaxon to put an arm around Max and help him along the path. We arrive at a large brick building with big windows and Jaxon pushes open the heavy glass doors, standing aside for us to enter. The reception room is warmed by a proper fireplace. Two large desks – one spread with paperwork, the other with a map – form a small office space on the left, and on the right is a leather couch. Light, although dull, comes through a huge glass skylight. The dark red-brick walls are decorated with photographs of kids riding horses and abseiling; a poster acknowledges that we are on Dharawal Country and pays respect to the Wodiwodi people. The room is so … ordinary, probably no different to how it would have been before the winter. The only indicators that anything is amiss are the oil lamps. Jaxon walks behind the desks, unlocks a tall safe and puts his gun inside. He motions for us to sit on the couch.

'So, you've driven down from Sydney today?' He's like a hotel receptionist with a personal grooming problem. 'You came straight from Jeff's place?'

'Jeff?' Fin asks.

'Jeff Effrez.'

I would not have picked Mr Effrez as a Jeff. It's oddly disappointing. Jeff sounds like a golfer. Maybe someone who hosts barbecues and watches rugby league. A Jeff wouldn't have friends – he would have mates.

'Yeah, we came straight from his house.'

'Were you staying with him?'

'Only for one night,' Fin says. 'Before that we were hiding out in a car park in Sydney. We live in the Blue Mountains. My dad went out on the night of the missiles and never came home. I don't know what happened. Maybe he had a car accident.' Fin glances warily at Max. 'Or he couldn't get back home, I don't know …'

I block out Fin's voice as he summarises our story – his words will only drag me through the whole ordeal again.

'How long were you in Sydney?' Jaxon asks.

'About three weeks,' Fin says.

'Your mum works for the government? Doing what?'

'She's a disaster response strategist.'

'Sounds like her strategy didn't work.'

'Thanks for your feedback,' I say.

Jaxon looks at me with something like humour playing on his lips. He turns his attention back to Fin. 'Did you tell her where you were going? Does she know about this place?'

'Vaguely. I just told her Mr Effrez knew about it.'

'She'd be able to find him, presuming she's a government official – she'd have access to a database with information like that.'

'If you say so.'

'Anyone follow you down here?'

'No.'

'You sure about that?'

'We would have noticed,' Fin says.

'It's not exactly rush hour out there,' I add.

'Some people are pretty good at hiding. You absolutely sure no-one followed you?'

'We both kept an eye on Max in the back seat,' Fin says. 'We would have seen anyone trying to follow us.'

'Okay.' He doesn't sound convinced. He takes a manila folder and a notebook from the desk drawer and begins to take notes. 'What did you bring with you?'

Our haul of resources is precious. I'm unsure if we should tell him what we have, but I'm so tired and hungry. We need to cling to the fact that Mr Effrez trusts these people enough to send us here. 'Some sleeping bags. Some clothes.' I hesitate.

‘Food?’

None of us answers.

‘You bring food?’ Jaxon looks up from his notes. ‘I’ll be straight with you guys: we’re gonna search your car anyway.’

I glance at Fin.

He shrugs. ‘Yes. We have two small boxes.’

Jaxon notes this down. ‘Any weapons?’

Again, we don’t answer. This conversation is starting to feel like a preposterous gamble. We don’t know this person. I don’t want to lay our cards on the table but I feel we’ve run out of choices. Fin’s eyes tell me he feels the same way.

‘And we’re gonna search you,’ Jaxon adds.

‘One handgun,’ Fin says.

‘Can you tell me where it is? Save us pulling the whole car apart?’

‘It’s under the front passenger seat,’ he says.

‘No it’s not,’ Max whispers. His bottom lip quivers, but he lifts his chin.

Jaxon sits up straighter. ‘Where is it, bud?’

‘Max?’ Fin’s voice is wary.

Max raises his hands, looking at Fin. He stands up.

‘Max, buddy, can you slowly lift your shirt and show us where the gun is?’ Jaxon asks.

Max does so. The gun is tucked in the waistband of his jeans.

Fin smiles. ‘Bro, I’ve told you, you gotta stop nicking the gun.’

The corner of Max's mouth twitches just a fraction.

'Okay. Pop it on the table,' Jaxon says.

Max doesn't move.

'Come on, Max. It's cool,' says Fin. I'm not sure it is cool – this guy has a twinkle in his eye like Santa Claus, and who the hell trusts Santa Claus? But what's the alternative? We can't walk back out into this particular winter wonderland.

Max doesn't move.

'You're pretty scared, yeah?' Jaxon says. 'I know how scary this is. But you're safe. No-one's gonna hurt you. I make that promise to everyone at this camp. Part of keeping people safe is making sure we know where all the weapons are. You wouldn't wanna stay here if some people had guns hidden on them, would you?'

Max shakes his head.

'Me neither. Every gun here is accounted for; it's the only way to keep everyone safe. Put it on the table for now. I promise no-one's gonna hurt you.'

Max puts the gun on the table.

'Thanks, bud,' says Jaxon.

It's hard to reconcile this chummy guy who's a dab hand at dealing with traumatised children as the same one who moments ago was wearing a balaclava and pointing a weapon at my skull.

'Don't search our car,' I say. 'We don't have any more guns.'

'All due respect but how do I know that?' asks Jaxon.

'Mr Effrez sent us. You've seen the letter. Do you think we're going to try and, I don't know, rob you? While you've got machine guns or whatever?' I don't know why I've said it like that; I know they're not machine guns. Maybe it's an instinctive self-preservation device – play the silly girl who doesn't understand the important men's business. Maybe that angle will make me less of a threat to this guy.

Jaxon smirks. 'That's not a machine gun.'

'Thanks. But I don't care.'

'Lucy,' Fin says.

I keep my focus on Jaxon. 'We've been through months of total indignity; I don't know why you need to go through our things as well.'

'Lucy, I don't think Jaxon—'

'Can you just let me talk? Freaking hell, Fin.'

He's as stunned as I am by the way I've snapped at him – it's the anger hissing through the cracks in me. It doesn't want to be silenced. Fin shakes his head and looks away.

Jaxon smiles. 'Okay. I get it. I understand. We don't need to go through your car, but you will need to put your keys in the safe.'

'Why?' I glance at Fin – surely he sees the danger in giving up our only means of escape. 'Why would you need us to do that?'

'I don't know you. I need to keep the people here safe.'

'From who? A bunch of murderous teenagers? Is that

who you think we are? Or do you think we're going to steal your baked beans and drive off into the sunset? We watched two of our friends die in the snow.' I can hear the shake in my voice, like I'm hearing someone else's. 'They were shot when all we were trying to do was get to safety. We've lost everything; we've left our families, our homes, everything. We're the ones who need to be kept safe. Us.'

Max sways a little.

'Lucy,' Fin whispers.

I'm crying. I'm the crying, hysterical girl who hopes a big tough guy will make her safe. I want to put my fist through the wall.

'Lucy,' Fin says again. He reaches out to take my hand but I stand and go to the window. I have the keys in my fist.

'I understand,' Jaxon says. 'Come and sit down.'

Fin is staring at me.

I glare at Jaxon. 'Thank you, but I don't want to sit down.'

Jaxon's eyes remain locked on mine. The twinkle fades and I wonder if he's had much experience with the word no.

I pull the list of names out of my pocket and hold it up to Jaxon. 'This is the list of people at the camp Mr Effrez gave us. You're not on it. Who are these people? Are they here? I'd like to speak to one of them.'

He holds his hands up in surrender and rolls the swivel chair backwards. 'No-one's forcing you to stay. You may leave at any time. I've got my people; you've got your people. I'm just doing my job. If you don't like it, please, I won't stop you from leaving – the door's right there.'

'Tell me where these people are.'

Jaxon holds out his hand for the list and I give it to him. When he reads it he lets out a slow breath and his shoulders drop.

'Okay. Susan is here – she does the rosters and runs the kitchen. Raahel is here with her children. Chandy never came here to begin with; he was overseas. Tom is here – he was out the front actually.'

Comforting.

'Elliot and Mary … They died before I arrived.' He rubs the back of his neck and looks away. 'They were killed out in the bush.' When he turns back to me his expression is pained, almost kind. 'I know it's not safe out there. I know you need shelter.'

He scrunches up the paper and tosses it into a rubbish bin.

Fin has not moved at all; he's watching Max, who looks even worse than he did in the car. I want to speak to Fin in private and I'm about to suggest it when the glass door opens and Ms Strong walks in. She's still holding the letter.

Jaxon smiles. 'Lucy, Fin, Max, this is Esther. Esther Effrez.'

FIVE

Esther does not waste time with pleasantries – there's no point asking how we are because it is clear we are shit.

'The letter's legit,' Esther says. 'It's my dad's handwriting. He says he's going to wait a few weeks in case I show up in Sydney, then he'll come down.' Esther turns to me. 'It would have been better if he came with you.'

'Why haven't you gone to get him?' I try not to sound accusatory.

'I ran out of fuel. I drove up from Melbourne and made it within about fifty kilometres of here. Walked the rest of the way. You had space in your car for him.'

'He wouldn't come with us,' Fin says. 'He was waiting for you. I don't think we have enough fuel to get there and back again. Actually, I know we don't.'

Esther turns to Jaxon. 'I want to ride up with Tom.'

Jaxon shakes his head. 'Not safe, Es. You know that. He said he will wait a few weeks then try and come here. So we wait too. We're good at that.' He turns his attention back to us. 'You understand the priority of the settlement is sustainability. The more people here, the more mouths to feed.'

'We've just come from Sydney,' Fin says. 'We know the problem of having mouths to feed. Food shortages make people do crazy things like throw tear gas at crowds lining up for food and then shoot them. We were there. That's what we're trying to get away from.'

Jaxon nods. 'Sorry, bud. I know. That was insensitive. I'm just tryin' to say that we need to look out for the people who're already here.'

'We're reasonably well-fed enough to be useful. We can help with whatever needs doing. You're hunting?' asks Fin.

'Yeah.'

'We could help with that.'

'What's your aim like?'

'We're fast learners,' I say.

Jaxon chuckles.

'Jaxon, let's discuss it with Tom,' Esther says.

He thinks for a moment. 'Have something to eat. Stay the night if you want. Then we'll make a decision. In the meantime you have to leave your gun in the safe.' Jaxon points his thumb to the gun safe. 'I'll unlock it. You put the gun in.'

'I'm not comfortable with that.'

Jaxon folds his arms and contemplates me. 'We've been through this. I don't have a gun on me. You don't need one on you. It's bad manners.'

'Ha. How do we know you're not going to grab it, shoot us and take our food?'

'Well, if I shoot you Esther's going to be pretty pissed.

She's scary when she's angry.'

Esther rolls her eyes.

'That's not enough of a guarantee, I'm afraid.'

'Lucy, just let him have the gun,' Fin says.

'If you're going to stay here,' Jaxon speaks with the tone of a preschool teacher, 'and that's *if* – you cannot keep a gun on you. You cannot be armed in any way. It's policy. Love it or leave it. Look, I'll tell you what. You put the gun in the safe, Esther will close the door and change the code, so only she knows it. She's Jeff's daughter and is unlikely to shoot you, not today anyway – she can be moody.'

Instinct has kept us alive so far. It's like a compass and I tune in to the needle often: trust/don't trust, run/stay. The winter has brought out the animal within all of us and we teeter between predator and prey, trying to find the balance of humanity between the two. I can't read the needle right now. The warmth of the room is clouding my judgement.

He swivels his chair around and unlocks the safe again.

I pick the gun up off the table and put it in the safe. Esther walks over, closes the door and punches some numbers.

'All good?' Jaxon asks.

She nods.

'See? Too easy.' Jaxon smiles. 'Come on, I'll show you inside.'

'Thank you,' Fin says. I get the impression he wants to wrap this up and move on to the bit where we are given food and shelter.

SIX

Jaxon opens a door that leads into the main building and we follow him in.

Max slips his hand into mine and I give it a squeeze. The space is cavernous, with a high vaulted ceiling that's strutted with exposed timber beams. Along one wall firewood is stacked to almost shoulder height. Large windows let in dull light. Months without electricity have not quite erased my immediate expectation that Jaxon will switch the lights on. Rows of mattresses and sleeping bags are set up near a large fireplace still glowing with embers. The room is very warm. Living in the car park taught me that huddling beside an outdoor fire warms one side of your body but not the other, like a steak that needs to be turned on a barbecue – this is different. At the other end of the room are an assortment of couches, beanbags, a bookshelf and a few coffee tables.

There's a piano.

'This is the rec hall and also the sleeping quarters. Obviously,' Jaxon says. 'Advantage of being at a place like this is that there was already a heap of bedding. They brought all the mattresses across from the cabins, along with blankets and pillows. In the back corner over there is the area we use for school lessons for the little kids, and that' – he points to a strange set of steel doors, like hatch doors, in the floor near the teaching space – 'is the door to the bunker. If at any time you hear the words "Code red" and/or a whistle, you run in here and go into the bunker. Now, I know it's a pain in the arse but we have strict rules about leaving the building at night. Basically you can't leave unless you are with your group. We have a system.' He sighs and looks the three of us over, as if he's a bit disappointed. 'If you want to sleep now we can set up some beds for you. Lunch will be in an hour or so.'

'Jaxon, is there a place we can have a wash?' Fin asks. 'Max still hasn't had one since … since our friend died. He has his blood …' Fin can't finish the sentence.

'Yeah, come with me. I'll show you the shower block so you can have a wash and I'll get you some clean clothes. Lucy, you can help Esther with the beds.'

They leave through a door on the other side of the room. I expect Esther to show me where I might be able to wash as well but instead she asks me to help her carry mattresses from a stack in the corner of the room and gives me sheets and blankets to make up our beds. Perhaps I don't stink as badly as I thought I did. We do our thing in silence until Esther takes a deep breath and asks me how her dad was.

'Pretty good, actually,' I tell her. 'He has lots of food,

like tinned kippers and sardines. He seems to like all the food other people don't.'

She smiles but it fades quickly. 'You should have made him come with you,' Esther says. 'I really don't get it. He would know there was no way I would turn up now.'

'You don't believe us?'

She straightens the doona on one of our beds. 'That should be warm enough. If you need more pillows or anything let me or Susan know.'

'I don't think anyone could make your dad do anything. You read the letter. We haven't made all of this up.'

Esther won't meet my eyes. She turns away, going outside then returning with firewood which she adds to the stack against the wall. I sit on a mattress and feel strangely uneasy being separated from Fin and Max. When they come back, both of them washed and in fresh clothes, I notice I've been gripping the bed with both hands.

'Have a rest,' Esther says, looking at Max in particular.

'Can I have a wash too?' It's been a long, long time since I've had a shower. I can feel the grime of our squalid existence layered on my skin.

Esther looks me up and down in that special way women have of belittling each other. 'There's a small bathroom in the hall where you can wash your face. I don't have time to get a guard to take you to the shower block. Perhaps someone can take you after.' She's out of the room before I can open my mouth to protest.

Fin raises an eyebrow. 'What did you do?'

'Unclear. I might have breathed without asking. Or perhaps we left her father behind in a desecrated wasteland.'

'I don't know what else we could have done.'

Max looks panicked again. 'Do you think Mr Effrez is going to starve?'

'Max, you saw the amount of weird canned fish he has,' I say. 'He's fine. You're not, you need to lie down.'

He lies down on the bed and I cover him with a blanket. His eyes remain wide and glazed, looking at nothing.

I stroke his hair back from his forehead the way my mother used to with mine. 'It's okay. We're going to be okay now.'

Max looks at me, tears in his eyes. 'I want Dad,' he whispers.

I tuck the blankets in tight around him. 'Close your eyes.'

I lie down in my own bed and feel the softness enveloping my tired body. The pillow smells of laundry detergent. It's all so civilised. I should feel like I'm at a luxury resort, but I don't sleep. My head is a white room full of evenly proportioned white boxes that I keep things in: the dead bodies at the gates to Sydney, the lines on my mother's palms, the plans I had, the songs I've written. My sister. The white room in my head has a single cold fluorescent light on the ceiling, the kind that is so bright you can't block it out. Even when you close your eyes the light pushes through your eyelids and you see red, red, red when all you want is black. I know why the light is like that – it's the light of the hospital room where my sister was when her organs began to fail and we were sure she was going to die. What a cruel thing for her to escape death only to be dropped into this living nightmare, where even though she would eat there is nothing for her. I shove my thoughts of Bit away – they take up almost all the space in the storage room of my head. I have left her behind. My mother thought I was the one with the best chance of survival in Sydney. We both knew she was right and now I might never see my sister or my parents again.

After a while a bell rings and a woman in an apron comes in and introduces herself as Raahel. She has a warm smile and a long plait of thick black hair that reaches her waist. It's shiny; they have shampoo here. She tells us lunch is ready. Fin has to coax Max out of bed. With his hair still damp and fuzzy from washing he looks impossibly young. Raahel leads us into a large room with an industrial-looking kitchen at the back. Rows of dining tables are lit by oil lamps and some of them have glass jars holding sprigs of gum leaves – someone has made an effort to make the place homely. About thirty adults and seven children have congregated for lunch. There are more men than women and some wear camouflaged clothing.

The dining hall is filled with chatter. People are relaxed here, smiling and joking. It's an environment alien to me. Some of the kids are squealing and laughing as they chase each other around the tables. The conversation quietens and people turn to look at us. The kids stare, curious. Everyone has colour in their cheeks and a brightness to their eyes – in comparison to the faces we are used to seeing, they seem photoshopped. Nobody here has been surviving on red frogs and dry Sultana Bran.

Some look at us with scepticism, some semi-commit to a smile. Jaxon gets up and walks to the front of the room.

'Listen up. You all probably know we received some visitors this morning. This is Fin, Lucy and Max. They are friends of Esther's dad, Jeff, who you know was supposed to be joining us some time ago. He's still in Sydney, but he sent these guys here. They've come from the Blue Mountains, via Sydney, so you know they've seen a lot of shit.' (This would normally be the time when Max would say 'Literally' and have a laugh at his own joke. I don't know if we have that Max anymore.) 'They're staying the night with us. Make them feel welcome.' Jaxon turns to us, rubbing his palms together. 'I'm not even gonna ask if you're hungry.'

SEVEN

We line up at the kitchen window and a gruff man with weather-beaten skin serves us hot food. He looks like the kind of person who would have a thirty-year-old Driza-Bone coat in his wardrobe and not much else. I can recognise someone from the country a mile off.

'You were with Jeff?' he says quietly. 'He's okay?'

'Yes.'

'That's good news.'

He has lines on his cheeks, as if he smiled a lot once. He puts a piece of roast meat on my plate without asking if I want it. I haven't eaten meat for two years (I don't think the chicken flavouring in the instant noodles I ate in the car park counts as meat) but I'm sure I'll seem brattish to these people if I leave anything on my plate. I follow the line along to a little table where a middle-aged woman with neat blonde hair pours me a glass of water. She welcomes me with a smile and says her name is Susan.

Raahel comes to join us at the table. I'm so relieved to be with people whose names were on the list. A girl of about three with the same big dark eyes and thick black hair as Raahel climbs onto her lap and picks up a piece of flatbread from Raahel's plate. She stares at me as she chews.

The man who served us food takes the seat next to Raahel. He has greying hair cut in the style of someone who had access to scissors but not a hairdresser. He clears his throat and introduces himself with a brief smile and the simple statement of his name: Tom – also on the list.

'What's the situation in Sydney?' he asks.

'Not fabulous,' I say.

'The army are distributing rations,' Fin says. 'No-one from outside the city is allowed in. No information about what's happened, no government plan besides choosing who lives and who starves.'

'What about outside the city? You came from the Blue Mountains?'

'Yeah. The army came once when we were up there. They said they would come back but they never did.'

'Did people start fighting over food? Is it violent?'

The smell of blood and sweat and the sound of my heart pounding in my ears. The room is dark, lit only by the wobbly light of Fin's torch as it rolls across the floor. Starvos looms over Fin's curled body, kicking him again and again. I'm behind him. The cricket bat is heavy. I grip it with both hands and step closer. He has no idea I'm there or what I'm about to do.

My uncle told me Starvos was still alive after I hit him. He was probably trying to protect me from the truth.

Fin clears his throat. 'Some. In Sydney it was a more organised operation.' He moves on quickly. 'Tuesday was ration day. We'd have to sneak out of the car park so no-one knew that's where we were hiding. You had to line up and they randomly checked IDs. If you didn't have ID they would take you away.'

'And then what?'

'And then you didn't come back,' I say.

'They were killing people?'

'We saw people get shot trying to cross the border and when lining up for food. We were with others in the car park and people were mostly just looking out for each other.'

Opposite me Max looks at his plate like it's an object he doesn't recognise. His fork remains untouched.

An older girl chases the little ones around our table – she is quick and when she catches them they giggle and squeal. She smiles at me as she dashes past, the golden smile of a child with no care except for catching her sister.

'That's my Elia,' Raahel says. 'She's seven. Saramma is three.'

'They're beautiful.'

'Thank you. They're a nightmare. They miss their father and it makes them naughty. Or maybe they're just naturally naughty! I don't know.'

'Is he here?' Fin asks.

'Chandy worked ... He was a diplomat.' She is holding back tears. 'He was over there. He sacrificed everything trying to stop this.'

'I'm sorry.'

'It's okay. I am very proud of him.' She gives me a small smile. 'I want everyone to know what he did. He was one of the founders here. We began preparing a long time ago. Everyone thought we were idiots, but my husband was like Noah building the ark. He knew. Those weapons were wielded by little boys pretending to be men.' She flicks her gaze away – it takes only a second for her to recompose. 'Can I ask how is it that you came to be alone? What has happened to your parents? Did they send you to Sydney?'

I don't expect Fin to answer straightaway but he does in a casual way, as if he's commenting on the unfortunate weather. 'My dad went out on the night of the blasts after an argument with his wife.' Fin pauses. 'My step-mum, not my mum. Anyway, he never came back. I don't know what happened to him. My mum is in Sydney. We thought she could help us. She couldn't.' Fin doesn't say anything more.

I drain my glass of water. It's my turn. 'My mum thought it would be best for me to go with Fin and Max. And Noll.' Breathe, Lucy.

'Who's Noll?'

'Our friend. He died in Sydney. When we were leaving.'

Worry creases Raahel's forehead.

'He and another friend, Matt, died trying to get fuel so we could drive here. We've also lost Alan, an old guy we lived with in the car park. He got sick and died.' I'm telling her more than I normally would a stranger.

'Oh my goodness. I'm so sorry. That's too much for anyone to take on, let alone someone your age.'

'We had to do something with … his body. We carried him to Circular Quay and put him into the water. That was hard.' Understatement of the century.

Raahel has tears in her eyes. 'It must have been so scary to leave your family.' She's too gentle.

'I got to say goodbye to my mum. Not my dad or my sister. They were further up the mountains. I left quickly and didn't get to say goodbye to them.'

My sister should be with me. There was one more space in the car – Bit should have been in it. It's not her fault.

It's not her fault.

I have not survived this long without being careful with my memories of my sister. They don't give me strength. They scratch and tear at me if I bring them to the surface. I have to seal them up in the boxes and store them away. I've had years of practice.

'I'm sorry, I can see it's very difficult,' Raahel says. 'I won't ask you more questions.' She notices the meat left on my plate. 'You are vegetarian?'

I nod, ashamed to be rejecting food that must be in very short supply.

'Maybe it's time for a rethink? You need to be careful of your iron levels.'

'Okay.'

Saramma comes to whisper something in her ear.

Raahel stands up. 'You must excuse me. This little one needs the toilet. I will see you later.'

'It was nice to meet you.'

Raahel places a hand on my shoulder. 'You too. I'm glad you have come.'

Fin has finished his food and he sits holding the table with both hands as if he is trying to ground himself. He eyes Max, who still hasn't touched his meal. 'Why aren't you eating? Come on, you need to eat.'

Max doesn't respond.

'Do you feel any better?' I ask him.

He gives a little shrug.

'Max?'

He looks up at me, his eyes watery.

'We're safe now.'

'Are we?'

Fin's eyes move, restless, around the room. 'I think so, buddy.' He does the thing he did in the car over and over, taking his beanie off and rubbing his head. I miss his hair. He had beautiful thick, dark, wavy hair until I went at it with a pair of scissors like he was a hedge in need of pruning. I did it so he could wear Matt's uniform and pretend to be a soldier, so he could get into the crisis response headquarters at Sydney Town Hall to see his mother. The stubble on Fin's cheeks is longer than his hair. He has a different look about him now. He was always serious but since Alan died there has been a heaviness to him.

'You really should eat,' I say to Max. 'This is à la carte by car-park standards.'

'I'd rather be hiding with Noll.'

There is nothing to say in response. I feel like we traded Noll's life for this place too.

An absent look comes across Max's face then he turns from the table and vomits onto the linoleum floor. A few people at the surrounding tables turn to look. They seem concerned, which is somewhat comforting – perhaps they don't want to shut us out of the camp just yet. Then my brain clicks over to the memory of Alan vomiting – we were certain he died of radiation poisoning.

'Max, Max.' Fin takes his brother by the shoulders and tries to sit him up straight again. Max vomited in the car park after Noll was killed, but we thought it was just shock.

Raahel comes back into the room and rushes over to us. 'Max, do you think you can stay sitting up? Or do you feel like you might pass out?'

He nods.

'Might pass out?'

He nods again.

'Okay. It's okay. Don't worry. We might lie you on the ground, save you bumping your head. You don't need a concussion as well!'

Fin is frozen, so I help Raahel move Max to the floor. I take my jumper off and put it under his head.

Raahel kneels down and takes Max's hand. 'Not feeling too good? Can you tell me what's going on?'

'I don't know. I'm dizzy.'

'It's okay. I can check you out and see if we can find out what's wrong. Don't worry.' She turns to Fin. 'I'm a doctor.'

A doctor. It feels as if she has said she's a magical fairy who can make all our dreams come true.

'Fin, go and get him some water,' I say, but Fin just stands there staring at Max. 'Here, sit down with him. I'll get him some water. Fin. Sit.'

He sits and takes Max's hand in an awkward guy way.

I go to the kitchen, where Tom is talking to Susan while she washes the dishes. I find a cup and half fill it from the big water dispenser on the bench. I'm well practised at conserving it.

'Take more,' says Tom. 'The boy needs it.'

EIGHT

Raahel leaves the room and comes back with a medical bag. She takes out a stethoscope and blood pressure monitor and wraps the cuff around Max's upper arm. She pumps up the cuff and notes down the reading. Then she shakes a thermometer – an old-fashioned one, no digital reading – and asks him to open his mouth so she can place it under his tongue.

'38.5,' she says.

'He's sick?' asks Fin.

'Do you have cramps in your tummy?' Raahel asks Max.

He nods.

'All right. I'm going to press on your tummy and I want you to tell me if it hurts.'

I stand beside Fin. I should touch him – hug him or hold his hand or something. I know I should. Instead I look out the window at the tree branches swaying in the wind and feel myself drift from him and the scene and the room.

Raahel takes us away from Max so we can talk without him overhearing. 'I think he's okay,' she says. 'Might just be an upset stomach. And he's still in shock.'

'It's radiation poisoning,' Fin says.

'Fin, we are a long way from the blasts and they happened too long ago for it to be from the radiation. It's best to treat him for dehydration, get him eating some good food and monitor him for a few days. Then we'll see where things are at.'

'But we've been drinking the water. We had to; we didn't have a choice. What if there was uranium in the water?'

'The water treatment plants stopped working when all the electricity went down. That would have caused a lot of illness.'

'So what are you drinking here?'

Raahel lowers her voice. 'We have clean water from … a safe source. Sometimes people get viruses because of poor sanitation in situations like this. Simple things cause disease to spread, like lack of hand soap, cooking utensils that haven't been washed properly because of lack of detergent. No antibiotics. Not to mention food poisoning.'

'Food poisoning?'

'Yep. Food isn't being stored properly without refrigeration. Rice is usually the culprit. You can get food poisoning from rice very easily if you're cooking it and eating it later.'

'You're telling me he's not going to die?'

'I don't think there's cause for panic.' Raahel pats Fin on the shoulder. 'Stay with him. Lucy, come with me to the medic room.'

Raahel takes me down a corridor next to the rec hall. I'm a slow mover thanks to my ankle injury and she asks me multiple times if I'm okay. I grimace through the discomfort and tell her I am. We reach a door and she pulls some keys from her pocket.

'I'm going to need you to wait outside the door; Jaxon's very … security conscious,' she says over her shoulder. 'I'll give you some things to take back for Max.'

I take the opportunity to look out a window and see more of the camp set-up. There's a path leading to a row of cabins on the left, presumably accommodation back when this place was actually a camp. On the right of the path are a few sheds, the kind that would have been filled with handy things like canoes and archery equipment. Beyond the sheds is a small paddock, where, swaddled in thick rugs, there's a horse with a tail the same colour as the ghost gums. A tall fence with a spiral of razor wire coiled around the top surrounds the property as far as I can see. It's around three metres high and I spot a figure walking along the outer perimeter. He carries an assault rifle and is dressed in camo gear.

'Raahel?' Jaxon is walking up the corridor to the medic room. He gives me a cold stare. 'Move away from the door,' he says and walks straight into the room. The only thing I catch before he closes the door is him asking Raahel what she's giving Max.

A few moments pass before they come out. Raahel wheels a drip stand, which she passes to me without eye contact. I wonder if she's deliberately giving me something to lean on as I walk. She carries a plastic box with a handle and a clear bag of fluid.

When Jaxon walks past me he doesn't say a word but radiates that particular aggressive energy that males seem to have easy access to, something indelible in their movement, something that doesn't require any sound to express itself.

Raahel opens the IV kit with surgical-gloved hands and removes a needle from its sterile plastic packaging. Max lies back on his mattress in the rec hall propped on several pillows and Raahel wipes the back of his hand with an alcohol swab. When she inserts the needle Max winces and scrunches his eyes shut.

'Sorry. I know it hurts. We need to rehydrate you really fast.'

When she is done she strokes Max's forehead and stands up to speak to Fin. 'We'll see how he's going once his fluids are up. His body has been through months of malnutrition; it's tougher on children. I need to check you both over as well.'

A corner of the room is partitioned off with privacy screens. Raahel invites me to take a seat in a plastic chair then checks my blood pressure and asks me a few questions about how I've been feeling.

'I don't have a way to test your iron here, but given your age … Are you having your period?'

'No.'

I'm pretty sure my period stopped because of stress and lack of food. My body's putting up a great big block on bringing offspring into this crazy world. Perhaps now that I'm eating – if we stay – my period will come back. I'm not really looking forward to that. Seriously, ladies, nuclear winter ain't good for feminine hygiene.

'Well, in that case eat all the food you can,' Raahel says.

I see my sister in her hospital bed as clearly as if she was right in front of me.

'Lucy? Are you okay?'

I'm alive but I don't know if that's enough anymore.

'Yes. Sorry. I think I'm just tired.'

Raahel takes off her stethoscope. She ducks her head down and tries to meet my eyes. 'If you want to talk about anything, anytime, I'm a good listener.'

I can only nod.

She looks at my ankle. 'What happened here?' she asks.

'We were going out at night to find petrol.' Stealing, Lucy. You were stealing petrol. 'I slipped on some ice. I'd already injured it – someone trod on it in a riot at a food line. I slipped. I couldn't walk, so Fin took me back to the car park. Noll, Max and Matt kept going. That's when it happened. When Noll and Matt died.'

I stare at my ankle but all I see is blood and snow. I wasn't even there when it happened, but that's what I see – bright red blood on white snow. Just like I see

Starvos's blood on the concrete floor, even though in reality I never did.

I want to know what Fin found when he went to Noll. I want to know if Noll died quickly. Matt turned his gun on himself, I know that much. He felt responsible for Noll being shot by a soldier. But Noll? I know nothing except that he was shot and now he is dead. That's not enough.

'Lucy, I am concerned for you.'

'I'm okay.'

'I don't know if that's possible after all you've been through.'

I turn my face away from her. 'I'm okay.' My words sound blunt.

'Well, I don't think you have a serious injury, so that's good news. Rest it. But …' she trails off.

'What?'

'You might have to try and use it again as soon as you can. I'm going to do whatever I can but Jaxon and Tom make the decisions now and they haven't allowed anyone new in for some time. They say it's important that everyone here contributes.'

'Has it always been like that?'

Raahel takes her time before answering. 'Not always, but … the situation is always evolving.'

'Those two guys make all the decisions?'

'There used to be a committee of sorts, but it's not an effective way of running things apparently. Two is better. Decisions are made more quickly, and Jaxon and Tom know a lot about running a place like this. We are safe, we have food and shelter. Tom is a good man.'

'What about Jaxon?'

'Things are more stable since he arrived. No more of us have died outside Wattlewood. It's difficult to argue with that.'

After checking Fin, Raahel pronounces us both dehydrated, exhausted, malnourished and in shock. Basically we're crap but not headed for impending doom. She instructs us to drink a lot of water, which she leaves for us beside our beds, and rest.

Max is still asleep when the dinner bell rings. Raahel brings us some food so we can stay with him while we eat. She has included meat on my plate and winks when she hands it to me.

'Welcome to the Stone Age,' Fin says. 'I guess you're one of us Neanderthals now.'

'What do you think it is?' I ask, examining the brown slab on my plate.

'Could be dolphin. Baby seal. Mutant koala, perhaps.'

'I wouldn't joke about that.'

'You reckon there's an army of mutant koalas out there?'

'I think there's all sorts of things out there.'

After dinner, Esther allocates Fin and me to small groups to use the shower block. I am in Esther's group and I'm given a stack of clean clothes and a bag with pyjamas, a towel, a bar of soap, a toothbrush and toothpaste. The water pumps stopped running here a while ago, so I also have a bucket half filled with water. I'm introduced to Rob, the guard who will accompany us. He is fat-necked and gives me only half a glance. I get the vibe that he likes that he's allowed to carry around a big gun. Our group walks (I hobble) by lamplight to the shower block, and other than Rob holding his rifle at the ready it feels like school camp.

Esther sets the lamp on the bathroom tiles and points to one of the four cubicles.

'Don't take too long; everyone else is waiting.' Her tone is brusque and she doesn't look at me when she talks. She goes into a cubicle, closing the door behind her.

The water is so cold it feels like it's slicing through my skin. I'm used to washing with a bucket – I dry and dress quickly, and then follow the others back to the rec hall. Actually on reflection the bathroom experience feels less like school camp and more like prison. In the rec hall it's different; it's cosy with the firelight flickering on the walls and the sound of easy chatter. There's a cupboard full of board games next to the beanbags. Fin finds a Scrabble box and tips the pieces out onto the carpet.

'Might surprise you to know that I'm the Scrabble master,' he says, as he begins turning the letters face down and shuffling them around. I make an effort to relax and tell myself everything is okay.

'I would be surprised if it were true, which it's not because I am the Scrabble master,' I say.

'Ha. I doubt it.'

'Then you take your life in your own hands, my friend.'

'My own life? What crazy-arse rules do you play with?'

'You lose, you do a nudie run outside in the nuclear winter.'

A mischievous grin creeps onto Fin's lips. For a little while we will ignore the horror of what we have seen in the past months and the grief for our friends – it's our long-practised strategy for survival.

'And if you lose?' he asks.

'Pointless talking about it. It won't happen.'

'You're in for a rude shock.'

'Well yeah – it will be rude and shocking to see you running nude.'

Fin tries to fight his smile as he finishes turning the tiles. I start choosing mine when Jaxon walks in with a guitar. He's met with whistles and applause around the room.

'Thank you, thank you very much,' says Jaxon in a faux-Elvis voice.

Max wakes up. He's too weak to walk so Fin carries him over to sit with us on the beanbags.

'This one is called "Esther" and it goes out to my special girl ... Stephanie.' Laughter and more whistles. 'No, it's for Maddie. No, Esther. It's for Esther. Here goes.' Jaxon starts strumming the guitar.

Esther, Esthhhhhher
If you ever met herrrr
You'd rememberrrrr
'Cause she's the most beautiful girl in the world
The most beautiful girl in the world
Sha la la something something la

Esther, Estherrrrr
She's so beautifoooool
She makes me act like a toooooool
When I'm around herrrr
Sha la something lala

Everyone laughs and turns to look at Esther at the back of the room. She smiles and rolls her eyes like she thinks it's adorable, but when the song is finished she has disappeared.

At lights out I curl up next to Fin with my head on his chest and listen to his heart beating. Within the white room in my head, on top of the boxes, is the compass. Safe/unsafe, run/stay, trust/don't trust. I can't let myself sleep; I have to monitor it. When we were sleeping in the car park I knew every exit, every corner; I knew how many steps in the stairwell, how many strides it took to run up the ramp and how many seconds on average it took to do it. I was prepared for a speedy evacuation. I was prepared for the dark. Here, I know nothing. We are locked in a room full of strangers who have easy access to firearms. I should feel safe, shouldn't I? Mr Effrez sent us here – he wouldn't send us somewhere dangerous. I tell myself this over and over, waiting for it to comfort me. But Noll is dead. Matt is dead. The soldier we passed on the way here is buried in the snow and his family don't know what has happened to him, just like I don't know about mine.

I don't know if Bit is alive or dead. I keep her memory in a box stacked so high I can hardly reach her.

NINE

For years I expected to lose my sister, but not like this. I try to picture her as she was on the last normal day we had together – the morning before the missiles.

We were attempting to share the space in front of the bathroom mirror. She had just spat out her toothpaste, a flick of which got on my shirt.

'Bit! You moll! Look what you did!' I said.

'Oh dear. Sorry, love. And on your big date day too. What a bitch.'

'Yeah. You are.'

'You're spending a long time on your hair. Looks hot … if you're into Star Wars. Oh God, he's not a Star Wars nerd is he?'

'No.'

'Because you've been there and you know it doesn't end well.'

'Shut up, Bit.'

My sister's name was – is – Penelope. But we went through a phase a few years ago where we would give each other stupid nicknames which got progressively more ridiculous and obscure. It worked like this:

Penelope
Loppy
Lop
Lop-eared Rabbit
Rabbit
It
Itty Bitty
Bit

Following this bizarre logic, I became 'Fru':
Lucy
Goosey
Juicy
Juicy Fruit
Fruit
Fru

Sometimes she called me Fru, sometimes Lucy. But she was always 'Bit' to me from that time onward. Maybe because I needed a part of her that was all mine – a name that wasn't recorded on hospital records and used in psychiatrists' notes.

She was my Bit of Penelope, and on that morning she was well. That's how our family always talked about her, almost how we talked about our lives. Bit was either well(!) or unwell. What we really meant was Bit was either eating normally or starving herself, thus she had divided her existence into two modes that she, and by extension the rest of us, slid between.

It wasn't her fault. We repeated it over and over; a mantra for each hospital visit, for each kilo lost. It's not her fault. It's not her fault. It's not her fault.

At that time, just before the missiles, Mum, Dad and I almost felt we could exhale. Almost. There were still blips, but Bit hadn't been in hospital for almost two years. It was a big deal. She had just got a job as a receptionist at an orthodontic practice, and was going to night school to get her high school certificate. She'd been too sick to stay in school back when she was supposed to do it.

Bit is three years older than me. She turned twenty-one last month, when we were living in the car park. I saw the date on the calendar Alan kept. I saw it and I spent the rest of the day pretending I hadn't.

When Bit was well our shapes were the same: narrow shoulders – narrow everything – barely any boobs to speak of, and about three inches shorter than we'd both like to be. But we were like identical line drawings that had been coloured in differently. I have dark hair, and her hair is fair, so fair in fact that the long hairs she shed when she was sick seemed almost transparent, like she was in danger of fading away; all her lines disappearing. That's how I imagined the illness would take her in the end: she would get thinner and thinner, paler and paler until she dissolved completely.

After covering me in toothpaste splatter she elbowed her way in front of the mirror to brush her hair. It was one of the ways we could tell how well she was – she didn't seem to mind seeing her reflection. Not too much.

'What's his name again? Frank? Fred? Ferdinand?'

'Fin.'

'Ahhhhh. Of course. Fin. As in flipper. I think I'll just call him Flip. That cool with you?'

'Fine with me. You'll never meet him anyway. As if I'd introduce him to you. Ugh.'

'And what are you doing? On your *date*.'

I didn't answer.

'What are you doing?'

'Nothing much, just …'

'Yes? Still waiting.'

'We're going to the library. We've got an essay due. History.'

'You're going to the *LIBRARY*?! Oh my gosh.' She clung to the bathroom door as if in danger of passing out with laughter. 'Oh you're adorable.' She leant into the mirror to apply her lipstick. 'I'm going to work. Let me know if he proposes.' She gave me a big kiss on the cheek, smearing me with red lipstick.

'Oh. Thanks very much.'

She hesitated and her eyes changed. 'He's a good guy, isn't he?'

'Yes, Bit. He's a good guy.'

Her smile faded and she held my gaze. 'You're sure.'

'I'm sure.'

'Tell me you'll be careful.'

'He's one of the good ones.'

'If it wasn't for Dad I wouldn't think any good ones existed.'

'I know. But you have to trust me. I'm being careful. It's just the library.'

'I want to meet him.'

'I don't think we're at that point yet. Trust me, Bit. I'm careful.'

She nodded. A little smirk crossed her face. 'Love you, Fru.' She left the bathroom.

'Oh my goodness, did you just *fart*?' I shouted after her.

'He-he. See ya, sucker.'

I heard the front door close behind her. And that was it. Our last normal conversation. Done. She never did meet Fin after all.

When I fall asleep I dream of the bat in my hands and Starvos's body falling.

And when I wake up in the morning it takes me a moment to realise it's not Bit sleeping beside me.

Bit, Starvos, my violence.

Each of them connected.

TEN

The rec hall is still in the black of night when the morning bell rings. Fin tries to coax Max out of bed but he rolls away and curls into a ball.

'Max, you should have breakfast. Raahel said you have to eat. Come on.' Fin pulls back the covers and takes Max by the arm. 'Come on!'

'Leave him. It won't work,' I say.

Fin looks helpless. 'He needs to eat. He's not all right. Max, stop it. We have food. Don't be stupid.'

Max sits up, his face inches from Fin's. 'There's no point eating. There's no point being alive. Mum doesn't care if we are or not. Why should I?'

The people around us try to avoid staring but they've noticed his outburst. It's not a good look to create this much disturbance but his hurt is so sharp he doesn't care.

'Max … don't say that,' Fin says, and I can hear in his voice how close he is to breaking.

'I can say what I want!'

Fin grabs his clothes from the end of the bed and leaves. A piece of him probably feels the same as his little brother. Max curls up again.

I can't try to comfort him – I don't have the energy.

I follow Fin out to join my group and get changed in the bathrooms. The clothes we have been given are … interesting. I have brown, flared corduroy jeans, a mohair turtleneck jumper in an alarming shade of lime green (Fin said I look like I'm on my way to Woodstock) and a boys' size twelve snowboarding jacket with a kick-arse skull on the back. Fin did a little better, even scoring a pair of coolish skinny jeans, although he's also wearing a turquoise blue ski jacket from before we were born.

In the dining hall we're given a bowl of porridge with stewed fruit. I notice a timetable and roster tacked to the dining hall wall that lists things like kitchen clean-up, border patrol, hunting and food preparation.

'Do you want to go and eat with Max?' I ask Fin.

He shakes his head, pulls a plastic chair out and sits down. I sit next to him and pull my chair up as close as I can so we can talk without being overheard.

'What do you think of this place?' I ask him.

'Well, there's no gym facilities or heated pool, but no-one tried to kill us overnight. A definite plus.'

'And there's breakfast included.'

'Bonus.'

Fin scrapes the sides of his bowl with his spoon. 'It's all pointless if Max won't eat, though.'

'He's traumatised.'

'I know he is. But I can't let it kill him.'

The spoon feels very cold in my hand and my mouth goes dry. I have a mouthful of porridge but don't taste anything.

'Do you think they'll let us stay here?' I ask. 'I thought Mr Effrez's letter was a golden ticket.'

'Same.'

'So we just eat as much as we can until we get kicked out?' I joke.

'Good plan.' He stands and holds out his hand for my empty bowl. I want to take his hand and press it to my cheek. I want to cry and I want him to hug me and tell me it will be okay. Ask me, Fin, please ask me to tell you what is really wrong underneath the jokes and all the bullshit I say. Please ask me because I don't know how to ask for help.

I hand him my bowl and he takes it into the kitchen.

Fin's hands were the first things that I noticed about him. When I walked into his modern history class the teacher told me to sit next to him because he was her 'star pupil'. He moved his stuff over on the desk to make way for mine. He had nice wrists (which I know isn't the kind of thing most girls would go weak at the knees over) and his sleeves were rolled up to his elbows, showing the lines of taut veins beneath his smooth golden skin. His fingers had a beautiful shape and were smudged with graphite – he had drawn in all the margins of his textbook. I had planned to never talk to a guy again. I was done with them. They were all arseholes.

But I couldn't ignore him.

He glanced at me when I sat down. He gave me a shy half-smile and I noticed that he was blushing a little. I also noticed that he had lovely eyes. I willed myself not to engage with him at all. I told myself guys are liars and scum and this one smells really, really … good. I went through all the reasons why I should definitely leave him alone, and was even congratulating myself on such a comprehensive list, when I leant over and wrote on his textbook, *Number one? I'm going to kick your arse.* I felt slightly sick after doing it and immediately wished I hadn't. He was going to think I was some sort of freakish nerd. But he slid my book to his side of the desk and wrote, *I'd like to see you try.*

On the afternoon of the missiles Fin had taken me home. He'd helped me carry the canned food we'd bought from the supermarket. He walked with me up the front steps and handed me the grocery bag. I took it from him and my hand brushed his.

I could have told him I was scared and I wasn't good at being scared and asked if he could stay for a little while. I could have let someone look after me, just for a bit. He would have. I was so tired of dealing with fear all on my own.

I didn't say any of it.

Our house was empty, of course. I went into the autopilot mode I'd refined so well over the years: I filled my time with chores in an attempt to stop the whirring in my brain. When you have a sibling with a chronic illness you learn early on how to keep your head down and pitch in. You don't make your mum more upset by refusing to clean up your room or empty the rubbish bin. You learn to peel vegetables and how much detergent to put in the washing machine. You smooth out wrinkles in a day so your parents don't have to. You become self-sufficient. You're never the kid who talks back, who makes trouble, who sees the line and crosses straight over it. You're careful. All. The. Time.

The internet was down and the pictures on TV were terrifying, so I did some piano practice to distract myself. I folded washing; clean undies for the apocalypse. Cute. The light outside faded. I sliced vegetables and made eggplant lasagne. I waited. None of the messages I sent to Mum, Dad and Bit seemed to go anywhere so I stopped trying. At seven thirty no-one was home. Mum's shift at the hospital was supposed to finish at five. Normally Dad was home by six thirty. I took the lasagne out of the oven. After that I ran out of jobs to do so I sat on the couch and stared out the window at the starless sky.

Finally I heard voices outside and the sound of the key in the door.

'Lucy?' called Dad. He was laden with shopping bags. Bit was carrying a fifteen-litre container of water and was muttering swear words at the effort of it.

'You should have let me carry that for you, Penelope,' Mum said.

'I'm fine. I'm completely fine.' My sister said those words so often that she should have had them printed on a T-shirt. It would have saved her a lot of time (and it's harder for everyone else to detect a lie when it's written down).

'Where have you been?' I asked as I took the water from Bit and put it on the bench.

'Sorry, sweetie,' said Mum. 'I had to go and get Penelope.'

'From the city?'

'Yes. I didn't want her getting stuck on the train somewhere.'

'You should have texted me, or called the school or something. I didn't know why you weren't here.'

'I'm sorry, darling. I tried. And your dad went to the outdoor supplies place.'

'Water purification tablets, dehydrated meals,' Dad said as he unpacked items from the bags. 'Oh look, you've already bought some non-perishables. Wise girl.'

'Did you put the lasagne in?' Mum asked.

'Yes. And I took it out again. This is going to get bad, isn't it?'

Bit sat down on the couch, looking like she might cry.

'I think it's a bit early to panic,' Dad said. 'We'll sit tight until we hear more. Worst case scenario – the power goes out. I'll find the torches. Charge your phone and laptop.'

'Didn't you see the pictures? It's bad, Dad. Really bad. Like, miles and miles of dust.'

'Darling,' Mum said in a let's-not-upset-your-sister way. 'I know it looks bad, but let's just wait and see. It happened a long way from here.'

We went to bed that night hoping the world would be back to normal the next day. In the middle of the night Bit crept into my room and slipped into bed beside me.

'Can't sleep,' she said. 'I've got a terrible feeling the world might be ending.'

'Yeah? Well, I was actually sleeping.'

'Show-off.' She gripped my hand in hers. 'I'm scared, Lucy.'

'I know.'

ELEVEN

Jaxon pulls Fin and I aside when we are leaving the dining hall, saying he needs to speak with us. We go with him into the reception area and sit on the couch. Jaxon spreads some papers over the desk. We wait in silence as he reads something, turns over a sheet and writes some notes.

'Me and Tom met this morning. You have to understand that we have a very tight community here. We work hard to keep each other safe and maintain sustainability. But, Jeff Effrez has close friends here. And Esther.' Jaxon rubs his eyes. 'I've spoken to several people who believe that, if Jeff sent you, you should be allowed to stay. So, you can stay for a month then me and Tom will review your case. I pushed for longer, but that's as good as it's gonna get. We'll put you on the rosters and get you trained up hunting and patrolling, Fin.'

'And me?' I interrupt.

'You'll mostly be on the domestic roster.'

'That's bullshit.' It's an instinctive but unwise reaction – this is the guy who'll be deciding our fate. It does feel good to say it, though.

His eyes harden. 'The people out there are animals.

I don't like having women outside at all, and they certainly don't leave camp unaccompanied. The only way you'll be going hunting is on horseback and that's not gonna work unless you can ride a horse.'

'I can.' I want to add, 'you dick' but I bite my tongue this time. 'I grew up with horses.'

Fin gives me a shocked look, as if I've said I can fly a spaceship. 'How did I not know this?'

'I'm extremely accomplished for my age,' I tell him. Turning back to Jaxon I add, 'My performance on the pianoforte is exquisite,' but I doubt he gets the *Pride and Prejudice* reference. Shame, we've been getting along so well.

'We'll have to see how good you are before I even consider letting you out there with Tom and Esther.'

Rather than saying what I'd like to, I look at the smiling kids abseiling in the picture on the wall.

'If, after a month, it looks like you're both pulling your weight, you can stay longer.'

'We're on probation?' Fin asks.

'Think of it more like a trial, for both of us. You might decide this place isn't right for you.'

'We decided getting shot or starving to death isn't for us. That's why we're here,' I say.

Fin flicks me a warning look.

Jaxon gives a broad smile which doesn't seem to reach his eyes. 'Give it your best shot then. Come on, I'll show you around outside.'

*

Despite the cold air on my cheeks it's good to be outside among the trees that surround the building. The bed of leaves on the ground is soft and squishy underfoot. Some of the gums here are different to the ones in the mountains; their bark is like watercolour painting – dusty apricot and burgundy. Leaves of leek-green. I don't know the names of these ones. The ghost gums are familiar; they are how they sound, pale curving whispers of grey. Limbs of smoke.

Jaxon points through the trees towards the cabins adjacent to the rec hall. 'Those are storage: tools, clothes, bedding, towels – that sort of thing. That paddock has three horses and there are a few stables. We lock them up at night. The fence runs all the way around the camp. It's patrolled. The bush beyond the fence line slopes down to a river where we set rabbit traps. About five kilometres west there's farmland where we ride out to hunt roos. Tom is a good tracker and marksman, so he's in charge of that.' Jaxon looks at me directly. 'Maybe he'll let you go with him and Esther, like I said, if you have the skills. They could use another set of eyes.' He looks down at my ankle. 'You're going to need to get over that quickly.'

'Noted.'

Jaxon leads us along the side of the rec hall and around the corner where there is a long white plastic tent with a curved roof and a huge shed. 'Greenhouse for growing seedlings, compost shed with worm farms. The fertiliser they produce feeds the mushrooms we grow in a disused mine shaft about a kilometre or so north of here. We're in coal country and not by accident. We've got a lot of mushrooms, and I mean a lot. Oyster mushrooms, wood ears and, best of all, Velvet Shank – they can withstand frost.'

'Where do you get the apples from? For the stewed fruit?'

'Before the winter we stewed as much fruit as we could. We've got stores of it, along with the sauerkraut, but we're getting low. Hopefully we'll have enough in store until the temperatures rise and the trees start producing fruit again.'

Jaxon says 'we' as if he was one of the camp's founders.

'You think the temperature will rise again?' I ask.

'Yeah. We've got several guys here who've looked into data modelling from various projected scenarios. This place isn't an afterthought. It's not a kneejerk reaction like what they're doing in Sydney. The people who had the idea to start this place saw what was coming. They stored food and worked out how to survive long term. It's just a shame they didn't have the management skills to operate the camp safely.

'It's hard not knowing the size or exact location of the blasts, but by measuring the temperature drop against the blast location and stuff, our guys have had a crack at working out when it will warm up. They reckon about three or four months from the blasts – which is around now – the temperature should start to climb.'

‘I don’t think it was snowing on our drive down,’ Fin says.

‘It’s been five days since we’ve had any overnight falls here.’

‘So the sun could come out again?’ I ask.

‘Maybe.’

‘How long has this place been here? Raahel said her husband did a lot of the work.’

‘A long time. Some of the guys here are internationals: two Americans who worked at the Pentagon and a British secret service bloke. They picked Australia because we’re far from the blast zones. But it wasn’t in good shape when I turned up. They were analysts, not strategists. I’ve had to do a lot of security work to keep the camp safe. There’s a lot of people out there.’ He points into the trees beyond the fence. ‘Who want what we’ve got. So you don’t wander around on your own.’ Jaxon looks at me. ‘Especially you. Hate to point out the obvious but you’re a girl and you’re small. We’ll teach you some self-defence but at the end of the day a guy could overpower you. There are others out there and they’re animals.’

‘What about Esther?’ I ask. ‘She was at the gates with you when we arrived.’

‘Under my watch. And she’s strong – she trains every day. Plus, she’s nearly six feet tall. You’re tiny.’

‘Lucy can handle herself,’ Fin says, but his words are weakened by the fact I have a bandaged ankle.

Jaxon looks me up and down. ‘We might wait till you

can walk properly. See how well you can handle yourself then.'

Back when we were on our journey from the Blue Mountains to Sydney, we came across a demountable building on the highway. It had been set up by the State Emergency Service, but obviously abandoned when it became apparent this particular variety of emergency couldn't be remedied and no emergency service on the planet was going to be of much use. The demountable had been reclaimed as a shelter and we stopped to see if anyone there had seen Fin's dad. I can still see the man who opened the door when we knocked, I can smell the stench of the unwashed men within it and hear the words that make my chest feel like it's going to collapse. '*Why don't you come inside – you might like it.*' It was like his eyes left a stain on me. I feel the same thing now and I hate it. I hate that I slipped in the snow and Fin had to pull me away from those men. I hate Jaxon's words and what they do to my head, how they reduce me to someone weak who needs protection.

And I hate the relief I feel now that I won't have to protect myself anymore.

TWELVE

I grew up in a country town called Wagga Wagga. Bit and I had a storybook childhood: a cubby house, chickens, pony club – the full wholesome ensemble. The worst thing that ever happened to us was losing my grandfather to cancer. Yes, it was awful, but it was also the only suffering we knew. How spoilt we were.

Before she was sick Bit got a job in the supermarket and started going out with a guy she met there, Declan Flemming. He was two years older than her and had the sort of face and body that would get him a lead actor gig on sight – with the right lighting and soundtrack anyone would believe he was capable of saving the world. Plus he always held the door open for Bit when he picked her up in his dad's Mercedes, he called my mum Mrs Tenningworth and he used good table manners.

I realised much later that there was something slick about him I had always found unnerving; he would hold my gaze a little too long, and when I got uncomfortable and looked away, he would laugh and say I was cute. He would tell me that my school skirt was too short and I thought I was supposed to find that sweet, like he was looking out for me, so I ignored the way his eyes made me feel uncomfortable. In a totally confusing way I liked that he paid me any attention at all; I wanted his tick of approval.

Mum and Dad wouldn't let Bit go over to his house if his parents weren't home and the same rule applied for our house. It was a pointless rule because Bit said they would just go and park his (dad's) car somewhere anyway. I asked her if they had sex and she shook her head. Her cheeks went rosy. 'I'm so not ready for that,' she said.

'Does he send you pictures of his privates?'

'His *privates*?' she laughed and shoved my arm. 'How old are you? Like, three? No. He's not like that. And I would totally dump him. Ew.'

'I thought that's what guys did.'

'Only creepy losers, Lucy. Stay away from the creepy losers.'

It went without saying that Declan wasn't a creepy loser – he was too funny and good-looking.

One afternoon I was at home alone and Declan's (dad's) Mercedes pulled up in the driveway. I watched out my window as the passenger door opened and Bit got out, clutching her schoolbag to her chest. She ran up the path and the car sped off before she even made it to the front door.

She tried to push past me when I met her at the door, but I grabbed her by the wrist.

'Don't touch me! God, Lucy!' Mascara was running

down her cheeks. I dropped my hand and she ran down the hall and locked herself in the bathroom.

I tried to talk to her through the door. I could hear her crying.

'Bit, are you okay? What happened? Bit? Open the door.'

She didn't, so I sat on the floor, leant against the door and waited. After half an hour I heard the lock click and I opened the door. She was sitting on the edge of the bath, staring straight ahead. Her shoes and socks were off and I noticed a fleck of blood on her ankle.

'Can you get me some clean underwear and my pyjamas. I have to change before Mum and Dad get home.'

'Bit, what happened? Why is there blood on you?'

'JUST DO IT!'

I backed away, went into her bedroom and got her pyjamas from under her pillow. They had unicorns and rainbows on them. When I came back she was running the shower. 'I'm going to give you my undies and my skirt. You have to put them in a bag and throw it in the bin.'

'Did your period come? Didn't you have any pads?' I think I knew that wasn't what had happened – I was just hoping.

She was breathing hard, sucking in air and wiping her eyes again and again.

'Bit, what happened?'

'It was my fault. It was my fault.'

'What?'

'I'm going to have a shower and go to bed. Tell Mum I threw up. I'm sick.'

'Bit?'

'Lucy, do it.' She pushed me out of the bathroom and locked the door.

I stood in the hallway as she showered. When she came out of the bathroom she gave me her skirt and undies in a bundle. Her undies were covered in blood, and when I looked at her face I saw all the light within her was gone.

I did what she told me and put her undies and skirt in a plastic bag. After I tied it and threw it in the bin outside I had to wash the blood off my hands.

There was no doubt in my mind that if Declan Flemming came to our front door that afternoon I would have picked up a kitchen knife and plunged it into his chest.

Is that why I swung the bat so hard at Starvos's skull?

THIRTEEN

After the conversation with Jaxon about our one-month probation, Fin and I go out to the car to bring in the things we want to keep safe. Jaxon tells us that there is no guarantee anything we leave in the car won't be looted if the camp is broken into. I pull out everything in my bag – most of my clothes are so filthy I don't see any reason to keep them, except for the red cardigan my mum gave me for Christmas. I also keep the squirrel hairclip Bit gave me. If I'm going to live through the apocalypse I may as well be accessorised. I feel around the side pocket of the bag and find the one thing that is probably the most useless of all: my mobile phone.

'You still have that?' Fin asks.

'It has photos on it.'

'But isn't it dead?'

'I turned it off ages ago, but yeah. Probably.' I press the button and to my surprise the phone wakes up. I'm greeted by my wallpaper photo of Bit and me, our faces pressed together, filling the frame. She has her eyes crossed and her tongue poking out, and her hair is whipped over my face by the wind. I'm laughing. The picture was taken at a music festival in the summer before the missiles. The little triangle in the top right of the screen is empty: no coverage. Seventeen per cent battery. I wish I'd never turned it on.

'Are you okay?' he asks.

'Yep.'

He puts his hand on my shoulder. I shrug him off.

'I'm fine – I just want to keep it. Otherwise one day I'll forget what they look like.'

'Totally. Here.' He finds Max's backpack in the boot and empties everything out of it. I turn the phone off again. Looking at it won't bring me anything good, but leaving it behind where it could be stolen feels like a goodbye I'm not ready to say. I put it in the backpack next to Fin's sketchbook.

I'm locking up the car when Fin tells me to wait. He opens the front passenger door and reaches under the seat. When he stands up again he's holding Noll's Bible.

'Can I have a look?' I open the book and leaf through its delicate pages. Noll has underlined words and passages and written notes in the margins.

'It didn't do him much good in the end, did it?' I say.

'What do you mean?'

'Well, it didn't save him. God didn't look after him and make sure he was safe.'

'I don't think Noll would have seen it like that.' Fin looks like he's going to say something more but he stops himself, picks up the bag and begins walking back to the building.

'He was full of grace.'

Fin stops walking and turns around. 'What do you mean?'

'I went to a Catholic school, in Wagga. We used to say a prayer: *Hail Mary, full of Grace.* I never really knew what that meant. I just thought it meant she was graceful. But that was Noll, wasn't it? Full of grace for people he should have hated.'

'Yes. It was.'

'You think he got it from here?' I hold up the book.

'He must have got it from somewhere.'

I look at the heavy, tattered book in my hands and trace the faded gold lettering on the cover with my fingertip. 'I had an argument with him about the Bible. Well, not so much an argument – I was arguing but he was calm and patient. I said it was full of crap about how women were rubbish and should be subservient to men. I said that if God existed he was a misogynist.'

'Have you ever read it?'

'No. And I thought Noll would laugh at that and ridicule me, but he just smiled and said that the women who hung around with Jesus were fearless. They shouldn't have even been talking to a guy who wasn't their father or brother – they could have been stoned for that. But instead they were following Jesus around and having him over for meals. Noll said women are some of the bravest people in the whole thing.'

Fin is quiet for a moment. He looks at me for so long I'm the one who starts to blush.

'Well, you're the bravest person I know.'

His words put a lump in my throat and I have to turn away from him. 'Come on, it's cold out here.'

FOURTEEN

After three days at Wattlewood it feels like I'm re-entering society; there is no scramble, no cloud of immediate danger, no spending the earliest hours of the morning trying to gather the strength to get through another day and survive the night. We don't need to check the car clock and sound the horn to let everyone know the time to make sure we don't feel like subjects in some inhumane deprivation experiment.

But I can't relax. Max still isn't eating and every time I hobble anywhere I feel eyes on me weighing my value. Am I worth a piece of damper? A portion of the meat that makes me gag and takes an age to get through? One day in the corridor I actually hear someone murmur, 'Apparently she can ride a horse though.'

I push through the discomfort when I walk.

Fin and I are given jobs on the roster. To be more accurate, I am given jobs: cleaning the kitchen, mopping the terrible vinyl floor, washing laundry. Fin attends training sessions where he learns to shoot things. He's told that once he improves his skills with weapons and starts to put on weight he will be rostered on border patrol.

That afternoon before dinner, while Fin is trying to convince Max of the merits of food consumption, I slip outside and go for a walk. I know I'm not supposed to but I feel caged. For the most part there is only about fifty metres between the buildings and the high boundary fence, except for a section of the property that seems to take in some of the bushland. There's a path leading into it and someone is walking along pushing a wheelbarrow that holds a large plastic water container. I look to the north and spot a gate secured with heavy chain and multiple padlocks. A guard stands by the gate – he's holding a rifle like the soldiers in Sydney had, but is looking outwards and doesn't see me. I head across to the small horse paddock. It's more of a large yard than a paddock and holds three horses. One of them, the big grey, raises his head, ears pricked, and watches me as I approach. He snorts and comes over to the fence. I hold out my hand for him to sniff and he lowers his head – a sign of acceptance in horse language. He seems to like it when I scratch behind his ears and I stay for a little while talking to him.

When I feel the hand on my shoulder I jump with fright. It's Jaxon, dressed in the same charming outfit he was wearing when we arrived: camo gear accessorised with a rifle.

'What are you doing?'

I try to get my breath back. 'I went for a walk. I'm just looking at the horses.'

'You can't be here on your own. I told you that.'

'I didn't go past the fence. Not that I could anyway – we're kind of locked in here.'

'Are you stupid?'

'What?'

'I said: Are. You. Stupid.'

I try to keep my chin up. I feel so small. 'No.'

'Because you seem to have trouble understanding the rules.'

'I don't. I thought you meant we couldn't be on our own out there, past the fence.'

His scowl softens. 'I don't want anything bad to happen to you. You can't move around on your own without permission. Do we understand each other?'

'Okay. Yes.'

'Now go inside and get some dinner – there won't be any left if the guys go back for seconds.'

At dinner Fin leaves Max in the rec hall and comes to sit with me. I tell him quietly what Jaxon said. Fin eats his food and doesn't say anything.

'Fin, he called me stupid.'

'Did he actually say that?'

'Well, he said "Are you stupid?", which is basically the same thing.'

'I don't think it is. He's looking out for you, Lucy. We need to listen to him. And you shouldn't have been out there.'

'Oh, so you think I'm stupid too?'

'Lucy.'

'How're you going with the guns? Feeling empowered?'

'Shit, Lucy. What's wrong with you?'

I want to swallow the words; I can see Starvos falling in front of me. Please just ask me what's wrong, Fin. Not what's wrong with me. I force the meat down my throat and take my empty plate to the kitchen. Raahel sees me and gives me a smile but something about her expression shows that she knows I'm not okay. I smile back.

Fin and I don't speak much for the rest of the evening and at bedtime, when he moves closer to me, I move away.

FIFTEEN

When I wake in the morning Fin is crouching next to Max's bed, touching Max's forehead and cheeks with the back of his hand. He turns to me with panic in his eyes. 'He has a fever.'

I rub the sleep from my eyes. 'You should get Raahel – she's probably already up.'

'Can you get her? I want to stay with him.'

I'm tired and I don't want to wander around looking for Raahel in my pyjamas so I get out of bed and look at Max. He's a bit pale but doesn't look as bad as he has in the past few days. I put my palm to his forehead. 'He's fine, Fin. He doesn't have a fever.'

'You don't think?'

'No. He's fine.'

'Maybe just get her in case.'

'Fin, he's really okay.'

He's not convinced and there is a trace of annoyance in his face. My group is gathering near the door, ready for the bathroom excursion, so I pick up my coat and pull it on over my pyjamas.

'Luce, can't you see he's not okay? Don't you care?'

'Of course I care, but it's not worth panicking over.' I know I sound dismissive.

Fin turns away from me and back to Max.

I smile at Esther when I meet her at the door. She doesn't return it.

'Jaxon said you can ride?' she says.

'Hi, Esther.'

'Can you?'

'Yes.'

She looks at me with scepticism. 'As soon as we're done in the bathrooms I'll take you down to the horses. Tom needs to see if you're any good.'

Esther is waiting when I finish getting dressed. I follow her down the path towards the paddock; she has the efficient stride of someone with very long legs and she doesn't slow down as I try to catch up with her. As we approach the stables a barrage of barking begins.

'Seamus, shush,' Esther commands. I follow her through the gate and an unnaturally large German shepherd gallops towards us. It barks at me again. Esther gives a sharp whistle and the dog halts at her feet and sits down; it fixes me with a glare and snarls.

'He seems friendly,' I say. She doesn't make any effort to reassure me.

A row of four stables – cobbled together with sheets of corrugated iron and mismatched timber beams – are beside the paddock. The grey horse pokes his head out over the stable gate.

'That's Jack Frost,' Esther says.

He snorts and his breath mists in the air. Another horse, smaller in size and dark grey, comes to put its head out too.

'That's my mare, Cloudy.'

'Were their names chosen especially for the apocalypse?'

Esther takes a slow deep breath, indicating her lack of patience for my dumb jokes. 'There's also Red in the next stable.'

'Where are they from?'

'Cloudy is a leftover from the trail ride horses originally on the property. Red is Tom's. Jaxon found Jack Frost and a lot of feed abandoned at a property near here. His *name* was on his rug. He was probably a well-trained sport horse, but he is toey in the bush – spooks easily. We've kept him on in case one of the others is injured.' Esther turns to me. 'He'll be yours, if you can handle him. We ride to hunt in the mornings – mostly kangaroo now. I'm not told a lot, but I know from Tom that food stores are running low.' She gives me a pointed look. 'Especially now that three more people who need food have turned up. If you can ride well, you're an asset. If you can't, you're a liability. Liabilities put everyone in danger and no food on the table.' Her final few words sound cold and practised, as if they are someone else's.

'Esther, please understand, we don't want to be

difficult. But it was your dad who sent us here. We haven't come to take what's not ours. We are just trying to survive.'

In the silence after my words I don't know whether she is going to scream or cry. Perhaps she doesn't know either. She turns away, walks past the other stables, and rounds the corner. I follow and find her crouching to unlock an old shipping container.

'You always have to make sure you lock up the shed,' she says. 'We have a lot of feed and it's valuable. You'll be on the roster to muck out the stables, rug the horses, clean their feet, groom and feed them. There'll always be a guard.' Her firmness and intensity mirror her dad's. 'But don't get complacent.'

'I haven't been complacent about anything for a long time. That's why I'm still alive.'

'Have you ever killed anything?'

I feel disconnected from my body, like I have stepped outside of myself. I can hear the crack of the cricket bat against Starvos's skull. 'I don't know.'

'That's a strange answer.'

'It was a strange situation.'

'You have to take every opportunity to prove yourself here.'

'I'm aware of that.'

'Good. Go inside and get Jack Frost's gear. It's labelled. There's also boots and helmets.'

*

I find a helmet that fits, but my feet swim in all the boots so I find the smallest size and do my best to ignore the terrible fit. When I return with Jack Frost's saddle and bridle to his stable, he raises his head and regards me. He flares his nostrils to detect whether I have a carrot or an apple he can snaffle. I have neither but he nuzzles my pockets to be sure.

'Hey, Jack Frost. I'm Lucy. Can I call you Frosty? Can we be friends?' His head is higher than mine. I reach out a hand and he sniffs it, his breath warm on my cold skin. I feel a comfort I haven't felt for years.

My family had to move away from Wagga when I was fifteen so we could be closer to the Sydney hospital with the eating disorder unit. It almost sent Mum and Dad broke. We lived in the western suburbs, which was severely lacking in horse paddocks anyway so even if we could have afforded to keep our horses, there was nowhere to put them. I didn't make many friends at the new school; I didn't know how to explain to anyone that we'd moved because my sister was starving herself to death. If I did they would ask why. I couldn't tell anyone why, not even my parents. I'd promised Bit and we never broke our promises. I kept chatting with my old friends, but conversations dry up when you're not seeing each other regularly or doing similar things. I don't think my parents or Bit ever saw me crying – I was pretty good at scheduling it for after bedtime. And what sort of spoilt brat cries over losing her pony when her sister is dying? That's one you want to keep to yourself.

Things changed when Mum got a job in the Blue Mountains. At the beginning of year eleven I left the Catholic girls' school in the city and started at the selective high school in the mountains. I had no plans to make any friends.

But then I sat down in that first modern history class.

And there was Fin.

Jack Frost connects me to a part of myself I thought was gone. I can picture Bit ahead of me as we canter across the grass. She's laughing. No-one can catch her. I lean my forehead against Jack Frost's neck. He sighs and shifts his weight. I like him – he had a past life like me.

He stands still and obedient while I saddle him, but when I lead him out of the stable he raises his head, ears pricked.

'Esther says you're toey. Are you going to look after me? I don't want to get heavy, but my life may well depend on it, my friend. Please look after me.'

SIXTEEN

Teenage girls are not powerful. Huge portions of the population view girls as baby-making machines, cooks, cleaners. In some countries, when you're born, you want to hope to hell you're not a girl so you don't get put out with the garbage. Literally. Even if we don't have to deal with that shit personally we know that only two generations ago girls weren't encouraged to stay at school beyond year nine or ten. Get a job, ladies, and wait for someone to marry you. Oh, and to add to that, there's like a 90 per cent chance you'll be sexually harassed or assaulted, so whatever you do, don't walk around outside on your own at night. At least not until you're big enough to put up a fight. And if you are outside on the street, maybe walking to your friend's house, and you hear footsteps behind you, fucking run. And go to the gym, not only so that you *can* run but to keep yourself hot. Bonus. Don't eat that cupcake. Don't forget to pluck your eyebrows. Don't wear jeans too much, because guys won't be able to see your legs. But it's okay if those jeans are tight because at least then they can look at your butt and maybe one of them will ask you out. But if you do shave your legs and wear a skirt, don't make it too short. Because then you look like a slut. Even if it lets you run faster.

Sure, I'm lucky to have been born in a country where girls aren't thrown away like garbage, but my sister almost died because a guy treated her as though she was.

Lastly, and I really mean it, don't go wandering around in the bush by yourself.

Unless you're on a horse.

I don't think it's a coincidence that so many girls love horses. A horse is a big, fast animal. It can outrun a guy no problem.

Jack Frost and I follow Esther south from the stable block down the track to a clearing. Various logs and tree branches are set up as jumps along with two rusted oil barrels lying on their sides and a large stack of truck tyres.

'You built these?' I ask.

She shrugs. 'I like to jump. Warm him up first. Take your time – he'll be spooky at first but he settles once he's busy. Do whatever you can – some jumps, a gallop. It doesn't matter really. You just have to prove that you can handle him and yourself. Tom will decide if you can join us on the hunts.' She nods in the direction of the hall and I see Tom standing there with arms folded, watching.

'Well, come on, Frosty,' I say. 'Let's do this.'

I have to mount from the ground; it's not like there will be any mounting blocks out in the bush. It's not easy and as soon as I'm in the saddle he tosses his head and trots forward, swerving his hindquarters sideways when I pull him up.

'Frosty, you're going to have to do better, my friend.'

He pulls forward again when I ask for a walk and it takes a good few metres to slow him. I'm too tense and he feels it. When I shush to reassure him I'm also attempting to reassure myself. Nothing good will come of me pushing him too soon and pretending I can handle anything. I can't. I'm tired and I'm scared and my ankle still hurts. I long for the sun on my back instead of this inescapable chill.

Calm the farm, Lucy.

'Do you know what's going on here, Frosty? It's just the strangest thing that we're even here at all. And here I am, the crazy girl talking to a horse. They're watching us, Frosty. Try and look after me, okay?'

A squeeze of my lower leg and he slips into a trot. I rise and fall in the saddle, feeling the rhythm, and he drops his nose and accepts the bit, as if he remembers how it's done. He's listening to me now. We trot large circles to the left, large circles to the right. I forget the eyes on us and when we are both loose and ready I nudge him into a canter. His strides are smooth and rocking; he would have won ribbons in his past life.

I block the rest of our frozen world out and line him up for one of the smaller jumps: two thick tree trunks stacked on top of each other. He takes it easily and does the same with the following two. Next we move on to the oil drums. I can hear the soft rhythmic thud of his hooves on the ground. He lifts over the obstacle with a faultless jump and steady landing. Not a hoof out of place. I guide him around to a larger jump made from logs and some car tyres, and I glance to where Tom stands watching. His expression gives nothing away.

One, two, three strides. On the fourth, as I am leaning forward, ready to lift my seat for the jump, he swerves to the side. Time slows as it always has when I've fallen and in the split second before I hit the ground I note two things: one, I am about to cop some serious mud to my face; and two, I better get back on fast if I want to pass this test. I hit the mud hard and feel a blow to my diaphragm as the breath is knocked from my lungs. I scramble to find traction but my palms skid in the cold slush and my cheek hits the mud again. Esther has caught Jack Frost and leads him back to me. I get to my feet and try to ignore the sloshing feeling in my stomach.

I don't say anything but take the reins from her and throw them back over Jack Frost's head. My legs wobble as I put my left foot in the stirrup.

'Lucy.'

'Yes?'

'Breathe.'

My legs have no strength. Tom looks on and Jaxon has joined him.

Esther grips the reins beneath Jack Frost's chin to steady him and somehow I'm able to get back in the saddle.

It takes everything I have to block the world out when we approach the jump again. I remember what my coach used to say: the horse has eyes of its own to see the jump; you have to keep yours ahead and focus on the following one. Jack Frost clears the jump. His forelegs land on the soft earth and I feel a sun that isn't there warm me. I ride a circle and bring Jack Frost back to the jump from the opposite direction. After I've made my point I steer him to the edge of the field, click my tongue and nudge him with my heels. He springs forward into a gallop and I lean over his neck, giving him full rein. At the far end of the clearing I slow him to a walk and pat his neck, but in my head we keep going, we gallop on. We jump the gates of the camp and we run away.

SEVENTEEN

My clothes are covered in mud and I can feel it smeared across my cheek. Jaxon turns away and walks back up to the building, and Tom takes Jack Frost from me without a word and leads him back to the stables. Esther walks with me to the rec hall. 'Do you think I did okay?' I ask her.

'It's not my decision.'

'But if it was?'

She pulls her woollen scarf tighter around her neck, keeping her focus on the building ahead. 'You did well. He's not an easy horse.'

Raahel meets us at the door. 'Lucy, are you okay? I heard that you fell.'

'News travels fast around here.'

'I'll check you over to make sure you haven't damaged anything.'

We head to the examination space where she asks me to sit on the chair and take my jacket and top off.

'Tell me what hurts.'

'My cheek. My shoulder.'

She lifts my arm and moves it around. I try to do an effective job of masking my pain. 'It's fine,' I say.

'It needs ice, which of course we don't have.'

She presses my clavicle and I wince. 'And you need a sling. I do have one of those.'

'No. I can't wear a sling, Raahel.'

'It will heal faster. You will be very uncomfortable without one.'

'I'll put up with it.'

She purses her lips in frustration but we both know why a sling isn't a good look. 'Okay. I'll bring you some clean clothes and take you to wash off.'

'Raahel?'

'Yes?'

'Can I ask you a random medical question?'

'That's what I'm here for.'

'How long does it take a person to starve to death?'

Raahel pushes a stray lock of black hair behind her ear. 'Are you worried about Max?'

'It's not Max. It's …' I can't say her name. 'What if a person was already unwell, or … had starved themselves intentionally in the past, enough to damage their organs?'

Raahel must be concerned about my question, but she takes her time to think, as if it's a hypothetical. 'It depends. If that was the situation, such a person wouldn't have the resilience an otherwise healthy person might have.' She puts her medical bag down and clasps her hands in thought. 'But it's difficult to say for certain. Is there someone else you are worried about?'

‘I’m … It’s … my sister.’ You cannot cry, Lucy. You might not stop.

‘It’s important to hold on to hope.’

I open my eyes.

‘Now can I ask you a random question?’

‘Yes.’

‘Do you mind if I pray for your sister? I’ll add her to my list. It’s quite long.’

Tears. Shit. ‘Noll used to pray. He’s dead.’

‘You could pray.’

‘No. I’m too angry.’

‘I don’t think God minds a bit of anger. He prefers it to silence. But I can do it for you if you like.’

‘Thank you.’

‘I’m concerned for you. You’ve been through a lot.’

I don’t know how to answer.

‘It can be hard when you stop after being constantly on alert for danger. Less scramble means more thinking time. And you probably won’t be prepared for those thoughts. I know from experience.’

Raahel leaves a space for me to respond. I don’t know where to start. All I can do is nod.

‘I think you three are amazing. I can’t believe you’ve been through all of this on your own. If you do want to talk about anything you can come and find me.’ She smiles. ‘Everyone’s too healthy at the moment and I don’t have much to do.’

‘We might not be allowed to stay.’

'I'm going to do everything I can. No child should be turned away.' She doesn't look confident – she looks sad.

I haven't thought of myself as a child for a long, long time.

'Lucy.'

I can't look at her. I squeeze my hands into fists to stop the shaking.

'Lucy. I'm here. I'm with you.'

It doesn't work. I start to cry and it makes me so angry – it's going to be difficult to pull myself up again. I turn away from her and press my forehead against the wall.

'I'm going to do everything I can,' she repeats.

'Please just leave me.'

'Okay.'

I'm not sure if she's still there or if she can hear me. 'Thank you,' I whisper.

Fin is waiting for me when I come out from behind the partitions.

'Are you hurt? I saw you come off. Are you okay?' He must notice the blotchy evidence of tears.

'I'm fine. Is Max okay? Did Raahel check on him?'

'You were right. He doesn't have a fever … I was worried about you out there.'

'I'm fine.'

'You're a bit shaky.' He's trying to meet my eyes but I won't look at him. 'You got back on and did that big jump. That was crazy. There's no way I would do that – it was kind of amazing.'

'I wasn't trying to be amazing. I was just trying to earn a place here. My capacity for collecting dead things depends on my ability to ride a horse. The collection of dead things is important for survival here. Can you shoot yet?'

I try to phrase it in a humorous way because I've found that being deadpan about things is an effective method of maintaining emotional distance from the horrors of reality, and I need all the distance I can get. But the images of the dead, our dead, are slipping out of their boxes in my mind.

Fin has been talking but I haven't heard a word.

He shakes his head – he looks so vulnerable and exhausted. 'I'm okay at it, actually. But you're right, it's hard not to feel pressure.'

The thoughts I'm having are probably in his head too. I should ask him if he thinks of Noll when he holds the gun.

'They'll give you time to learn,' I say. 'You're already useful. You could do all sorts of things.'

'If you were scared you shouldn't have done that jump.'

'Scared isn't an excuse for anything anymore.'

'Lucy, I think we're going to be all right. We're safe.'

'Are we?'

'Um, there's a big frigging fence all around the place, no-one can get in.'

*

Raahel brings me a stack of fresh clothes and tells me Rob will take me to the shower block. When I meet him at the door he doesn't look me in the eye. He has his gun.

This does not make me feel safer.

I stand on the cold tiles and sluice the icy water over my skin, washing away the mud and grit. The muddy water swirls at my feet and gurgles down the drain. It's impossible to ever feel properly clean when you're only washing from a bucket, but it's better than nothing. My skin prickles with the chill and I get it over with quickly. I used to want to get this whole disaster over quickly. I thought of our situation as a slice of life that would pass and become a memory. Now I am beginning to understand that this isn't a slice at all. This is going to be the whole frigging pie. Our dream since the blasts has narrowed. It began full and wide ranging: electricity restored, infrastructure repaired, pancakes, hot chips, Netflix. Life would be changed a little, but we would form back into a civilised society. We would learn valuable lessons and buy toilet paper.

Then the dream was honed a little further: families reunited.

Now it has been whittled down into a fine point: the sun will shine and I will be the sort of person who survives in this new world.

The towers of white boxes in my head are swaying.

Declan Flemming holding the door open for my sister.

The men leering and snarling at me from the demountable.

Jaxon: '*Are. You. Stupid?*'

A violent man and me with a cricket bat in my hand.

I didn't even hesitate.

I will have what it takes to stop feeling when I need to. I will.

EIGHTEEN

Dinner is a portion of roast kangaroo two-thirds the size of my hand and a cup of couscous with herbs. For the first time since he got sick, Max is at the table with us, but he looks at the food with hostility.

'Max, can you please try to eat,' says Fin.

Max kicks the leg of the chair next to him over and over. And over. Someone at the next table glances at us.

'Max, stop,' I say, and he does.

'Please eat dinner,' Fin repeats.

'I'm not hungry.'

'You're not hungry? We came here because we were going to end up shot over a bag of rice and you're not hungry? Eat.'

It's not going to work, Fin. The look in Max's eyes is familiar – it's the look of someone who doesn't care if they are dead or alive.

I remember taking a Mars Bar with me when I visited Bit in hospital. They are her favourite. When we were little she never wanted Easter eggs from the Easter bunny, only Mars Bars. I sat on her bed and held it out to her, but she wouldn't even touch it.

'Just eat it, Bit. It'll be delicious.'

She shook her head.

'Eat it.'

'No.'

'EAT IT.'

'NO!'

I threw it across the room right as Mum and Dad walked in the door. Mum looked at me and pointed to the door. 'Get out.'

It's not going to work, Fin. Even if we did have a Mars Bar to give him.

Later, by the fire, I spend some time in the white room of my mind where the fluorescent light buzzes and I try to put all the lids back on the boxes. In an attempt at mindfulness, I focus on the excruciatingly mundane task of building a real house of cards, hoping to distract myself from the disintegration of my sanity. It's difficult and a complete waste of time. Fin's chosen method of distraction is to draw the scene around him, including me and my pathetic attempt at card engineering.

'Being watched closely isn't really helping my stress levels, Fin.'

'I have to draw everyday life,' he says. 'It's the only record we'll have of this time. No-one's taking photos. I feel called to the noble pursuit of recording life's precious everyday moments.'

'In the hope someone will care one day?'

'Yes. They could put my drawings in museums and shit.'

'A museum of shit drawings,' says Max. There's no humour in it like there would have been before. I wonder if I should risk saying to him that he's a real downer these days, but he doesn't look like he remembers what a joke is. Every night Fin has to coax him just to go to the bathrooms and wash. Raahel has told us that he isn't physically sick anymore. She says it's psychological. I'm sure that if he doesn't get better and start contributing to the camp, we won't be allowed to stay.

'Maybe you could mess with the historians,' I say to Fin. 'Draw the mutant koalas attacking us.'

'Good idea. I can already see the history class exam: Which mutant animal ate most of the population during the Great Nuclear Winter: a) three-headed koala, b) two-metre bilby, or c) …'

'Tiny but very hungry spotted quoll with laser eyes?'

'Perfect. I'll get started on the diagrams.'

Max watches us. This is exactly the sort of banter he is excellent at. He says nothing.

Jaxon comes over and takes a seat on the floor next to Max. I have kept my distance from him since the 'stupid' incident at the horses.

'How's it going, Max?'

A shrug.

'Can you deal me in?'

I'm insulted that he can't tell I'm using the cards for building.

'We're not really playing,' I say, right at the same time Fin says yes. I gather the cards and hand them to Max to deal.

Jaxon looks at his cards and chuckles. 'This is going to be painful,' he says. 'It's good to see you're still alive, Max. It'd be a waste if you died 'cause you're too skinny to eat.'

Max smiles a fraction.

'And I heard you don't like the cooking much. Don't know why. Canned cabbage with a side of dried roo is my favourite. Tell you what, I know where there's a stash of chocolate. You eat breakfast tomorrow and I'll give you a square.'

Max's jaw drops. 'Serious?'

'Serious.'

'Are you allowed to do that?'

'Mate, I'm the boss of the chocolate. And hey, are you good with animals? Sometimes we let the dogs have time off to play. I thought I could teach you some commands, show you how to handle them.'

Max's eyes widen in excitement. 'Really? I'm awesome with dogs!'

Fin looks like he might object to his little brother playing with dogs who are trained to kill, but Jaxon gives him a reassuring smile.

'I'll teach him what he needs to know. It'll be good for him.'

Fin beams at him the way my mother would at Declan Flemming. Jaxon smiles at me too and I can't get my face to do what I'm certain it needs to if we want to stay here.

NINETEEN

Three days pass with no word on whether I have passed the riding test. I'm like a girl scout waiting to be awarded her special badge. I mop floors, clean toilets and wash dishes while Fin, who I hardly see during the day, is shown the outside borders of the camp and shoots things, interspersed with doing push-ups and squats, and running laps of the grass clearing. He gets an extra serving of meat each night.

Finally Tom finds me one day after breakfast. He puts his hands on his hips, and I can see a handgun holstered on his belt.

'Come on. I'll show you the ropes for ride outs.'

'I passed the test?'

'You passed the test.'

'Is Esther coming?'

'Yes. Be friendly.'

'I'm always friendly; maybe it's her who needs to put in some effort?'

'She's having a hard time without her dad. Be nice to her.'

I now have a job. I can be useful. And the nerves could make me spew all over Tom's boots.

Outside, Tom walks with one hand resting on the gun and doesn't say anything more. When we arrive at the stables Esther is clearing up after the morning feeding. Tom, giving instructions while walking around and checking the surroundings, tells me to put a stock saddle on Jack Frost. They're mainly used for farm work, not for prissy pony club, but I don't mention that I have hardly ever ridden with one.

Tom points to Jack Frost. 'He's yours.'

'Okay. Thank you.'

'I'm not doing you a bloody favour – he's a pain in the arse. Red knows what I want before I have to ask him.'

'Sure. But he's better than the horse I have at the moment.'

Tom stops and gives me a questioning look.

'I don't have a horse at the moment.'

He looks at me like I'm an idiot and shakes his head.

'Sorry.'

'Go to the tack shed – there's a camo jacket and a balaclava that you can wear under your helmet. Pale face like yours will scare the deer.'

'Well, thank you. I appreciate the help. My complexion can be startling.'

He pauses again. 'You always like this?'

'I try to be consistent.'

'Gawd help us,' he mutters.

*

Tom rides with the relaxed and steady seat of someone who knows horses well. He holds his reins in one hand and is able to manoeuvre Red with imperceptible movements of his hands and heels. Esther rides Cloudy in silence behind me and I wonder if she's going to be taking notes on my performance. Jack Frost is alert – head up, ears pricked as if he's looking for the next jump. Tom is right, I have to concentrate and be firm with him, which is difficult when your shoulder is throbbing and you're riding into a wilderness full of people who might kill you. At least in a car there's a barrier between you and the world.

'What does he do if he's spooked or unhappy? Is he a bolter? Does he buck? Rear? What should I expect?' I ask.

'All of it. But it's only happened once or twice … He's only been out once or twice.' He looks back at me. 'I'm pulling your leg. He'll have a tantrum, throw his head about, dance around. Haven't seen anything really nasty.'

As we ride up the track beside the fence line my chest feels tighter and tighter. When we get close to the gate Jack Frost jolts into a trot and I overreact, pulling him up too fast so he throws his head. Tom halts Red, but Esther and Cloudy keep walking.

'I'm not taking you out if you're a Nervous Nellie.'

I am not a frigging Nervous Nellie. The anger and shame pushes out of my chest – I feel it pulsing in my fingertips.

'I'm fine.'

'You handled him with the jumps. Relax or he'll tense up too.'

Right. Although, funnily enough when you're ordered to relax it's difficult to have much success. Tom shakes his head and walks on. I follow him and try to sink into the saddle to ground myself.

Rob is guarding the gate. He greets Tom and Esther with a tip of his head and me with a hostile glance. He has a look of extreme self-importance and the posture to match.

'Any movement overnight, Rob?' Tom asks.

'Nope. Haven't seen anyone since last week.'

'Didn't fall asleep, did you?'

'Ha. No, it didn't snow but it's still too bloody cold to sleep out here.'

Rob takes a ring of keys from his belt and jiggles one of them in the fat padlock. When it's unlocked he unloops the chain and pulls the narrow gate open just wide enough for the horses to walk through.

'New recruit?' He directs the question to Tom, as though I'm not even there.

'We'll see.'

'Good luck.'

I can't be sure who he's talking to, but I'm pretty sure it isn't me.

Riding through the gate feels like crossing a threshold – it's a true transition into the wilderness. The snow, even though it's now stopped, has slowed the undergrowth, but the tall eucalypts and twisting banksias are thick and adaptable. It feels far, far away from civilisation, or what's left of it. It's a place that was home for people for thousands and thousands of years, but it doesn't feel like we are visitors; it feels like we are aliens. Tom has a rifle with a telescopic lens slung across his back (I wasn't offered a weapon to go with my outfit) and a large knife of the variety which my dad used to make Crocodile Dundee jokes about. He explains that my job is to follow him and be another pair of eyes. Whenever he shoots I'm to dismount and collect the bullet shells from the ground so they can be reloaded with gunpowder back at the camp. It's also my job to help load the 'kills' (aka freshly dead animals) onto the horses and act as lookout when he's stalking or collecting a kill. I ask him what I'm looking out for.

'Some other bugger who wants our kill, our horses, our weapons, us.'

'And what if I see someone?' It takes a bit of effort to keep my voice smooth and light.

'You let me know.' His tone suggests he thinks I'm a bit dense to be asking that question.

'But then what?'

'If we have time we get the hell out of there.'

'And if we don't?'

'Then I sort it out.'

I know he means shoot them.

Around us the trees are like towering sentries: still and

silent. The sky so heavy with sooty grey that barely any light comes through the canopy. My mouth is dry. I don't need to see any more people being shot. I don't want to be attacked either. And here I am out in the bush with a woman who resents me and a man with a knife and a gun.

Soon the track meets a wide dirt road cut through the bush – a fire trail. Tom urges Red into a trot and Esther and I follow him.

'Keep your eye out; sometimes roos jump out across the trail. That horse'll go ballistic.'

Comforting.

'Back when we used to have fuel we'd take the truck out and shoot deer,' Tom says. 'Now we have to go on horseback and there's no way we'd get a deer onto a horse's back – they're almost the same size. We had to start hunting more and looking further afield. There'll be kangaroos out in the paddocks. We'll see what we can get, load it and bingo. Dinner.'

'Have you seen other people out here?'

'Yes.'

'Where?'

'All around. They used to try and get through the boundary fence before we started the night patrols. People are ruthless. It's all well and good to think everyone's gonna give everyone a hand in tough times, but if there's one thing I've learnt it's that when the chips are down, you put you and your own first.'

'Has anyone from the camp been attacked?'

He says nothing for a moment. And then, 'There were two who had been here right from the start, Elliot and Mary. They went out one day, not so long ago, and didn't come back. We went out to search for them the next day, thought maybe one had been injured and hadn't been able to walk back. They'd been injured all right. We buried them up at the bush chapel near the camp.'

'Someone killed them?'

'Did a good job of it too. Elliot had been armed and all. Wasn't anymore, that's for sure.'

'Have you had to shoot someone?'

Tom pulls Red around so he's facing me. Jack Frost comes to a halt.

'You got any more bloody questions?'

'I just—'

'I've told you your job. That's all you need to know.' He eyes me with an expression that tells me I'm not welcome to respond. He wheels Red back around and continues along the track. I glance at Esther and she pretends not to notice.

After an age of riding through bushland, we get to a low paddock fence. The wire has been cut and we ride through into a field on the edge of the farmland. A few large gums are scattered through the paddock and there's a dam in the distance. The grass is mostly brown and slushy. We trot along the fence line until Tom gives a quick, low whistle, raises his hand and pulls Red to a halt. A small mob of kangaroos graze about five hundred metres away. Tom dismounts and gives me Red's reins. He approaches, crouched low, each footstep precise and deliberate. Two kangaroos pause and lift their heads – watching, ears twitching – but Tom has stepped behind a tree, out of sight. The roos see me and the horses but don't think of us as a threat; we're too far away. They lower their heads again and continue grazing. It's reassuring to see that animals have just carried on, perhaps oblivious to what humans have done to the world. I find myself wanting them to scare, to take off into the trees and escape the bullet. But I know we need this meat, and I need to be instrumental in getting it.

Tom steps out from behind the tree and inches closer. His camo ensemble blends into his surrounds and he makes it to a tree about eighty metres from the mob. They lift their heads again, sensing a closer presence, but again don't seem too troubled by it. Hidden behind the tree, Tom takes the rifle from his back and lines up the shot. In a movement that seems so simple for the damage it will inflict he pulls the trigger.

You'd expect a significant reaction from an animal upon being shot – maybe a screech of pain. Instead the kangaroo shudders for a moment, bounds three times then drops to the ground, by which time its friends have evacuated without so much as a backward glance. Only after the job is done do I notice I have been holding my breath. Tom slings the gun over his back and walks towards the kangaroo – its legs are thrashing about. He picks up a big rock, runs at the kangaroo and throws it, smashing the animal's head. The kangaroo stills.

'Why doesn't he just shoot it in the head or slash its throat?!' I ask Esther.

'Waste of a bullet. And did you see its kick? You can't get near enough to use a knife,' she says before riding off in the direction of Tom. I'm stunned.

Tom turns to me and shouts, 'You waiting for an invite?' I trot Jack Frost over, leading Red beside us. I wonder how many dead animals the horses have carried back to camp. Do they recognise the scent of blood, of death? Did it frighten them the first couple of times? Are they used to it now?

Will I get used to it?

The kangaroo isn't big. It lies on its side so I can't really see its head. Its coat looks unbearably soft, like a souvenir plush toy's. Tom crouches beside the roo and pulls some cord from his pocket, which he ties around the rear legs. He then hauls the kangaroo away from where it fell.

Esther glares at me. 'Get off and find the shell,' she hisses through her teeth. I dismount quickly and give her Red's reins to hold. Keeping hold of Jack Frost I collect the shell and slip it into my pocket.

On the way back I see the kangaroo's smashed skull. Flies begin to gather.

Do not vomit, Lucy. Do not vomit. I turn away and spew my breakfast into the soggy grass.

Tom is less than impressed. 'You'll have to get used to this. And you're going to have to pay more attention; you took too long to get over here. I'm not risking my arse if you're no good at your job.'

'Sorry.'

'You will be if one of them comes for us.' His voice softens. 'Now help me load this kill.'

Tom instructs me to hold the front of the animal so he can lift the hind legs and secure them to the back of his saddle. I grasp one paw in each hand and lift the dead roo as high as I can, which isn't very high. Its half-head lolls to the side.

'You're too small,' Tom grunts.

My arms ache, but I stand on tiptoes, trying to lift higher.

'Esther, you'll have to do it,' Tom says. 'Lucy, get on the horse – keep a lookout and for gawd's sake if you see someone tell us quick.'

Esther dismounts and hands me her reins so I now have three horses to keep hold of. If they all decide to have a tantrum I won't be able to control any of them. Tom hoists the hind legs high over Red's rump so the roo is slung over the horse. He produces another cord and secures the legs to the saddle. On the other side Esther does the same with the forelegs. Tom's back in the saddle before I've even had time to think about it; I'm distracted by the blood from the roo's head trickling in a narrow line down the side of Red's hindquarters.

Tom watches me with the disapproval of a teacher waiting for silence in a rowdy class.

'Sorry.'

'Like I said, you've got a job to do. Three is only better than two if you do your job. If you can't do it, it's useless having you out here.'

Esther and I mount up again.

Tom nudges Red into a trot. 'Hurry up,' he yells to me over his shoulder.

TWENTY

We don't arrive back at the camp until after lunch. Tom tells me to stay at the stables with Rob and take care of the horses while he and Esther carry the dead kangaroo up to the back of the main building for draining and skinning. Rob and I don't talk to each other – he just stands there with his gun and watches the bush while I brush Jack Frost and Cloudy before rugging them to turn them out. Red requires more work. I scoop water from the trough with a bucket and sponge the blood off his hindquarters. Red flinches under the cold touch of the water.

'Sorry, my friend, cold baths for all of us.'

When I squeeze water from the sponge it dribbles scarlet through my fingers.

Tom returns as I am throwing Red's rug over his back. He pulls something from his pocket and offers it to Red.

'There ya go, mate.' He scratches the horse on its neck. 'Salted liquorice,' Tom says to me. 'You tell Jaxon I've got a stash and I'll kill you.'

I meet Fin up at the main building. 'So?' he asks me. 'How'd you go?'

'Okay.'

'You don't sound overly confident.'

'Tom doesn't dish out compliments. He told me to do my job and not ask any questions.'

'Ah. I know which one you'd struggle with.'

I punch him on the arm.

'Careful, I've been learning self-defence. You can't beat me up anymore.'

'Ha. What did you do today?'

'Worked on my shooting skills. I even hit some things.'

'Things you were supposed to hit?'

'Yep. If it were at a fair I could have won you a big teddy bear.'

'Wow. If only.' Keep it light, Lucy, keep it light.

'They've rostered me on bush patrols and clearing traps for now,' he says.

'They're trapping people out there? How big are the cages?'

'Rabbits. The traps are for rabbits.'

'Right. Well that's a relief, but less impressive. You'll have to find more ways to charm me.'

'I'd give you flowers but strangely there aren't any around.'

'Drats. Have you been all around the camp?'

'Yeah, the only part I haven't seen is that really bushy section on the inside of the fence. There's always someone guarding around there.'

'Maybe it's something to do with the water. It could be

a bore. Are you on the welcoming committee at the front gates?'

'No. And I'm kind of glad about that.'

Jaxon comes around the corner and interrupts us. 'Follow me, you need to learn something. You can come too, Lucy.'

Behind the building the kangaroo lies on the ground beside a big gum tree. Tom grabs the roo by the shoulders as Jaxon takes the rear legs and hoists it up, hooking its thigh onto a metal hook that hangs from the tree. Jaxon calls it a gambrel – a blunt, violent sounding word.

He looks pointedly at me. 'This isn't going to be pretty.'

'I've seen a lot of things that aren't pretty lately. I'll be fine. Thanks for your concern.'

He smiles like a TV chef and takes a large knife from a sheath on his belt. 'Goodo. So, you want to peel the hide off in one piece. You take the blade and slice along the curve of the hams, like this.' The rear legs aren't legs anymore, they're hams. An arbitrary label informed by whether a body – not a body, a carcass – is going to be eaten or not. Whether its final destination will be a grave or a plate.

I watch, determined to keep my expression passive. At first it isn't so bad, until Jaxon slips the blade sideways under the skin.

'When you've got enough to grip, roll the hair side under itself and start pulling. Use force – it's not going to tear.'

The skin underneath is pink and glistening, like polished marble. I saw this creature alive just hours ago – nibbling grass, feeling safe – and here it is with its skin being peeled off. I fight the urge to look away and I will the colour not to drain from my face. I won't be the queasy girl again. Beside me, Fin also looks like he is trying not to pass out. I'm envious of him. Yes, he's a guy and the pressure on him to act tough is high, but in this he's not the representative of his entire sex – the only thing he's risking is his ego. He might cop a joke at his expense, or a snigger at worst. Me? If I faint, especially after the vomiting incident, it will reinforce the almost universal belief that girls are weak and best left to cleaning up after big strong men who do the real work.

'Right,' Jaxon continues. 'You want to skin all the way to the throat. You can leave a cape of hide around the neck if you want to keep the head to mount on your wall, otherwise you're going to saw the head off.' Jaxon wipes his knife with a cloth and returns it to his belt. Then he picks up a saw.

I breathe.

'Lucy, you'll probably just be doing rabbits, but the principle's the same. Any questions?'

'Do you need to keep the meat cold?' Fin asks.

'Yeah. So we'll wash it with cold water, dry it then leave it out here. It'll keep all right. Whatever we don't eat tonight we'll salt or smoke.'

Fin and I have remained conscious. We have passed this test.

I go to the shower block – with Rob as my guard – so I can wash off the dirt and the blood. My jacket will need a wash too otherwise the blood will start to stink. Afterwards, Fin and I go to the rec hall and sit on the floor with Max. Fin begins shuffling the cards one-handed.

'How did I not know of *this* skill?' I ask. 'Shooting, doing push-ups, and now this fancy stuff – be still my beating heart.'

Fin glances at me. Sky-blue eyes. For a second I am back in history class sitting beside him. But he doesn't smile at my joke this time.

'Alan taught me,' Fin says. He tries to lighten the moment with a wink. 'I've been saving it for when I've run out of ways to impress you.'

'Consider me impressed. Until I beat you, that is.'

Max's eyes are fixed on the cards in Fin's hand. He is terribly thin but the fact that he is engaged in anything at all is an improvement.

'Hey, Max,' I say.

'Hey.'

'How was your day?'

I expect him to roll his eyes but instead I get the hint of a smile. 'Jaxon showed me the dogs. There's a guard dog called Seamus; he's a really good sniffer dog too. I'm teaching him to bark on command. He really likes me.'

'That's someone at least. Keep working on the people.'

Fin deals the cards then nods to the piano. 'Hey, you should play something. Your performance in the shopping centre was excellent. This will be a sellout.'

I remember how nervous I felt when I imagined my audition for a place at the Sydney Conservatorium. I'd pictured it from the age of ten, and had even planned my outfit. A dated ski jacket and ill-fitting jeans probably wouldn't make the cut. Not that it matters.

I've missed my audition date – something came up. I'd planned to move to Sydney if I was offered a place. It wasn't a decision so much as the knowledge that that's what I would do – I would move out and be independent. And, hidden beneath all of that, I would leave Bit and her suffering behind.

The guilt stabs me through.

'Lucy?'

'No. Not now.'

'Just one song? These people are deprived – they believe Jaxon is a musician. Have pity on them.'

If I could just get up and play a song on the piano, the moment of light between Fin and I would stretch. But I can't even look at the piano. It's a particle of my life that lingers like the dust particles that weigh down the sky.

'I don't want to.'

'Are you okay?'

'I just don't feel like it, Fin.'

He opens his mouth to respond but Jaxon comes over and crouches down next to Max.

'How's it goin'?'

'Okay.'

'You ate breakfast?'

'Yeah,' says Max. 'It was gross but I ate it.'

'You joking? Three months of chicken instant noodles and our breakfast isn't good enough for you?'

'I have standards.'

'Standards for being annoying,' laughs Fin.

I glance at Fin. This is more than Max has said to either of us.

'You can make it yourself then,' says Jaxon. 'Start tonight. See how you go cutting up potatoes for forty people.'

'Maybe I will.'

Jaxon laughs. 'I don't trust you with the potatoes. You reckon you could come out tomorrow, help me and Fin get firewood? You reckon he could do that, Fin?'

'Yep. He's pretty handy with an axe, aren't ya, Max?'

'Oh yeah?' asks Jaxon.

'There was this cop that came to our house and tried to take our food,' Max says. 'He was totally going to shoot Fin—'

'He was going to hit me. He didn't have a gun, Max.'

'He was going to attack Fin with his club—'

'It was a baton, Max.'

'With his baton, and I got the axe and totally threatened

to cut his head off if he didn't let Fin go.'

Fin beams with pride – the broadest smile I've seen from him since the missiles. I can see the dimple in his left cheek. The sight of it makes my chest ache and I want to kiss him.

'For real? Maybe I shouldn't give you an axe after all,' Jaxon says. 'You might stage a revolt.'

'And you know Lucy hit a guy with a cricket bat?' Max says. 'Probably killed him.'

Jaxon looks at me and laughs. It's an odd response. I try to sort my hand of cards but I can't focus on them.

'How do you know we've been eating chicken instant noodles?' I ask Jaxon.

His smile falters for just a moment.

'You said you wouldn't search the car.'

He holds his hands up in defence. 'I saw a packet through the window. Have mercy, your honour.'

I know we made sure all our food was well hidden when we set off from Sydney. We would have been an easy target if it was visible. Fin knows it too but his face gives nothing away.

TWENTY-ONE

Two days pass before my next ride out. Fin has target practice and also learns how to effectively perform a headlock. My focus is folding laundry (a community of forty people produces quite a lot of washing) and preparing meals. I learn how to make damper, I cut bits of rabbit into tiny chunks for stew, and I wash mushrooms in a bucket of water Susan gives me. The highlight of my day is caring for the horses, despite being treated to Rob's less-than-glittering company – he stands outside the stables holding his rifle and staring at the bush, perhaps reminiscing about his former life as a used-car salesman or accounts manager. He pays me so little attention that I wonder if he has forgotten I'm there.

By the time Tom comes to get Esther and me for another ride out I'm desperate for an escape from the compound. Once we are well away from camp Tom tells us to halt and asks Esther to dismount. They both give me their reins and walk a little further down the track. Tom hands Esther a pair of earmuffs and the rifle. He points to a spot among the trees.

'I want you to hit that *X* carved into the tree trunk.

Like we talked about: lean on this tree to steady yourself, line up the sight, take a deep breath, exhale and squeeze the trigger. A squeeze, not a pull. No need to rush.'

Esther does what he says and shoots. I don't know how long Tom has been teaching her, but she's very accurate. She does it again and again, hitting her mark every time.

'Good. Grab the shells and we'll get going,' Tom says to her.

'Oi!' She grins. 'I'm doing the shooting, that means you have to get the shells!'

'Is that how this works? Gawd help me.' Tom shakes his head and collects the shells.

When he returns to his horses he gives me a stern look. 'This stays between us, right? Not a word to anyone.'

'Right. You don't have liquorice and you don't let Esther use a gun.'

He watches me for a moment and I catch just the slightest twitch in the corner of his mouth.

For the first kill Tom shoots and Esther helps him load the carcass onto Red while I'm on lookout. But when Tom shoots our second kangaroo he looks up at me and jerks his head to the side, signalling for me to dismount. Once I'm closer to the roo I can see where the bullet hit it in the shoulder. The animal's chest is rising and falling with each desperate breath and its long legs are thrashing.

Tom holds out a rock.

'You need to be able to do this and you need to do it

quick.' His tone is soft and kind, like when he talks to Red. 'Get as close as you can and throw it as hard as you can.'

I look to Esther for reassurance, but she looks away. I take the rock from Tom.

We've been here just over three weeks and our month's deadline is looming.

The cricket bat cracks into Starvos's bald head like a spoon into an eggshell. Blood that I never saw in reality pours from the hole. I shake my head, drop the rock in the grass and walk away.

'Lucy.'

I can't turn back and face them. The trees in the distance blur with the stupid tears welling in my eyes. Stupid weak tiny girl. I can kill a man like some psycho but not a wounded, hurting animal.

'Lucy.'

'You do it! It's in pain. Do it!'

'You have to do it.'

I turn around. 'I'm not doing it!' I've never heard my voice sound quite like this; I didn't know it could be so loud. 'You shot it! You fucking kill it! Kick me out of the camp – I don't give a shit!' I do give a shit – of course I do. I keep walking, with no plan for where I'll go.

Tom grabs my upper arm and I spin around again. The punch I throw gets him in the jaw but I'm guessing it's more the shock of it than the force that makes him take a step backwards.

'Don't touch me! Don't fucking touch me!' My throat burns from screaming. The three horses prick their ears and watch for the next move.

Tom raises both palms in surrender. 'I'm not going to hurt you, Lucy. I just don't want you wandering off. Come on, let's get on the horses and we'll go back to camp.'

'You need to kill it. It's in pain. It's scared.'

'I've already done it, Lucy. It's done. Come on, mate.'

Suddenly I'm so tired I just want to sit down and curl in a ball.

When Esther leads Jack Frost over to me there is a soft understanding in her eyes. I get on the horse and wait while Tom and Esther load the kangaroo behind Cloudy's saddle. The ride back to the compound is slow and quiet.

TWENTY-TWO

In the late afternoon I'm on laundry duty again in one of the cabins, but this time Fin is my rostered guard, looking out for people who might want to nick our doona covers. It's his first time with his newly allocated gun, which he holds with both hands in the same way the border guards used to hold theirs in Sydney. The mattresses have been removed from the bunks in the cabin and taken to the rec hall, so the frames serve as shelving for neat piles of bedding and towels. I take my time folding pillowcases into neat squares with sharp corners – it's almost as mindful as the house of cards.

'Raahel says Max has put on nearly two kilos.' Fin leans back against the doorframe. He seems relaxed, looser, but he watches the trees while he talks to me.

'Hmm.'

'He loves being with the dogs. He's got one that follows him all over the place.'

'Seamus? I met him. He's nearly bigger than Max is.' This isn't true. I say it because it's the kind of thing people normally say and I wonder if Fin will catch me out for faking.

He just laughs.

'You have a gun, Max gets an attack dog and I'm given a pile of pillowcases.'

'You get a horse!'

'Yeah, so I can go out and be bossed around by a man who also has a gun. Actually, you know Tom was teaching Esther to shoot today. He told me not to tell anyone. Seems it's against the rules to give a girl a gun around here.'

'He was?'

'Yep.' I place the pillowcase on the stack.

'I think it's a good sign I've been given a weapon. Jaxon wouldn't do that if he thought I'd stage a mutiny—'

'Don't you have to be on a ship to stage a mutiny?'

'Yeah. A coup?'

'Or treason – it feels like Jaxon wears the crown here.'

'Ha. Maybe. My point is, I don't think we're going to be kicked out.'

I make a really nice corner in my fold. One of my best.

Fin looks at me over his shoulder. 'I know that face, what's wrong?'

'Nothing.'

'Did something happen?'

'Sometimes you go down to clear the traps near the creek, don't you?'

'Yeah. Why?'

'What do you do when you collect the rabbits from

the traps? They're still alive, aren't they? How do you kill them?'

Fin stands up. He's not supposed to take his attention from the lookout but he turns to face me. 'Why?'

'How do you kill them?'

'We … um … we have to break their necks. It's quick – it doesn't hurt them. They die straightaway.'

'You think I'm asking if it hurts?'

'Aren't you?'

Another pillowcase on the pile. I get the next one from the basket.

'I've screwed it up. I was supposed to smash a kangaroo in the head with a rock and I couldn't do it.'

Fin takes a moment too long to reply. 'It's okay.'

'It's not okay.'

He comes closer and takes my hand to pull me into his arms. He has such lovely hands. I don't let him. 'I don't think they're going to kick you out over one thing, Luce.'

'Mr Effrez should be here by now, don't you think? It would be better if he would just show up.'

'I know, but we have to make it work until he gets here. Was Tom angry with you?'

I shake my head.

'Then there's probably nothing to worry about.'

'Not for you. You're useful – you can do all sorts of things. You can protect the camp with your gun, you can kill things, cut wood, go out on your own. What can I do? I didn't have a choice with that jump and I didn't have a choice today. I'm a small girl and I think they already have enough housekeepers. The only valuable skill I bring is the ability to ride a horse, but I was useless out there today because I couldn't kill a kangaroo that was in pain.'

'Lucy.'

'What? You haven't thought about that? It's not "if one stays we all stay"; you and I aren't a package deal. I have to wait and see if a couple of men will allow me outside. You'll be fine.'

'I'm hardly going to stay here if they want to kick you out. That's why I didn't stay with my mum.'

'Really? You'd leave and take Max back out there?' I point to the shadowy trees beyond the boundary fence.

'I wouldn't let you go out there on your own.'

It's like he's stepped on a landmine.

'You wouldn't *let* me?'

'I don't mean it like that. You know what I mean. I'm not going to just sit back if Jaxon and Tom decide you can't stay.'

'Do you know how that makes me feel though? It totally, completely sucks because I'm helpless. We're in the frigging Stone Age again. You've got no idea. You think you do, but you don't and you can't. How many conversations do you have in a day with other guys knowing, deep down in the back of your mind, that they could kill you if they wanted? Look at you! You're twice the size of me; how come you get the gun? Any guy could kill me out there and any guy could kill me in here!'

All I can see is Declan Flemming smiling at my sister as he holds the door to his father's Mercedes open while she gets in.

'Women are in danger around *all* men. You can do whatever you want—'

'You think you're in danger around me? How could you think I would ever do anything to hurt you?'

'I'm not talking about *would*. I'm talking about *could*. You have the physical means to overpower someone, even to protect yourself. I don't have that. Just imagine for a moment what that's like.'

'Lucy, I—'

'You want me to be safe, I know. Safe from what? From the women out there lurking in the bush? No, from the men. The men keep the women safe from the men. I'm sorry if I'm coming across a little unhinged, but I'm kind of over being in this situation.'

He's turned pale. Shocked at my outburst. He's one of the good ones and he can't comprehend how he could ever not be. He's hurt and it's like I've shut him out without realising that's what I was doing. I want to tell him I'm so scared I killed a man and I can't get the sound out of my head. That I'm furious because I was too small and useless to stop Starvos any other way. That now I have nothing to defend myself with out in the bush and when I did have a job to do I couldn't do it. And I'm terrified that if I'm in that position again – if I have to kill something or someone so I can survive – I won't be able to do it.

I turn from him and resume folding the pillowcases. He steps outside the door and waits – eyes on the trees, watching for threats.

TWENTY-THREE

The next two days are: laundry, meal prep, ride out with Tom and Esther, close my eyes when Tom smashes the kangaroos' heads, sit with Raahel at lunch and dinner, go to bed early and pretend to be asleep when Fin comes in.

When the Friday of our fourth week comes around, Tom and Jaxon announce that there will be a special dinner outside. Raahel says they hold dinners like this every now and then to help boost morale. Once the meal prep is finished and the campfire is lit outside, people gather in clusters, chatting and laughing over mugs of something Fin, Max and I aren't offered.

Jaxon brings out his guitar and the usual applause follows. He sits down on a tree trunk and sings:

Did you ever meet Max?
He was white like wax
And fell down stacks
But now he can eat
Big chunks of meat
And he can cheat
at caaaaards

I wonder when he gets a chance to write this stuff. The next one's for Esther and instead of humour Jaxon goes in for a slow ballad about how deep his love for her is. Apparently it is fast like a river and soars like a flower – not the most logical imagery. I make the mistake of laughing before I realise no-one else is and the song is supposedly heartfelt.

He's watching her while he sings, and she stands on the other side of the fire, hugging herself and looking at her feet. Something about her is off-centre, something in her posture. It looks like shame. I recognise it.

Later, when I go inside to get my gloves, I hear Jaxon's voice coming from the kitchen. I walk a little closer down the corridor and listen.

'I've been so patient with this crap, Esther. It's like you don't give a shit about anyone else.'

'I'm worried about him.'

'Yeah, yeah. You've said it a thousand times and it's doing my head in. You know you can't go out there – you'd put yourself, and everyone else, in danger. Stop being selfish and think of what's best for the camp, for us.'

'I do.'

'Don't you care about the extra stress this puts on me, trying to keep you safe and happy all the time?'

There's a pause.

'Can't you even apologise for the shit this puts me through? I love you so much and you do this over and over.'

'I'm sorry.'

'It's okay. I forgive you. But I don't want to hear this crap from you anymore.'

I get my gloves and go back out to the fire. Across from me Fin is sitting with Max and Seamus. Max is talking. His eyes are bright and he's moving his hands around a lot. Fin looks happy and relaxed. He says something and Max howls with laughter. Fin pulls him into a headlock and messes his hair up until Seamus barks and Fin lets him go. The talk around me drifts to the weather and the temperature: the ground is thawing. The sun hasn't exactly shone yet, but it's warm enough for us to shed a few layers of clothing. A temperature increase is excellent news for planting and there is talk of sowing potatoes.

Jaxon walks over to me. 'Max did good today,' he says, warming his hands on his mug. 'I took him out into the bush with Seamus to look for dead trees. He was tired by the time we got back, but he lasted ages out there. Looks like he's put on a bit of weight.'

'Hmm.'

I peer over into his mug. 'What's in that?'

He gives a sly grin and doesn't answer.

'You got a brewery here?' I do my best to be friendly and conversational.

'I wish.'

'What is it? Moonshine?'

'You're not getting any.'

'I can smell it. I don't want any.'

He laughs. 'Max is a funny kid,' Jaxon says after a while.

'Not as funny as he used to be.'

'He told me a bit about Noll and Matt.'

I don't like hearing Jaxon say their names. It's like he's taking something that isn't his.

'No wonder you guys are grieving.' He pauses. 'I regret what we did when you three arrived. I get so focused on my job here I forget …' He trails off.

'Forget what?'

'That most people aren't always on the lookout for danger, that not everyone is a threat. It's been my job for a long time.'

'You mean since before the winter? Were you in the army or something before this?'

'I discharged – Iraq does that to you.'

I remember Matt's nightmares when we were in the car park. He would scream in his sleep – if he slept at all. He told us it was the decisions he'd had to make as a soldier that got to him the most. Who would have ever predicted he'd experience such things in his own country.

'When were you there?'

'2007, 2008, 2010.'

'That's a lot.'

'It is. I've seen what happens when people are trying to survive. I know we're not in a good position. I knew from the start.'

'You mean after the blasts?'

'Yep. You could see how it would unfold. A war over resources was inevitable.'

'And you're certain that's what's happening – internationally, I mean.'

'It was commonly accepted in the defence force that conflict would break out over resources. Iraq was never about weapons. You can't even bet on the whole of Australia sticking together when it comes to resource policies.'

'You mean we could have a civil war?'

'Maybe.'

'Is that why you came here?'

'Yeah, I heard about this place and I thought helping here might be a way of actually helping, of making a real difference. That's what sucked in Iraq – I never felt I was making a difference. It was lucky I turned up when I did. This place was failing – there was no organisation, no strategy. A lack of leadership is a dangerous thing.' He looks away. 'I'll die before I let anything happen to the people here.'

'But things are a bit different now, aren't they? Everyone understands how to keep things working safely. Isn't it a good idea to spread the leadership out a bit, to have more of a democratic system? It would take some of the pressure off you.'

Jaxon's whole posture changes, and he seems to grow in height. I get a glimpse of Tom standing only metres away; he would be able to hear our conversation.

Jaxon takes his gaze from the fire – his expression is cold and it's only an inch but he moves closer to me. 'Don't talk to me about democracy. You topple the leader, you get chaos. Is that what you want?'

'I'm not talking about toppling anyone, I just mean—'

'I'm gonna cut you some slack 'cause you don't understand how things really work in the world. You'll learn in time that this is the best way. I only want what's best for everyone. I want peace. Can't argue with that.'

Tom comes over and clears his throat. 'I think it's time to let them know, don't you?'

Jaxon keeps his eyes on me for a moment, then looks at Tom with a smile. 'Sure thing.' He drains what is left from his mug, puts two fingers in his mouth and makes a loud whistle. The chatter quietens.

'Hey, everyone.' His charming smile broadens. 'Just an announcement – if you've grown attached to this girl here' – he points to me – 'or Max and Fin, you'll be happy to hear they'll be staying with us.' He puts his arm around my shoulders and pulls me in close.

Everyone is watching. I keep the smile on my face.

TWENTY-FOUR

On Saturday afternoon everyone gathers down at the clearing near the horse jumps for a game of soccer. I'm crappy at team sports but I join in anyway – it's good to move for the purpose of fun rather than survival.

Esther is not in it for fun. She's serious and determined to win, barking instructions at her teammates (one of which I am not, thankfully) and it reminds me of when my class would hear Mr Effrez's voice booming through the wall from his room next door. The only person who gets a smile from her is Jaxon. Afterwards, when everyone else is walking back up to the main building, she stays behind and stretches. Jaxon sits on a log nearby and watches her as she takes a tyre from the side of the clearing and starts lifting, pushing and turning it over like I used to see fitness groups doing in the park on a Saturday morning. I stop by the side of the building and watch as she moves on to squats with a kettlebell.

Esther arrives at dinner freshly showered, her thick hair pulled up in a high knot.

I take a seat next to her. 'Hey, I'm just wondering ...'

She raises an eyebrow, again just like her dad.

'Did you say anything to Jaxon about the kangaroo and how I lost my cool?'

'By which you mean hit Tom.'

'And hit Tom. Precisely. Or not so precisely as it were.'

'Why would I mention anything about the kangaroo?'

'I'm not daft, as if it wasn't some kind of test.'

'You think we would like you better if you could bash an animal's head in without hesitation?'

'Perhaps not so much like as value.'

Esther puts her fork down and lowers her voice. 'I didn't say anything to Jaxon.'

'Thank you.'

'Do you wish you had done it?'

'I don't like that it suffered longer because I couldn't.'

'There's a big difference between wouldn't and couldn't.'

Esther has finished her stew now but she doesn't get up to walk away. Perhaps she wants to be friends, enjoy a little female camaraderie.

'You should have brought my dad with you.'

Perhaps not.

'I don't get how you could drive away and leave him behind in that … horror – if what you say about Sydney is true. I mean, if it was so dangerous why didn't you convince him to come with you? Does he even have enough petrol to drive down here on his own?'

'He was waiting for you.'

'But that's stupid. He would know that if I was ever going to make it to him I would have got there by now.'

'He had no idea you were going to be here. It's a horrible thing to let go … to stop hoping.' The fluorescent light in my head flickers. I have to press the lids down on the boxes. 'We tried to get him to come, Esther, but it was his decision to stay behind. He was waiting for you.'

'You should have made him come with you.'

'Ha! *Made him?* I don't think anyone could make your dad do anything.'

Esther looks away.

'Why don't you go to him? You have a horse, so you don't need fuel.'

As I say the words I realise I'm not just telling Esther she should find her family, I'm telling myself. I've found safety – that's what I left them behind for. I've found it and I'm here eating and sleeping in the warmth while my parents and Bit – if they're still alive – are starving.

'I can't.'

'Why?'

'It's not safe.'

'Esther, you'd be on horseback and you can take a big frigging gun. I know Jaxon goes on about scary people out there, but most of them don't have guns. Certainly not the fancy-arse weapons you guys have here. Besides, you were part of the welcoming committee who met us out front when we arrived. I don't get why he would allow that and not let you go out with a horse and a gun to find your dad. Doesn't he want to know what's going on in Sydney anyway? That would be useful for the camp.'

'Firstly, I'm not part of the patrol groups anymore and I don't go to the gates. He's taken me off that roster because he worries about me. Secondly, two people died from here. Before Jaxon came. They were beautiful, kind people. It was awful. Tom was the one who found them and he hasn't been the same since.'

'Sure, not a great sign, but how long ago was that? And were they walking or on horseback?'

'Walking. And it wasn't long after the winter started.'

'Things might be different now. And like I said, you can move faster on a horse.'

'Who are you trying to convince here, Lucy? Me or yourself?' Esther flinches suddenly.

Jaxon has appeared behind us and puts a hand on her shoulder. 'You two look intense. What you talking about?'

Esther shifts in her seat. 'Nothing. It's not important.'

'Esther should go to Sydney and get her dad,' I say.

Jaxon folds his arms. 'That's what you think, is it?' He laughs. 'I wasn't aware you're the one around here who makes the decisions.'

'It's not my decision. It's not anyone's except Esther's. If she wants to go she should.'

'Riiiight. And what happens when someone grabs her and takes her hostage? When they demand stuff from here? Or worse.' Jaxon walks around the table and sits down opposite us. He slumps back in the chair and crosses his ankles, reminding me of the way boys at school would try to prove their superiority over substitute teachers – usually female. He places his hand on Esther's.

'We just talked about that. First of all, she can ride. Horses are quick – if she runs into any trouble she can just take off. Also, you have quite a few weapons here, Jaxon. Everyone patrolling the border has one. You said she can handle herself. You could even send a team of people. I'd be happy to go.'

Jaxon leans forward. 'One thing I know for certain is that you don't understand the full situation.' He jabs a finger at me. 'Don't even think of putting Esther's life on the line so you can try to prove how clever you are.'

'I'm not proving anything.' I feel sick in the stomach with him looking at me like this, like I'm tiny and insignificant, but it only makes me keep going. 'And Esther's right here, you don't have to talk about her as if she isn't,' I say.

Jaxon stands up. 'We're done. I hope you're making yourself useful out there with Tom, because that's the only reason we're letting you stay. To be useful. This' – he draws a little circle in the air with his finger, putting Esther and me in one loop – 'isn't useful. This is a waste of time. If you care at all about Esther you'll stop messing with her about this—'

'I'm not messing with her, I'm—'

'Can't you see what you're doing to her? She's really upset. She's grieving her dad. Esther, I think you should go clear your head, babe. It's okay. Everything's gonna be okay.'

Esther picks up her bowl and I watch her walk away.

Jaxon glowers at me. 'I'm watching you. Don't forget it.'

TWENTY-FIVE

Around midday on Monday, when I'm done shovelling horse poo, I push the wheelbarrow out the stable door and onto the path that leads to the compost. And then I see it: my shadow. I stop walking and stare. It isn't sharp – it is dull and undefined – but it is there. When I look up at the sky, I have to shield my eyes from the glare; the sun is swathed in haze yet it shines through. I drop the wheelbarrow and run.

Outside the rec hall two people who had been chopping wood have stopped their work and are also staring at the sky.

'The sun!' I yell.

I run into the rec hall to find Fin, but he isn't there. Raahel and Susan are mending clothes.

'Have you seen it?!'

They look up from their work, puzzled.

'The sun! The sun's out.'

Raahel widens her eyes and Susan starts clapping.

'Come see.'

By the time we get back outside people are gathering and looking at the sky. They are laughing and hugging each other. I savour the sunlight and the precious moment of hope and relief and joy it brings. Fin and Max join the group and Fin wraps his arms around me and kisses the top of my head.

'Things will change,' he whispers. 'Things will get better now.'

The ground has been prepared ever since it stopped snowing, but now the intensity of work increases. It will only be a matter of days until there is enough warmth from the sun to grow seedlings for crops, and with the current winds the science guys predict that it won't be long until it shines unfiltered. I'm put on the gardening roster with Raahel, and the following day she and I are in the greenhouse together potting seeds.

'How are you doing?' she asks.

'It's good the sun's out. And I'm glad we can stay, obviously.'

'I've been wondering what it must be like for you here, on your own. I have my children. Fin has his brother.'

I can't think of what to say to her.

'I'm sorry, I don't mean to pry.'

'No, it's fine. I try not to think about my family.'

Raahel nods and gently brushes loose soil from a seed punnet.

'It was a quick decision to leave them. My mum really thought I'd be safer in Sydney.'

Safer. Just like Noll thought he'd be safer in Sydney. Maybe the picture of Noll's death in my head is worse than the reality. But how could that be? I need to know if it was quick. He'd already been through too much pain. He loved God. What kind of God would let that happen? I don't say any of these things, I just push the black soil over the little white seed.

'Fin ended up leaving his mum anyway,' I say. 'She wouldn't help us all so …' I shrug.

'Fin wouldn't leave you behind?'

'No.'

I expect her to say how wonderful he is. What a great boyfriend.

'That must put a lot of pressure on you. And your relationship. You're still very young – that's a lot.'

It's more than a lot – it's too, too much and I feel the crush around my lungs when I try to take a breath. I turn away from her and pick up another little punnet.

'We went on one date. One. That's all. But he's so wonderful.' My voice wobbles and I try to breathe through it. 'He's told me he loves me.'

'Do you love him?'

'Maybe if all this had never happened, if we were just a guy and a girl in high school, maybe then I could let myself … do that. I try not to.'

'I can understand that. Loving someone is a risky thing to do. It makes you vulnerable and I'm sure you already feel vulnerable enough.'

'I thought about him so much after the missiles, when the winter started. I wanted to go and look for him, but I didn't know where he lived. You know he was robbing the local supermarket when I found him again? I went over there because I saw someone being attacked. I didn't know it was him and Max. The supermarket owner, Mr Starvos, was kicking him over and over. He stopped and put a gun to Fin's head, so I hit Mr Starvos on the back of the head with a cricket bat. I didn't even think about it. Or I suppose I did think about it; I thought I should use as much force as I could.'

I give up on the seed punnets and sit on an upturned milk crate.

'What if I killed him, Raahel?'

'I don't think you set out to kill anyone, did you? Lucy, you're a child.'

'I'm nearly eighteen. I don't think that makes much difference.'

I want to ask her about Declan Flemming and what she thinks of me wanting to hurt him. But what if she thinks I'm a raging violent sociopath?

'It's okay to feel upset about what's happened to you,' Raahel says.

'I made jokes about hitting Mr Starvos.'

'I don't think you would have joked about it to be funny. That's a typical strategy for dealing with trauma.'

'Maybe.' I stand and brush the soil from my clothes. Fine black particles, like soot, are stuck under my fingernails. It takes five minutes of scrubbing in the bucket of freezing water to get them out and I remember Mr Effrez yelling Lady Macbeth's lines. *Out, damned spot. Out.*

But it can't be done. I have Starvos's blood on me and it will be there forever.

TWENTY-SIX

In the weeks after the sun comes out the atmosphere in the camp lifts. I had thought that morale was already good, definitely in comparison to the car-park days, but now people smile and laugh more readily. Our world is thawing. The meticulously sown wheat, which Tom, Esther and I monitor, is pushing through the soil. We had to use some of the precious fuel to drive out to the crop fields. Now the fields have rows of ordered stalks. It will be a substantial harvest if the sun continues to shine. We see more and more kangaroos when we ride out on hunts. Spring has arrived.

But Mr Effrez hasn't.

I have seen Esther talking to Jaxon from time to time, and each time she looks more agitated, but I haven't heard of a plan to go and get her dad.

One morning I ask Fin to be my guard while I go to the cabin where all the clothes and shoes are kept. He stands at the door as I sort through a large crate of sneakers in varying sizes and states of disrepair.

'Wardrobe update? But I like those flared jeans. And your jacket's really grown on me,' Fin says.

'I'm going to train with Esther. I've always wanted to be a body builder and now I finally have the time.' I find one shoe that looks in good condition and set about searching for its mate.

'Yeah, not convinced. What are you really doing?' His tone shifts to poorly concealed concern.

I spot the second shoe and then begin looking through the crates of clothing for something resembling activewear. A Spider-Man T-shirt and a pair of red tracksuit pants are the best I can find – no stretch pants here. I'll look like I'm dressed for a book-week parade.

'Esther's got way more freedom than I do because she's strong.'

I commence a fantastical search for a sports bra but soon give up. Maybe I can rig something up with gaffer tape. For the first time in my life I'm thankful for my small boobs.

'Jaxon's been keeping her closer lately. I haven't seen her out much – she hasn't been clearing traps or anything,' says Fin. 'And when are you going to work out? You need to have someone else down there with you.'

I ignore him and pull my jacket off so I can try on the T-shirt.

'I've always thought of you more like Batgirl,' Fin says with a smile. Dimples. Blue eyes. He's always been so gentle and tentative but now he steps forward, takes my face in his hands and kisses me hard. I'm kind of stunned by his urgency. His hands move under my T-shirt.

'Guess what I spotted,' he whispers, pointing to a mattress under two crates of clothing. 'Behold, fairy maiden, for I, Sir Chopping-Wood-a-Lot have—'

'Fairy maiden?'

'Yeah?'

'It's fair maiden.'

'Fair maiden?'

'Yup.'

'I like fairy maiden better.'

'Then find another girl.'

He laughs and kisses my neck. I pull away and press my palms flat on his chest. He leans in again but I shake my head.

'We can go back to Batgirl if you want. Or Spider Man is fine too. I mean, it's confusing on a number of levels but I'm willing to try anything,' he says.

I pick my coat up and pull it on.

His dimples disappear. 'We've got ages, Lucy. No-one cares where we are right now.' He takes my hand and laces his long fingers through mine. 'I miss you,' he says. 'You're right here but I miss you.'

Say something, Lucy. Anything.

'What's going on? I know something's wrong.'

I pick up the clothes and shoes I've found.

'Can you talk to me?' Fin asks. 'Have I done something?'

'You haven't done anything.' I can't look at him. Does this make me a bitch? It's such a horrible little word. Like a sharp spit.

'Wait. You can't walk back on your own.'

'Oh, I forgot I need a man to protect me.' Bitch. Bitch. Bitch.

'Can you please talk to me?'

'It's not you, Fin.'

'Whoa. Nice line. Classic.'

I turn around and look him right in the face. 'I don't want to have sex. Are you okay with that? Or is that all you want from me?'

He's wounded. It's as if I've punched him in the stomach.

'No. It's not. I'm sorry.'

'You want to know why I'm going to get fit? Because I'm going to go and find my family. I'll ride home. It won't take long to make it to the mountains.'

'On your own?'

'You're welcome to come along. We'll make a day of it.'

'Luce, no.' His tone is more scared than worried. 'It's less than a month since we've been given permission to stay. No-one's going to let you take a horse and a gun.'

'Mr Effrez hasn't come, and Jaxon won't let Esther go and find him. Don't you think that's weird?'

'No. I think it's smart.'

'Fin, I'm sorry but your mother and brother are alive and well. You have that. Esther has no-one. I have no-one, and I don't know what has happened to the people I love most in the world. I have an opportunity to find out.'

'You have me.'

I can't tell him that's not enough.

'I don't think … It's been a long time. It's unlikely they're still alive.'

I put his words in a little box and hide it in the back of the white room along with the image of my sister's hollow cheeks.

'Please, Lucy. I don't want to wake up one day and find you've gone. Lucy, look at me.'

I can't. If I look at him I'll see the gentle love in his eyes and I'll lose my nerve. 'I've found what I need. We should get back.'

I leave the cabin, pulling my coat tight around me against the chill.

We don't say much to each other for the rest of the day. It's not like we are angry – it's just that now there is a distance between us that has never been there before. After dinner he pulls his chair close to me. His knee touches mine, just like it would on the school bus when we were 'just friends' and the heat of electricity would thud in my chest the whole way to school.

'Are we okay?' he asks.

I don't know how to answer.

'I don't want anything bad to happen to you, Lucy. It would kill me. Maybe that makes me selfish and if it does I'm sorry.'

It will hurt to look at him, so I just nod.

*

Later we sit in our usual spot by the fire and I look at the pages of a novel without reading them. Fin draws and Max finds a nature encyclopaedia.

'The fingerprints of a koala are so similar to humans' that they have sometimes been confused at a crime scene,' Max reads aloud. 'Maybe archaeologists will find this place in a thousand years and think it was built by koalas.'

'Ha.' Fin doesn't even look up from his drawing.

All I can manage is a smile.

TWENTY-SEVEN

The next day I walk down to the field where Esther has set up a training circuit. She frowns when she sees me, eyeing my dodgy workout ensemble.

'What are you doing?' she asks.

'Can I join in?'

She's clearly not thrilled by the idea.

'I won't get in the way.'

Esther glances up the hill to the main building. Jaxon is leaning against the wall. Supervising. 'Whatever.' She jogs away from me.

I follow her and attempt to copy what she does. I'd like to imagine it as a slick and inspiring montage with an uplifting soundtrack, but in reality I'm a squishy slug compared to Esther. I struggle through the routine, maybe managing half the reps she does. I am doubled over, hands on my knees, trying to get my breath as she sprints past me, doing a final lap of the field.

'Don't overdo it,' she calls out. I'm not sure if she's trying to bait me or is genuinely concerned. When she goes to an old swing set near the trees and starts doing chin-ups, I don't even try.

Jaxon watches us walk back up the hill then disappears inside. Esther follows him with her eyes. I try to copy her stretches, but I can't make my legs do all the things hers can, so I eventually give up and just lean against the wall to prevent myself from collapsing.

'Is Jaxon pissed at you for some reason?' I ask.

'You shouldn't have said anything about me leaving. He's worried about me and he gets angry when he's worried.'

'How angry?'

She shoots me a glare. 'Keep out of it.'

Fin comes outside with two cups of water. He gives one to Esther and she looks at him gratefully like he's a species she's never encountered before. She downs the water and goes inside.

'I think she's warming to you,' he jokes and gives me the other cup. It's a peace offering. He stands beside me with his hands in his pockets and the hood of his jacket pulled over his head. His breath hangs in the air. I can sense that he's nervous.

'How did you do?'

'Unexpectedly well,' I lie.

Silence.

'Luce, I'm sorry I was blunt yesterday. About your family.'

'It's ...'

'You don't have to say it's okay.'

'Okay,' I say.

'Do you mean it's okay? Or okay you don't have to say it's okay?'

'I can't remember.' I finish the cup of water.

'Do … do you want another one? I can get you another one.'

'No, I'll get one.'

'It's fine, I'll go.'

'Fin.'

'What?'

'Stop it.'

'Okay.'

Silence.

'I'm sorry I kissed you,' he says. 'I didn't … I wasn't trying to make you do anything you don't want to.'

'I'm sorry too.'

'You just don't seem to want to be … I don't know. You don't want me near you.'

I close my eyes.

'We don't have to do this – we don't have to be, like, together or anything.' He sniffs. 'I mean, I understand if you don't want to be with me in that way.' His breath catches on his words and he swallows loudly. When we were in Sydney, Fin used to draw the ocean, with us in tiny boats that had sails made of chip packets. I feel like I've slipped inside one of those drawings. Each day rolls over me like a dark wave; I don't float on the top – I have to hold my breath, put my head down and wait for it to pass over me. Now, it's like he's slipping under the water beside me. I reach out, grasp his hand and scrunch my eyes closed. I can feel warm tears rolling down my cheeks.

'Fin, I don't feel safe.'

'You are, Lucy. You are safe.'

But I shake my head. My eyes are still shut tight and the tears haven't stopped. He takes my other hand and clasps them tightly in his.

'Lucy, look at me,' he whispers.

I open my eyes and look into his; the intensity of his gaze is unnerving.

'Try and trust this. I know it's really hard, but just try and trust it.'

'But it doesn't feel right here. I don't feel right around Jaxon.'

'Right how?'

'I don't know. I can't really describe it. I had a conversation with him about Esther going to Sydney and he … it was like he threatened me, like maybe if I didn't shut up about it I wouldn't be able to stay here.'

Fin doesn't respond, but I can tell he's holding something back.

'What? You want to say something – what is it?'

'Lucy, I understand. I get it. I know why you would want to go. But for now, if he's that agitated about it maybe you should just let everything settle. He's kept everyone here safe for a long time. He knows what he's doing.'

'He … Fin I can't explain it. I just don't like the power he has and how he treats Esther. And it's not just Esther and me – he upset Raahel when we first got here. He was angry at her for giving Max treatment or medicine or something.'

'What did he say?'

'I don't know. I didn't hear him. I just know Raahel was upset afterwards. He intimidates women.'

Fin is hearing me. I know he is because I can see the conflict in his face, the deep worry and pressure – it's the same look he had when his mother wouldn't take in Noll, Matt and me.

'Max is getting better and Jaxon's been … he's really good with him,' Fin says. 'I know it's not perfect, but we can't leave. We don't have anywhere else to go.'

He's right.

'No matter what Jaxon has said or done, we are safer here than out there. And I kind of agree with him that it's not safe for anyone to go to Sydney on their own. Or even with someone else. Lucy, please … we've already lost Noll.'

'Because I rolled my ankle and had to go back to the car park.'

'That's not what I'm saying.'

'But you've thought about it, haven't you?'

'No. I haven't … I was glad …'

'What?'

'I was glad you hurt your ankle and had to go back and

it wasn't you who …' He trails off. He looks fragile and almost defeated.

'Who what?'

'Who got killed.' He looks away. 'I was thankful it wasn't you and it wasn't Max. I don't regret leaving the city, or leaving my mum, because I got to stay with you. I know it's not perfect here, but this isn't for the rest of our lives. This is just for now.'

'And after now?'

'I don't know. I just know that we'll need to keep breathing if we're going to get there. I can't do this without you, Lucy. Please.'

His hands are still wrapped around mine. I step closer to him and lean my forehead on his chest. I cling to the boat.

TWENTY-EIGHT

On Saturday morning Jaxon has rostered me on laundry and Fin on wood collection but there's a line through both and Susan has moved us to clearing traps together. As we walk out of the compound gates the sun shines through the trees and I am struck by the pleasure of seeing something so pretty as the flitting shadows of leaves cast on the ground. There has been no space for marvelling at anything beautiful for so long. A soft breeze ruffles the branches and carries the chirp and chatter of birds. There is no sign that anything is amiss except for the fact that Fin is carrying a rifle, has a knife strapped to his belt and we are wearing clothing from a car-boot sale in 1995. I can still see my breath pluming when I speak, but it's not as cold as it has been.

Fin's hair has grown considerably and now it's thick and wavy like it was when I first met him.

He catches me looking at him. 'What?'

'Nothing.'

'Why are you looking at me like that?'

'Because you're hot.'

The tips of his ears redden. He grins but doesn't look at me. I need to feel connected to him.

'Wanna make out?' I ask.

He laughs, but keeps on walking.

'I'm serious.' I want to feel like I did in the weeks before the blasts. Just for a little bit. Just so I can keep going in this place. He stops walking and turns to me. He's pretty keen.

'Just don't mess up my clothes,' I say. 'These are my favourite acid wash boys' jeans.'

He takes my face in his hands and kisses me with crazy-level urgency. He pauses for a moment and pulls off his gloves so he can touch my cheek. 'I love you,' he whispers.

I remember the day on the bus I found the picture he drew of me. What kind of guy does that? How do guys like him even exist in the same universe as Declan fucking Flemming? Shit, shit, shit. Now I'm crying again.

Fin holds my face in his hands and wipes the tears with his thumbs. 'It's okay,' he whispers.

But it's not okay so I kiss him and run my fingers through his thick hair because what the hell else am I supposed to do? I have to find some way of getting back to the place we were before all this. He holds me tightly around my waist and I walk backwards, stopping against a tree trunk.

Fin takes off his coat and I wriggle out of mine. He pauses, breathless. 'Are you okay?'

I nod and pull his face back to mine. He tastes really, really good. We kiss more and I lift my jumper and two

T-shirts up and wriggle my arms out, dropping the clothes to the ground. I'm only in a bra (proper one, not gaffer tape) but I don't feel the cold. It's the most he's ever seen of me.

'Okay,' he says, staring at me. 'Well … Okay.'

'I'm really pale,' I whisper.

'You're really beautiful.' He pulls his top off. I haven't seen much of his body for a long time; there are always so many layers of clothing. It's pretty darn hot. Not hairless, which I've always thought a bit icky, so that's a win. The wood chopping is evident. But we've both got pants and shoes on. How's that going to work? Do we sit down and take our boots off? The ground is going to be cold and this is going to be messy. There's going to be blood because I haven't done it before.

Blood.

All over Bit's skirt.

I stop kissing him. I go cold all over.

Fin stops. 'Lucy?'

I can't move.

'Lucy, what's wrong?' He looks over his shoulder, wondering if I've seen something or someone.

'I can't … I can't do this.'

He steps back, breathless and a little shocked.

'I'm sorry.'

'It's okay.' He runs his hands over his head. 'I just need a minute,' he says and walks a few steps away.

'Sorry.'

'It's okay. You don't need to apologise. It's not really the right setting – I get that. Totally understand.'

I fold my arms across my chest and sink to the ground. I feel like the trees are closing in all around me.

Fin turns back and sees me huddled on the ground. He hurries to pick my clothes up and brings them to me but I can't move to take them off him.

'Lucy,' he whispers. 'I'm sorry – I thought you were into it. I didn't mean. God. I'm sorry.'

'It's okay. I was but …'

There is so much time to tell him about Bit but the words are all stuck inside me, sharp in my throat. Fin puts my jacket over me like a blanket. He picks his clothes up and gets dressed, then he sits next to me on the ground.

'We should probably do the job we're supposed to do,' I say after a while.

The traps are about five metres away from the edge of the creek. They are humane: little cages with a mechanism that shuts when the animal steps in to get whatever tasty morsel has been placed inside to lure it to its demise. Although, this is less about minimising cruelty and more about keeping the meat as fresh as possible. At least the animal gets to eat the food it has traded its life for.

The first trap has a small brown rabbit inside. It quivers in terror as we approach, backing into the rear corner as if it has any hope of escape. Fin sighs and I know that he will always be the sort of person who deep inside hopes that the cages are empty, even after the hunger we have experienced.

He crouches down and makes a clicking noise with his tongue. 'I'm sorry, little guy,' he says. Then he unlatches the cage, reaches in and grabs the rabbit by the scruff of its neck. It scrambles and kicks with its big plush-toy rear paws. Fin pulls it out and holds it up. He turns his head away, and with a single quick movement snaps the rabbit's neck with a twist of his hands. He drops its limp furry body into the sack. I watch him and in that moment we are not Fin and Lucy out walking in the bush anymore; we are two people clinging to the raft for survival.

By midday we have cleared ten traps. We walk the track south, back to the compound and are nearly at the fence when I hear leaves crunching behind us. We both spin around, and Fin puts his hand on my shoulder, pulling me towards him. He scans the surrounding trees frantically.

'There's someone there,' he whispers.

'It might be an animal.'

'Big frigging animal,' he says and takes the rifle from his shoulder.

I see movement – a dark shape. I whip around and think I see more. There's more rustling, from the other direction. Fin grabs my hand and pulls me behind the thick trunk of a tall gum. The trees all start to resemble figures.

Fin steps in front of me so I am between him and the tree. We both hold still. Moments pass but there is no movement. No more sounds except for the breath of wind through the treetops.

Someone comes sprinting towards us down the track – he's wearing camouflage clothes and a balaclava. And holding a rifle.

Fin flicks the safety off his gun, his actions smooth and quick.

'Lucy!'

It's Tom.

'Did you see them?' He stops running and looks left and right.

'We thought we saw something, someone,' says Fin. He points through the trees. 'That way.'

'I saw them too and raised the alarm. A woman – black coat, blue beanie.' Tom is puffed. He leans against a tree to get his breath. 'You both okay?'

'Yeah,' says Fin. 'Fine.'

Tom looks at me. 'Okay?'

'Yes.'

'Let's get back then. Fin, you cover behind.'

My heart pounds as we walk back to the compound in single file with Tom leading and Fin following me.

TWENTY-NINE

When we're back in the safety of the compound, Tom pulls his balaclava off. 'Rob and Jaxon are leading a team doing a sweep of the bush. I wanted to get you two in safely. Everyone needs to be back inside.'

'Shouldn't I go out too?' Fin asks.

'Jaxon said no. He wants you to stay here.'

Fin glances at me and shrugs.

'I was heading to the horses when I saw her. She was shadowing you both – about thirty or forty metres behind you.'

I feel sick at the thought of being followed – they could have been watching us the whole time. I'm slightly comforted knowing it was a woman, but there might have been others who saw the whole show.

'She was moving slowly. Don't know what she was doing. It was odd. Too close for comfort though – everyone not on security is being brought inside. Fin, you and I will cover the entries to the building.'

'We've never seen anyone out there on hunts,' I say. 'I was beginning to think maybe there wasn't anyone left who would try to get in, or try to get us ...'

'It happens from time to time.'

'You didn't try and shoot her?'

'She wasn't armed. Didn't look dangerous. I mean, it's hard to tell, but I don't like to go around shooting people unless I'm 90 per cent sure there's no other option.'

'Are you ever 100 per cent sure there's no other option?'

He looks at me directly. 'Never.'

I'm glad Fin's staying inside the compound but I still feel nervous at the thought of him outside the building. All but a few of the men are doing the security sweep, but with the lunch preparations in the kitchen and the noise of the schooling program in the rec hall, the atmosphere inside is almost normal. This is the first security issue since we arrived, but it obviously isn't totally unusual and I feel some of the tension leave my body. Max, who Fin recently decided was now well enough to resume his education, spots me and leaves the school group.

'Where's Fin?' he asks.

'Just outside. Don't worry – everything's probably fine.'

'They took Seamus.'

'He's the size of a bear. He can look after himself. What you learning over there?'

Max rolls his eyes. 'I made a collage gum tree and rewrote "Incy Wincy" with rude words.'

'There's a bit of an age gap between you and the others. Sorry.'

'Now I'm memorising the amphibian section of the

nature encyclopaedia. It's like a Stone-Age version of Google.'

'Excellent.'

'Lucy?'

'Yes, Max?'

'Everything's okay, isn't it?'

'Everything's fine. It's just precautions.'

Lunch is being served when Jaxon walks inside and declares us to be free of impending doom. Seamus trots in with him and lies down at Max's feet.

'See?' I say. 'I'm sure he would tear the limbs off anyone who tried to get to you. He's comforting like that.'

Max smiles and scratches the dog behind his ears.

After lunch Fin comes to find me.

'Jaxon's given me the arvo off,' he says. 'I heard he and Tom arguing about whether we should go into lockdown. Tom didn't want to, said there's not enough of a threat, just because someone is out there doesn't mean we need to.'

'But Jaxon wants to?'

'Big time. You should have heard him go off at Tom. Freakin' hell.'

'So why do you have the afternoon off patrols? That doesn't make sense.'

'Jaxon said he only wanted people with more experience on patrol, said there was a risk I'd be taken hostage. Tom didn't agree with any of it but let him take me off patrol. Anyway, I was wondering if you might want to come on a date with me. I'll take you to the bookshelves, just like the old days.' He's joking but there's something more serious behind his eyes – he's worried after what happened between us in the bush.

'Do you think it will end in global catastrophe like last time?'

'I don't really think things could get much worse.'

'True.'

Fin is going over a sketch he did of Tom skinning a kangaroo hanging from the gambrel, while I look through the books on the shelf. He doesn't draw any of the metaphorical stuff anymore, no oceans or boats. It's one of the changes in him since we left Sydney.

Fin pulls an eraser from his pocket and rubs at something on the page. Then he pauses and looks up at me. 'Are you okay? Like, after this morning? … Us?'

My sister was raped. My sister was raped. Just say the words, Lucy.

'No – yes. It's … I'm sorry.'

Why can't I just tell him?

'You don't have to say sorry,' he says. 'But … are you okay? I was thinking about you and what happened with that guy in the demountable on the highway, how he chased you. What he said to you. I think if I was you, that would mess me up a bit. Not that you're messed up. I'm not saying that. Please don't think I'm saying that.'

If I was you. He's so damn empathetic. I've told him he can never understand what it's like but he's trying. Neither of us say anything for a little while.

'Do you think about the rest of your family much? Do you think about your dad?' I ask him.

'A bit. You know what keeps coming back to me? I keep thinking about how he would walk me up to the supermarket and buy me lollies on Sunday afternoons.'

'Off Mr Starvos.'

'Yeah.'

I feel sick.

'I don't think about Kara much,' Fin says. 'She was an idiot. Not that she deserved to die.'

'I wonder who does. If anyone ever deserves to die.'

Fin gives me a look. He knows. 'You didn't have a choice with Starvos, Lucy.'

'But—'

'He would have shot me.'

'Yep.'

'I would be dead. You saved my life. I cannot believe that you – that anyone – could be so fearless and do what you did. You see it all the time in movies, on TV, heroes pulling off stuff like that all over the place, but in reality it's a totally different thing. I've never had to do it. All this time, I've never done anything like it.'

'You're lucky,' I whisper.

'I know.'

*

Jaxon cancels the ride out for the following day. My job instead is to shovel more horse poo. Tom comes down to the stables and asks if I can help him give Cloudy an injection, so I get her from the paddock and Tom pulls a piece of liquorice from his pocket as a bribe. I hold Cloudy steady while Tom injects an anti-inflammatory into her neck.

'Good girl, Cloud,' Tom says softly.

Out in the paddock Red spots Tom and raises his head, nickering. He walks to the fence and puts his head over the rail.

'Jealous,' Tom says, and walks over to his horse. He produces more liquorice and gives it to Red.

'How long have you had him?' I ask Tom.

'Seventeen years. He was born on our property.'

'He's seventeen?!'

'Yep. Don't tell him. He thinks he's three. He was my wife's favourite.'

I hadn't imagined that Tom might have a wife – he seems like a steady single entity.

'Is she still alive?' I shouldn't have asked; I know how he feels about questions. But he glances at me with a soft expression, as if he's realised we are both alone here in that way.

'Helen passed ten days before the winter. She was old friends with Jeff – they were at university together years ago. I got to know him through her, and we always kept in touch. Helen was sure this would happen. I didn't really think so, but she was the smartest person I'd ever met, so I didn't dare argue with her. We got involved with a few others setting this up, pooled money to buy the place. We let Jeff know about it, in case it all went to shit. That was about eighteen months ago.' Tom puts his hands on his hips and looks up at the treetops rustling in the breeze. 'But then Helen got sick. We were on our property up north, a cattle station. She wanted to stay there … She didn't have long to go. She wanted me to leave her and come here but I couldn't. I stayed with her and she died just before the crap hit the fan. God's a bloke I never had much time for, but I thank him for that. I took Red and fifteen head of cattle, loaded them into the truck with a tonne of feed, and came here.

'I hoped Jeff and Esther would turn up, but in the end only Esther came. We've been waiting for Jeff ever since. It was a bonus that Esther knew a little about horses and riding.'

'What about Jaxon?'

Tom turns away and crouches down to gather the bits from the vet kit. It's a few moments before he speaks. 'A month after the winter started he turned up with an army truck and half the bloody weapons in the country. I thought he was going to try and take the place off us, but it was the opposite – he wanted to help us get it back on track.'

'How did he get all the guns?'

'Mate, I don't want to know.'

'He stole them?'

'Like I said, I don't want to know. We're better off for it though.'

'Do you like him?'

'You and your bloody questions. You ever thought of a job in journalism when this is done? What does that matter? He does a job and he does it well.'

'What about with Esther? I don't think he's that … I don't like how he talks to her, how he treats her.'

Tom clips the plastic lid of the kit shut. I'm certain he's not going to answer the question, but then he sighs.

'I've heard him speak to her in a way that I don't appreciate. But that's not really any of my business – I don't want to go sticking my nose into other people's affairs. She's a grown woman, and a strong one too, so I would have thought that if she wasn't happy she'd break it off with him. I know there's been tension about her wanting to go to Sydney, but honestly I agree with Jaxon. It's too risky. I feel very responsible for her. I would have offered to go up with her, but we can't risk something happening and neither of us coming back – we need the horses to hunt. You can't carry a big kangaroo for fifteen kilometres.' Tom begins walking back to the tack shed and I follow him.

'But … she's her own person,' he says. 'When you three came here and said he was still alive and waiting for her I could understand why she would start thinking about going again. And I don't think there's as much of a threat out there anymore – other than the woman yesterday we haven't had an incident in months. But it's not worth causing conflict with Jaxon about. We need to work together.'

'Tom, the way he talks to her – he's been like that with me too.'

'Has he?' Tom looks surprised.

'Yes. And Raahel.'

'Hmm.' He frowns and rubs his chin.

'Tom?'

'I'll have a word.' He clears his throat. 'You're in here this afternoon? Doing the stables?'

'Yes.'

'You want lunch brought down here?'

'Please.'

I eat my rolled-up flatbread standing outside the stables where the sun can warm my legs and then get to work inside.

Rob must wonder what the hell I'm doing in there for hours on end, while he's standing outside. But he never asks a single question – it's pretty clear he has no desire to be buddies. The stables are the only place I can go and not be bothered by anyone. I keep the dirt floor so meticulously raked it's like a dusty Japanese rock garden, and the water troughs are so clean they could be baths, except that you'd have to break the thin film of ice on the surface before you could get in.

I'm crouched in a stable removing loose rusted nails from a plank on the wall when I hear voices outside. I recognise Jaxon's first, his barking words getting louder as he approaches. I don't know who he's shouting at or why he's coming down to the horses, but I feel sick at the thought that it could be Esther and I don't want him coming closer. They stop just outside the stables and I hear another voice – it's not Esther, it's Tom.

'All I'm saying is they weren't armed. And it wasn't a bloke, it was a woman – every attack we've had has been men. We can start thinking about opening up more now.'

'You don't know what you're talking about,' Jaxon spits. 'I'd bet anything she wasn't here to make friends.'

'How do you know?'

'Which one of us is trained in risk assessment? Did I miss something? Were you trained to deal with tactical situations on your bloody farm?'

'Mate, you need to learn some respect.' Tom's words are a growl. 'This was discussed before you even showed up here. The crops are already sprouting, we've got mushrooms coming out of our ears and the roos are coming back in droves. And this is just the beginning. We will be able to open this place up. Slowly, sure, but we're that much closer to—'

'We're not ready.'

'No, not yet—'

'So I'm done talking about it.'

I can hear the crunch of Jaxon's boots as he walks away, but Tom calls out to him.

'We're not done. You also need to watch yourself with the girls.'

'What the fuck are you talking about?'

'Mate, I've heard how you talk to Esther—'

'Whoa, who the hell do you think you are, Tom? What Esther and I talk about – and how – is none of your business.'

'But Lucy and Raahel are my business. I've got more years under my belt than you. I've known plenty of blokes who treat women like dirt. We're not having that here.'

'So now you decide what's allowed here? That's rich, mate, after all your bullshit about democracy. You need to mind your own bloody business. We're done here.'

It's only when Jaxon's gone that I realise I've barely drawn breath.

THIRTY

The following day I train with Esther again, then spend the rest of the morning cleaning the kitchen. In the afternoon I'm back in the laundry cabin, with Fin as guard. It's nearly dark and Fin is locking up the cabin when the dogs start barking down at the back gate near the horses. Barking, barking, barking. A shout. A gunshot.

Fin pushes me back inside the cabin. 'Stay here. I'll lock the door.'

'I don't want to be locked in here!'

'Stay here!' he shouts and slams the door shut. The lock clicks closed and it's just me and a lamp of dwindling oil moments from sundown. I can hear people running in the direction of the horse paddocks and more shouting. Another gunshot cracks through the twilight and a flock of cockatoos screech and squawk as they flee the trees. Someone shouts, 'Code red! Code red!'

Then I hear a key jangling at the door. Fin opens it and grabs me by the arm. He doesn't say anything, just pulls me along the path and into the rec hall where people are running to the hatch in the corner. He pushes me towards them and shouts, 'Go!' and then he's gone again.

I run to the hatch and clamber down the narrow metal ladder into a concrete passageway. A loud whistle sounds and I can hear the hatch closing behind me. At the end of the passage is a heavy metal door and I file through with the others into a space that's larger than I was expecting. Big plastic containers loaded with gas masks are stacked on one of the shelves. Beside them are crates marked 'hazmat suits' and 'children's hazmats'.

It's freezing and the kids are crying. I glimpse the red and white stripes of Max's beanie behind a cluster of people and weave through them to find him pushing himself into the corner as if he can hide there.

'It's okay. We're safe in here. It's okay.'

'Where's Fin?'

'Outside helping the guards.'

'What's happening?'

'I don't know. I was with Fin and we heard people yelling and running, and then he brought me here. He's gone out there again. It's his job.'

I try to hug Max but he pushes me away. 'I want to go out. I can help with Seamus.'

'You can't go out there.'

'What if Fin needs me?'

'He'd want you to stay safe. With me.'

Raahel comes to sit beside us with Elia and Saramma. The girls are both in tears.

'Do you know what's going on?' I ask Raahel.

'No, but there's probably been an incident at one of

the gates.'

'There were gunshots.'

She nods. 'It's not the first time.' Saramma climbs into her mum's arms. Raahel puts her arms around her daughters, talking quietly to them.

We wait in silence until the bunker door opens and Jaxon and Tom come in. Jaxon calls for quiet.

'We've secured the perimeter,' he says. 'I was at the front gates and a guy came at me with a knife when I had my back turned. My vest saved me.'

'Who was it?' someone at the back of the bunker asks.

'I don't know. I've never seen them before.'

'Will we go into lockdown?' Susan asks.

Jaxon opens his mouth to speak but Tom cuts him off.

'Jaxon says the intruder has been dealt with. We've done a thorough search of the surrounds and it seems he was acting alone – there's no-one else around the camp. For the moment it's safe for everyone to come up, but we have to remain cautious. There will be extra patrols tonight.'

'Did you shoot him?' Esther asks.

Jaxon walks away as if he hasn't heard her.

'Jaxon?' she calls after him. 'I said did you shoot him?'

He turns around briefly and smiles reassuringly. 'They're dealt with. They won't be coming back.'

Fin is waiting for Max and me at the top of the ladder. He looks rattled.

'Max, go and sit down. I want to talk to Lucy,' he says.

'No. You're going to talk about what happened and I want to know.'

Fin rolls his eyes and swears under his breath.

'Are you all right?' I ask him.

'Yeah. I didn't see anything. I just heard the gunshots and I don't know … maybe a car? I was heading to the gate after I took you to the bunker but Jaxon told me to stay up at the building. I think Jaxon shot the guy.' Fin pulls off his gloves and drops them to the floor. He rubs his face then looks at the ceiling. 'I thought we were done with this. I *am* done with this … You guys go have something to eat. I just need to be on my own for a minute.'

Max and I leave Fin and make our way to the dining hall. Out in the corridor I can hear voices from inside one of the storerooms. Or just one voice: Jaxon's.

'Max, you go start dinner. I'll be there in a sec.'

He shrugs and keeps walking to the dining hall.

When he's gone I press my ear to the door and I can just make out what Jaxon is saying.

'Do you get it now? Do you?' There's a thud, like a hand thumping a table or wall. 'Can you get it through your thick head and stop whining for your daddy? You're not going anywhere. Don't be a fucking idiot.'

I feel sick. I go into the bathroom and lock myself in a stall. Someone comes in after me and I hear water splashing in the bucket at the sink. When I come out I see Esther rinsing her face. Her skin is blotchy and her eyes are red.

'Are you okay?'

'Yes.'

'Are you sure?'

'Lucy, leave me alone.'

'Only if you're okay.'

She slaps her hand in the water in frustration. 'Piss off.'

'Esther, I heard what Jaxon said.'

'You were eavesdropping on us? Mind your own fucking business!'

'I'm just worried—'

Esther pushes past me, and slams the door after her.

THIRTY-ONE

The atmosphere of hope and relief brought by the sunshine is lost after the attack. Early the next day I'm rostered on at the greenhouse but I can't find Raahel, who usually gives me the key. I go to the reception room to ask Jaxon to unlock the greenhouse for me. The door is open and Tom and Jaxon are arguing but neither of them see me waiting there.

'That wasn't your decision to make,' Jaxon says.

'If the intruder was dealt with, and you say they were, there's no need for lockdown. We didn't find anyone else near here.'

I step away from the door, out of sight but still in earshot.

Jaxon's tone softens. 'Yeah, I said I dealt with him, but now I'm wondering if maybe I didn't do a good enough job. He was still alive. I didn't finish him off. I could've but I took pity on him, you know?'

'If you shot him and he doesn't get treatment he's as good as dead.'

'Either way, I don't want Esther or Lucy going on hunts,' Jaxon says.

'Mate, I'm not going on my own and those two are perfectly capable. They don't take unnecessary risks. We're fine. We need meat – we can't use any allocated rations unless we absolutely have to. You've said it yourself. I'm hunting today and Lucy and Esther are coming with me.'

'Okay. But you all wear balaclavas and stay away from the roads and the fire trails. Well away.'

'Sure, and Esther brings a gun.'

'No way.'

'If you're that worried, mate, give her a gun.'

'No! She hasn't had training.'

'Fine. Have it your way. You usually do.'

Tom leaves the room before I have a chance to move. It's obvious that I overheard them and Tom gives me a disapproving look but doesn't say anything until he's closed the door behind him.

'I'm going to pretend I didn't see you listening. Get your stuff together. We're going out before Jaxon has a hissy fit and locks the place down.'

As always, Tom leads, I'm in the middle and Esther rides behind me – she has a handgun, which I'm guessing Tom gave to her without Jaxon's approval. I hear every sound around us as if amplified.

We get our first wallaby in less than an hour and are heading east on the fire trail when the horses begin to feel edgy. Red, who normally plods along like he's daydreaming, keeps his head up, his ears flicking towards sounds we can't hear. Jack Frost has a lot of what horse people call 'forward movement', which means he could bolt if I even think of loosening the reins. I know he needs stillness from me to stay calm.

'The horses don't feel right,' I call out to the others.

Tom keeps his eyes on the track ahead and I don't think he has heard me until he murmurs, 'Nope.'

He doesn't give anything away but I can tell he is listening to the bush around us. He pulls Red up, dismounts and hands me the reins. Esther turns Cloudy around so she can keep watch behind us.

Tom examines the scrub at the edge of the trail. 'Someone's about,' he says. He puts his hands on his hips and looks around.

Jack Frost tosses his head and takes a few steps backwards.

Tom blows a fly from his lips, gives the scrub a final look over then takes back his reins and mounts up. He clicks his tongue and Esther and I follow as he urges Red into a trot. After about five hundred metres he drops back to a walk.

'Reckon we should head up to the north paddock.'

'Was someone back there?' Esther asks.

'Yeah, I reckon. We'll take the south-east track back when we're done – it'll give us a better view.'

We ride on in single file for a few minutes.

When a woman emerges from the bush up ahead, the jolt of Jack Frost's sideways movement almost unseats me.

Tom is quicker, pulling Red up before he has a chance to panic. He holds up his hand, signalling for Esther and me to halt.

The woman holds her palms up in surrender.

'Get behind me, girls,' Tom murmurs. 'Stay close.' His right hand moves towards the gun at his hip.

'Please don't shoot! We need help,' says the woman. Her voice is weary, like she doesn't see the point asking. She is wearing a grey ski jacket, jeans and a beanie with a green pompom. Her greasy brown hair is gathered around her chin and neck at the jacket collar. I've worn my hair like that too – it keeps your neck warm when you don't have a scarf.

'Please. Are you at the camp with the spring? There's guards who won't let us anywhere close.'

I've never heard of a spring. It explains the supply of fresh water. Tom shakes his head and looks away.

The woman raises her chin, a touch of defiance. 'Is that your lot? I know you hunt. And I know those are your traps by the creek. Can you spare anything at all? Please. We have nothing … We're starving.'

Tom is silent. I walk Jack Frost up beside him, ignoring the hand he raises to tell me to stop.

'Lucy, stay behind me.'

The woman fixes her gaze on Tom. 'I know you. You used to let us in for water. Why can't we come in anymore?'

The scrub beside her rustles. Tom moves to draw his

gun but then a girl with matted blonde hair and cheeks smudged with dirt emerges.

'Mummy?'

'It's okay, Polly. I'm okay.'

The girl turns towards us, brow furrowed. She stands as tall as she can and puts her hands on her hips. 'Go away! Don't hurt Mummy!'

I look at Tom. He is frozen as if he doesn't know what to do next.

'We have the wallaby,' I whisper. Tom draws the gun from his holster and my heart drops to my stomach. The woman grabs her daughter's hand and backs away.

'Get off. Give the wallaby to her – quickly,' Tom says. His eyes don't leave the woman. 'Esther, cover her.'

When I dismount I look back at Esther. She sits tall, and although it is only a woman and a little girl, she looks afraid. She rides up beside me and I give her Jack Frost's reins, then I untie the soft paws of the wallaby from the side of Red's saddle. The woman watches my every movement. I carry the wallaby by the base of its tail and its body knocks against my leg as I walk the fifteen metres to where the woman stands.

She lets out a breath as I hand it to her. Close up she looks so frail, almost brittle enough to break. Like Bit was.

'Thank you. Thank you.'

'You say you haven't been able to get to the spring?' I whisper to her. 'Talk quietly.'

'No. He used to let me through sometimes, in the early evenings.' Her eyes well up with tears. 'Now there's different guards. We've been threatened – they said to keep away.'

The little girl has dark circles under her eyes.

'Did the wallaby die?' she asks me.

'Yeah, it died. It's sad, I know.'

She gives a solemn nod and strokes the wallaby's fur.

I take off my backpack and pull out my water bottle, which is still full. I hand it to the woman.

'Oh thank you, thank you.' She gives it to the girl, who looks at me with wide eyes.

'It's okay,' I tell her. 'You can have it.'

She takes some mouthfuls and hands the bottle back to her mother.

'No, sweetheart. You have it all. I'm okay. You have it.'

The girl looks to me again and I nod. She tilts her head back and drinks the rest of the water with the urgency of a marathon runner.

I scan the bush around me. 'Is anyone else here with you and your mum?' I ask the little girl.

She shakes her head. 'We left Daddy at our house a long time ago. He's going to come soon and pick us up and then we're all going to go on a holiday.'

The girl's mother looks up at the sky to hide her tears from her daughter.

'I'm Lucy.'

'I'm Sarah,' the woman says. 'This is Polly.'

'I'm going to see if we can help you. Where are you if I need to come and find you?'

Sarah hesitates.

'Try to trust me – I know it's hard.'

Sarah turns to Polly and crouches down. 'Darling, can you go over there and see if you can find some nice big sticks for the fire? We need some really good ones. You're so good at finding them.'

Polly smiles and goes into the scrub.

'Three of us have been shot. How do I know you won't come after us?'

Tom calls me back. I put my backpack on.

'You don't. You might just have to take the risk. I've been in your shoes.'

'We're north-west from here. Up over the big hill there's a park ranger's cottage.'

'Okay. I'll see what I can do.'

THIRTY-TWO

I mount up again and Tom waits until Sarah and Polly have long since disappeared into the bush before he talks to me.

'What did she say to you?'

'She said that they haven't been able to get water from the spring. Apparently we're guarding it? She said you used to let her in.'

Tom opens his mouth to reply, maybe to tell me it's not true. But he closes it again.

'Why did you stop?'

He ignores my question. 'What else did she say?'

'Why did you stop?'

'Lucy!' he barks. 'Enough bloody questions. What else did she say?'

'That they have no food left.'

'And what did you say?'

'Maybe I should have taken notes.'

'Don't be a smart-arse, so help me God, girl. What did you say to her?'

'I said we can help.'

Tom lets out a long sigh. Esther looks away.

'Wish you hadn't said that, mate. It's not for you to decide.'

'Who gets to decide?'

'Did she say where they are living?'

I keep my mouth shut.

'Lucy? Answer me.'

'Yes.'

'Where?'

'I'm only telling you if we can go back and get them. Bring them to camp. Or at least share the water. It's a spring – they don't run dry.'

'We can't have people coming into camp.'

'The sun is out and we are starting to grow things. This is exactly the time when we should be bringing people in.'

'We can't. We have to keep the camp secure.' His words lack conviction.

'It's not a camp – it's a frigging compound.'

Tom shakes his head in frustration. 'Call it what you want, but it keeps you safe.'

'Exactly! No child should be out here. They should be safe too.' I look to Esther. 'Esther?' I plead.

'We have to keep the camp safe,' she whispers.

'From who? Little girls?'

'Lucy!' Tom yells. 'You're on thin ice, mate.'

'Why? Because I want to help other people? They're just like we were when we were trying to get into Sydney – on the wrong side of the fence. Didn't you see that little girl?

Her name's Polly, and she thinks her dad's going to come and get her and they're all going on a holiday.'

Tom's jaw tightens. 'You need to tell me where they are. Jaxon and I will go and check it out. Maybe take some food.'

'Only if I can come.'

Tom rolls his eyes. 'You're a pain in the arse.'

'Thank you.'

He urges Red forward. 'Get moving,' he says over his shoulder. 'Both of you. I don't want to be hanging around out here.'

We return to the compound empty-handed. When we reach the stables Tom says he will sort out the horses and sends Esther and me back up to the main building.

'Don't talk about this to anyone. Got it?' he says.

Esther walks quickly with her head down and arms folded. I have to jog to catch up to her.

'Have you seen anyone like that before?'

'A couple of times, but they've run away.'

'Did you know there were children out there? Families?'

'Jaxon has told me that the only people they've come into contact with are terrifying. Brutal.'

Now I can read her: she's not scared or worried, she's shocked.

'Did you know Tom was letting them use the spring?'

'No.'

'What should I do, Esther? Should I tell Jaxon and Tom where they are?'

'Jaxon's a good man. He takes good care of us. Anything I need ... he's always there.'

We walk on. Be brave, Lucy.

'What if what you need is to find your dad? If that woman is surviving out there it must be safe enough to go. Esther—'

She glares at me. 'What?'

'Have you ever thought that maybe he doesn't want your dad to come here?'

She freezes.

'Like, what do you think your dad would say about what's going on here? Jaxon wouldn't want to hear it.'

'I'm going inside,' she mutters.

'Should I tell them where Sarah is?'

Esther pauses. 'You can trust Tom,' she says and closes the door behind her.

I want to follow her inside but I hear Fin call my name as he walks over from the woodpile. I meet him halfway.

'How was the hunt? Did you find anything?' he asks.

I don't answer him; instead I take him by the arm and lead him further away from the building so I can tell him about Sarah and Polly without being overheard. 'They should be brought into the camp,' I say.

He nods but doesn't say anything. Not the reaction I was expecting.

'Have you seen them when you've been out there?'

'Someone's been stealing from our traps. We've had to go out even earlier to beat them to it. I thought I saw someone a few days ago, like you and I did when we were checking the traps. They were gone quick, though.'

'You didn't say anything.'

'I know. I—'

'Why wouldn't you tell me about it?'

'I thought it would upset you.'

'What the actual fu—'

'Lucy.'

'You've kept this from me? What else haven't you told me?'

'Calm down. We need to think about this.'

'I am thinking about it. I'm thinking there's children out there who can't get water because people here won't let them.'

'They're not just *people* here, Lucy. They're people who have let us in and are looking after us. People we are depending on. People who know what they're doing. Who are keeping this whole thing ticking over.'

'Who have you been talking to?'

'What?'

'This doesn't sound like you. You helped anyone you could before. You took Matt in when he was technically the enemy. And I've never heard you say "ticking over". Who have you been talking to about this? Jaxon?'

He looks away.

'I don't like it, Fin. They're starving and they don't have access to water.'

'I know, I don't like it either. But …'

'Did you tell Jaxon you'd seen someone near the traps?'

'Yes. He was glad I told him.'

'Glad "let's help them" glad? Or glad "we need to get rid of them" glad.'

'I don't know. The first one, I think.'

'I think Tom wants to help them. He said they could have our kill.'

'Tom did that?'

'Yes. He didn't seem to want to be involved and he doesn't want Esther or me to tell anyone about it. But still, he tried to help them. He's going to talk to Jaxon. I want to be there.'

'I think you should leave it to them, Lucy.'

'Why?'

'Because I don't want to overstep the mark. I've barely been doing any patrols – I don't know if I've done something wrong or what but Jaxon's been different with me and I really don't want to piss him off.'

'Different how?'

'He's gone a bit cold. I don't know.'

The bell for lunch sounds. I think of Susan and Polly lighting a fire to cook the meat. How many other people will they have to share it with?

'We should go and help. You and me. You have a gun. We can at least take them water and some more food. Or give them a few traps – show them where they can set them up.'

Fin frowns at the expanse of bush beyond the fence. 'Lucy, we can't.'

'Why not?'

'It will piss Jaxon off. We have nowhere else to go. I left my mum in Sydney to come here with you.'

'I know what you left there, Fin,' I whisper. 'Don't try and tell yourself or me it was solely for my sake. You left your *mother* because you couldn't live with the decisions that were being made. And now you're happy to say that woman and her little girl are the enemy? What has happened to you, Fin?'

'I'm not saying that ... I'm ... You want to know what's happened to me? I sat with Noll while his blood drained from his body. There was a bullet hole in his chest. It was an actual hole.' He shakes his head. 'So bizarre to see that. And his blood was pooling on the fabric of his coat.' It's like Fin is talking about something inane now, a little observation of a detail that he has seen, not his dead friend. He's been carrying this with him the way I've carried my memories of Bit and what happened to Mr Starvos. 'It was pooling because his jacket was waterproof. His blood didn't seep in – it just pooled and ran across the fabric. He was looking right at me, Luce. I held his hand and he looked right at me while he died. That's what happened to me.' Fin looks up into the sky. 'That can't happen again. I won't watch you die and I won't watch Max die. I won't let it happen.'

I reach out and touch his shoulder but now he's the one who moves away.

'I understand. I get that you're scared,' I say softly. 'But it doesn't mean you can tell me what to do. I want to do the right thing here, Fin. Tom wants me to tell him and Jaxon where they are, but I don't know if I can trust Jaxon.'

'Lucy, I don't know what to do. This wasn't the plan. I thought it would be our happy ending. Happyish ending. I thought once we had food and shelter and no-one coming after us or our things we'd be okay. I'm still scared, Luce. And I can still hear Noll …' Fin's voice cracks and he wipes his knuckles across his eyes. 'I can still hear him trying to breathe.'

My love for him hits me so quick and sharp I don't have time to block it. It fogs and blurs everything.

'I want to be a good guy, Lucy, but I don't know what that is anymore. Before it was clear: take care of Max, take care of you. Now I just don't know what to do. I'm sorry. I'm really sorry.'

'You are a good guy,' I whisper.

He looks me straight in the eye. 'To who? Because I want to be good to everyone. But I don't think that's possible.'

THIRTY-THREE

Jaxon and Tom walk past us and into the building. Through the window I see them go straight into the reception room and close the door.

Raahel comes outside. 'Are you okay, Lucy? I saw Esther and she looked upset. Has something happened?'

I lower my voice and tell her about Sarah and Polly. She turns pale.

'Raahel, should I tell Jaxon where they are?'

'Let me try and talk to Jaxon first.'

I watch her knock on the reception room door; it opens and she goes inside.

'Stay here a minute,' Fin says. He walks around the side of the building, closer to the office. I pretend to be casually standing around enjoying the view until he returns.

'There's some arguing but I couldn't hear much from outside,' he tells me.

They're in the office for a long time. Eventually we give up waiting and Fin comes to the greenhouse where I am rostered for the afternoon. It feels like a long time before Jaxon and Tom come and find me.

'Jaxon and I will go and look for them,' Tom says.

'How? Are you riding? I want to go with you.'

'We're going on foot. Don't worry, Lucy. I want to help as much as you do.'

'What are you going to do if you find them? Are you going to bring them here?'

Jaxon opens his mouth to answer but Tom speaks over the top of him. 'If we find them we will bring them back here.'

'Lucy, we need to know where they are,' Jaxon says.

If Noll were here right now he would pray. He would ask God to help him make the right decision. If God's real I'm not sure he would want to hear from me when I've ignored his existence for my entire life. I have to trust Tom.

'There's a park ranger's hut north-west of here, over the big hill. That's where they are.' I look Tom directly in the eye. 'You won't hurt them, will you?'

'I won't.'

'You've done the right thing, Lucy,' says Jaxon. 'Fin, can you help Tom get our packs ready? I'll wait here with Lucy while she finishes up.'

Fin hesitates. 'You go, Jaxon. I'll wait with Lucy – she's nearly done.'

'Nah, it's fine. Go on.'

Fin's only option is to stand up to Jaxon, to say he's not comfortable with the situation, or that he's sure I'd rather he stayed. I'm afraid of pissing Jaxon off when he's about to go to find Sarah and Polly, so I give Fin a small nod.

'See, mate? We're fine,' says Jaxon.

Fin gives me one last concerned glance but then follows Tom down the path.

Jaxon waits until Fin is out of earshot and then turns to me with a smile. 'I like you, Lucy. I think you're good value. But, once again, you need to mind your own fucking business.'

He takes a step closer to me, blocking the doorway.

I can't make my mouth move. Or any other part of me.

'I'm happy to go on this little walk with Tom. It's dangerous, but I can't handle the thought of a little kid out there right now. I'll do it. But I swear to God, if you keep getting in Esther's ear about finding her dad, I will lose my fucking patience. She's upset. She needs stability, not some little girl coming and telling her fairytales about riding off into the sunset and reuniting. Because the idea that her dad's still waiting for her is a fucking fairytale. I don't know what you're playing at. Maybe you're messed up. Maybe you're just bored. Who knows? But Esther is mine. If you think for a second she's gonna turn against me or leave, you're wrong. She's not goin' anywhere. Shut the hell up about it.'

Jaxon leaves the greenhouse. It's only after he's well away that I can move.

My hands are balled into tight fists at my sides and I can hear the crack of the bat on Starvos's skull. I didn't hesitate for a moment with Starvos – I just did what I had to do.

But with Jaxon I am frozen.

They are gone for hours. I stay in the greenhouse and try to put the things in my head in order, but the little boxes are toppling and everything is getting jumbled up. The blood on Bit's skirt, Jaxon's narrowed eyes, Polly's matted hair and the tears on Fin's cheeks. When Fin comes back he sits on the step with me while I work. I want to tell him what Jaxon said, but it would only make him more cautious about upsetting Jaxon. There's no way Esther or I can go and look for our families without jeopardising our place here. It will piss Jaxon off. And how would I even explain what happened with Jaxon? How do you describe that thing guys can do with their bodies – their posture, a tilt of the head – that can make a woman feel … less.

Jaxon and Tom still aren't back when the sky begins to darken.

At dinner, Max stares at his food but doesn't touch it. I can't eat either.

'What if something's happened to Jaxon?' Max whispers.

'It's a long walk there and back,' says Fin. 'Don't panic yet.'

It's almost lights out and there's still no word of their return. The rec hall is quiet – only the kids talk and laugh.

Then the door opens and Tom walks in. But he's alone.

'What happened?' I ask. 'Did you find them?'

'We split up to cover as much ground as possible. I got to the hut first but no-one was there. Jaxon was supposed to meet me. I waited for hours, but he didn't show. I've searched all around and couldn't find him; I thought he might have come back here. It's too late to go back out now – too dangerous in the dark.'

Talk ripples through the room. Everyone looks worried and Tom is hit with question after question about where exactly he searched, what he heard, what he saw. He looks tired and out of patience. Esther grabs him on his way out of the room. She looks distraught.

'Something bad's happened. I know it,' I say to Fin. 'We have to go and look for Sarah and Polly.'

'Tom is right – it's too dark. Let's wait until morning. We should try and sleep. It'll be okay.' He's trying to reassure himself as much as he is Max and me.

I barely sleep. I can't stop thinking about Sarah and Polly and why they weren't there, where they have gone. Jaxon I am less concerned about. Maybe it makes me an evil person to think this place might be better off without him. I wish I could talk to Noll.

I don't know what time it is when I hear the rec hall door open again. I sit up. It's still dark outside, so someone has lit the hurricane lamps. Jaxon is standing at the exit with people gathered around him. The unsteady light of the hurricane lamps illuminates a smear of blood on his face. He's holding a cloth to his forehead and his cheek is swollen and bruised.

Despite his injuries, his voice is steady. 'We need to lock down. Nobody leaves.'

I get out of bed and weave through the people to get to Jaxon. Esther is already at his side.

'Where are they? What happened?'

Jaxon shakes his head in anger at me. 'I don't need you involved. You've done enough damage. I'm going to the medic room.'

'He was attacked,' Esther says. 'He found some people and they turned on him. He was attacked because of you.' She points her finger at me. 'He could have died.' She shoves my shoulder. Fin tries to step between us, but she pushes past him. 'It's you and all your bullshit. I should have never listened to you.'

I back away from her. Jaxon looks at me with a strange expression on his face. Something close to smug.

I look for Tom and find him in the kitchen, filling a saucepan with water for Jaxon to wash with.

'Did he tell you what happened?'

'He didn't see the girl,' Tom says. 'He saw Sarah though. Seems she lured him into an ambush.'

'I don't—'

'Yeah?' Tom slams the saucepan down on the bench. The water sloshes back and forth like an angry sea. 'You don't what? What do you have to say, Lucy? Tell me, I'm all ears.'

'I don't think she would have—'

'How do you know?' His words are like a spit in my face. 'This is what happens. You let even the smallest amount of mercy in and you get fucked over.'

I've never heard him talk like this before. It's uncomfortable.

'We're done with hunts for now, you understand? Jaxon wants to lock the place down, so you can forget about going out there for a long time.'

'We'll run out of food.'

'Could have used that wallaby.'

'I'm sorry.'

Tom picks up the saucepan. The skin on his face is lined like the bark on a tree. It's impossible to tell whether it's from age or sun exposure. Probably both.

'It's not your fault,' his words are gruff, but softer. 'You're a kid. I should have known better. We have rations for three days. It will be okay.'

THIRTY-FOUR

Steel shutters come down over all the windows; forty of us locked into one small building. Even the skylights in the rec hall are deemed a possible entry point for intruders and are covered. Jaxon, patched up by Raahel, takes up residence in the reception room. We are to stay calm. We are to use the inside bathroom in the hall only, and go in pairs. Everyone must be accounted for at all times. The fences are no longer guarded – Jaxon says it would make us vulnerable to hostages being taken – only the building is patrolled. No natural light comes in for what we are told is three days. It's like being in the car park again – hiding in the dark, constantly on alert for attack. And the boredom of endless waiting for something, anything, to happen. If anyone is too loud, or if a child cries, Jaxon emerges and shouts at us. The only other person permitted entry to the reception room is Tom. They argue a lot – I'm sure it's about the lockdown – and we can all hear Jaxon's voice reverberating through the walls.

Early on the fourth morning of lockdown Jaxon summons Tom and me to the office. He looks over the maps spread across the desk.

'We're running out of meat, so you two need to go out. Where do you reckon you have the best shot so you'll be back quickly? We need two big roos.'

Tom frowns down at the map. He traces an area to the south-west of compound. 'That's our best bet – there's a few big clearings, camping grounds. There's usually a mob or two around there.'

'Which tracks will you take?'

Tom shows him on the map.

'Don't be out there too long. Be back here by midday.'

'We need Esther.'

'No. She stays here.'

Tom sighs. 'Fine. Then give us someone on foot. We're not going far, so there's no reason for us not to have at least one other armed person with us. We carry the kills on the horses. Simple.'

Jaxon hesitates. His eyes dart back and forth between us. 'It's not safe. No-one can outrun them if they come for you and the meat.'

'Well, in that case, Lucy needs a weapon too.'

'No way.'

'Why?'

'She can't use it. She doesn't know how.' Jaxon rubs his hands up and down on his jeans, as if trying to dry sweaty palms.

'Better than nothing.'

'No.'

'Mate, this isn't a negotiation. I'm giving her a gun.'

'No you're not!'

'You need to calm down.'

'Her horse is a psycho,' Jaxon hisses. 'How's it gonna go if she shoots a gun? Huh?'

He's always been so calm and – other than his anger – emotionless. Now it's like he's panicking.

'You need to go now,' he barks.

'Fine.' Tom turns to me. 'Get dressed. Get your boots.'

Fin catches up with us as we are leaving the rec hall. I tell him Jaxon's instructions.

'No.' His words are definite. 'You can't go out there, Lucy.'

'I have to. Tom can't do it on his own.'

'No.' Fin turns to Tom. 'Please. It's not safe. Take me. Take anyone else.'

'Can you ride a horse?' Tom asks.

'I'm a really fast learner.'

'Mate, I don't want this any more than you do, but I'm not going to let anything happen to her. I swear on my bloody life.'

Fin looks at me. 'I love you. You can do this. Okay? I love you.'

I nod.

Tom clears his throat. 'We have to go.'

I follow Tom to a storeroom door at the end of the corridor. He takes his keys from his belt and unlocks it. Inside there is a series of metal cabinets. He unlocks one and pulls out his rifle. He takes it to a small workbench in the centre of the room, where he opens a case of bullets and loads them into the cartridge. He slings the weapon over his shoulder and goes back to the cabinet. He takes a small handgun, loads it and lays it on the table along with a holster.

'Take off your jacket.'

I can't move.

Tom softens his voice. 'I need to fit this to you. It can go over your sweater, but it needs to be adjusted properly.'

I take my jacket off and Tom shows me how to put my arm through the holster so the gun will sit snuggly under my left arm. He gives me the gun and I push it in.

'I'll talk you through it out there. That's the best I can do. If Jaxon hears you practising he'll come out guns blazing.'

'Literally.'

'Yes.'

'Do you think it's safe for us to go out there?'

Tom adjusts his jacket and zips it up. He's nervous. I can't have Tom nervous; it will bring me undone.

'What if I can't do what I have to do – if I have to shoot someone, to kill them. I don't want to do that …' Again. I don't want to have to do it again. Do not cry, Lucy. Don't be that girl.

'You'll do what needs to be done.'

'Tom, I can't do this—'

'Yes, you can. Do you know how brave you are? Lucy, look at me. You are a strong person. You don't make it this far and go through what you've been through if you're weak. You've lost people. Lucy, look at me, you need to hear this. I've lost people too and it's the worst, loneliest thing, but you're still here. There are people who would say that this whole fight is a survival of the fittest thing – strong live, weak die. Fittest for what though? Fittest for letting a little kid starve to death?

'You're not a kid anymore. You're a bloody strong woman with a lot of fight in you. You think I let you go on hunts because you rode a horse nicely over some jumps? Mate, you fell headfirst into the mud.' Tom smiles and the lines around his eyes crinkle. 'You grabbed those reins off Esther and the look on your face! You were so pissed off! You got back on and I reckon it wouldn't have mattered how many times you came off – you would have kept going at that jump. If you'd fallen off ten times I still would've let you ride out because you've got fight.

'Keep your head up, eyes forward. Look down when you're riding and you're more likely to fall, aren't ya? Same with this. Eyes forward. I'll look out for you, you look out for me.'

Tom pulls a tissue out of his pocket and hands it to me.

'If I was your dad I'd be bloody proud of you. Keep your eyes forward, mate. You'll be all right.'

We leave the compound and ride to the spot where Tom taught Esther to shoot. He pulls Red up and dismounts.

'Get the gun but stay on the horse.'

I do what I'm told. The gun is warm.

'Hold the reins tight with your left hand. Gun in the right.' He arranges my fingers around the handle. 'Raise it up. Arm straight. Don't lock your elbow. Look through the little circle and make sure the line is centred. Squeeze the trigger a bit to load it – you'll hear a click. The next squeeze will fire a shot. It's difficult with one hand, but I don't trust this horse – you'll need to hold him. Don't pull the trigger; squeeze, it will help reduce the kickback. Your hand's probably still going to jolt. Don't panic. If you have to let go of the reins to take the safety off, fine. But pick them up to fire. Frosty is used to the sound of my gun, but this is louder. We'll just have to hope for the best.'

'Will do.'

'When I get off to make a kill, you take the gun out. Cover me.'

'Okay.'

'You'll be fine.'

'If you say so.'

When the sun comes up the light dips and flickers through the treetops. The only sound is the steady rhythm of the horses' hooves on the ground and the pounding of blood in my ears. We keep to a walk to minimise the possibility of kangaroos fleeing and it's at least two hours before Tom spots anything. He raises his left fist and pulls Red to a halt. I pull the handgun from under my coat to cover him. Once he's on the ground Tom hands me Red's reins and loads his rifle. It occurs to me that I'll have to hold Red and Jack Frost and fire a weapon all at once. It will be interesting at least. I watch as Tom takes slow, tentative steps into the scrub, pausing whenever one of the mob raises its head.

The shot cracks through the stoic trees and three black cockatoos the size of eagles evacuate screaming from the branches above.

'Luce! Hit,' Tom calls. Leading Red beside me, I manoeuvre Jack Frost through the trees, all the while trying to keep watch. It feels as though I don't take another breath until the kangaroo is loaded onto Red's hindquarters and Tom is back in the saddle.

'Good,' he murmurs. 'We're still alive.'

We don't come across anything else and by a quarter to twelve we are back on the north track heading home. I'm flooded with relief that it's almost over.

Tom turns to me and winks. 'Good job, Luce. I reckon we—'

A gunshot snaps through the silent bush. Another. Another.

'Lucy! Stay with me!' Tom kicks Red into a canter and I follow him. Another gunshot. Tom falls forward and Red pivots on his hindquarters. Tom comes out of the saddle, landing heavy on the ochre track. There's another ear-piercing noise and I realise it's my own screaming. Jack Frost dances to the side as I pull him up. I still have my gun but have no idea which direction I should aim it.

'Lucy, go, go,' Tom moans. 'Get away.'

Jack Frost swings around again, head in the air. Red stands still with his head lowered while Tom rolls onto his back, clutching his right bicep. Blood is seeping through the khaki fabric.

'Lucy, go!'

'No.'

'GET OUT OF HERE!'

I jump down from the saddle, put the gun away and take the lead rope from the back of my saddle. I clip it to Jack Frost's bridle and tie him to a low tree branch. I pray that if Red doesn't take off, neither will Frosty. Tom growls at me, his words now garbled.

'You have to get back on,' I tell him, looking into the bush around us. I pull off my scarf and knot it as tightly as I can above the bullet wound. 'I'm not leaving you out here.' I put my hands under his armpits.

'Leave me!' he screams.

'No!' I scream back at him.

He cries out in pain but I persist. Somehow he manages to get to his feet, stumbling forward when he takes the first steps. Red waits patiently as I give Tom a leg-up into the saddle. Tom slumps forward over Red's neck. I take a big chunk of Red's mane and close the fingers on Tom's good hand around it and the reins. When I untie Jack Frost he pulls back from me, so I yank on the reins and yell at him too. I keep hold of the lead rope and clip it onto Red's bridle. My legs shake so much I can barely get my foot in the stirrup to mount up. I had expected someone would emerge from the bush to take our kills or our horses or both, but the bush is silent again.

'You're losing blood. We're going to have to hurry. Do you think you can stay on at a canter?'

Tom straightens himself a little and nods.

'Red will just follow on, won't he?' I ask.

Another nod.

Tom's blood is seeping into the grey wool of my scarf. It only takes the slightest touch of my heels for Jack Frost to spring forward into a trot. Beside me, Tom is steady in the saddle, so I push Jack Frost into a canter.

'Do not fall off!' I yell at Tom.

The ride back seems to take longer than ever. The horses pull to a halt at the gate, tossing their heads. Tom tries to twist around to see if we've been followed, growling with pain. As he struggles to unhook the keys from his belt with his left hand, there's another gunshot in the distance and the horses scramble. I half fall, half dismount, just managing to keep hold of Jack Frost's reins.

'Lucy!' Tom tosses the keys to me.

'Code red!' I scream in the direction of the main building. 'Code red!'

I unlock the gate and it swings open. Spooked, Jack Frost pulls away from me and bolts up to the stables. I scream for help over and over so loudly I feel as though my throat must be bleeding. I pull Red through the gate and lock it behind me. People, including Fin, are running down the hill towards us. The arm of Tom's coat is soaked a rich burgundy. I try to re-tie the knot in the scarf tighter and the blood seeps warm through my gloves. I lead Red from the gate to the stables as quickly as I can.

Fin and Rob help Tom off the horse and take him inside one of the stables where they lay him on the dirt floor. Raahel, followed by two guards, arrives with the medical kit. She hands me a pair of scissors to cut Tom's sleeve open while she prepares an injection of painkiller. Tom's groans quieten and he stills. His eyes are half-closed.

'Stay with us, Tom,' Raahel says.

I stand there with no way of helping, my body shaking all over.

Fin puts his hands on my face. 'Are you okay?'

I nod, unable to talk. He wraps his arms around me and I sob, my face pressed against his chest.

THIRTY-FIVE

Once Raahel has stopped the bleeding, Tom is brought up to the building and put in the medic room. I've been wrapped in a space blanket but I shake it off and ignore Fin's plea to sit down.

'I need to see Tom,' I tell him.

The door to the corridor feels especially heavy when I pull it open. Esther is pacing in front of the medic room and she looks hopeful when she hears the door open but her expression turns sour when she sees it's me.

'What happened?' Her words are sharp.

'Someone shot at us.'

'You seem fine.'

'I'm not fine. I'm scared. And I want to see Tom.'

'Where's Jaxon?'

'I don't know. I thought he would be with Tom. Esther, what's happening in there? Is he okay?'

Raahel emerges from the medic room. She closes the door behind her and pulls the surgical mask down below her chin.

'Lucy, you're in shock. Go and sit down.'

'Is Tom okay?'

'Can you please go and sit down.'

Jaxon comes into the corridor; he seems to suck all the air from it. 'Raahel! What's happening with Tom?'

'The bullet went through his bicep. He has lost a lot of blood.' She's flustered. 'I need to look through the files and find a potential donor.'

'That's not … that can't be right.'

'He has been shot, Jaxon. I'm performing surgery in there, which I'm not trained to do.'

'Has he said anything?'

'He's unconscious.'

'I want to know as soon as he wakes up. He talks to me first. No-one else. What are you doing now?'

'I've stemmed the blood loss, but we need to give him a transfusion. I can't remember his blood type or who his matches are. I sent someone to get you earlier—'

'You can't remember? It's your job to remember! What the hell are you doing here if you can't remember how to do your bloody job? Move!' He shouts so loudly she flinches. Esther looks at her feet as Jaxon shoves his way into the room. Raahel follows him while Esther and I wait outside.

The sound of his cutting words.

Esther with her head in her hands.

Raahel comes out and whispers to me, 'Go into the office and open the filing cabinet.' Her hand trembles as she presses her keys into my palm. 'Look in the second drawer down: Shepherd, Tom Shepherd. Bring me the file.'

*

Tom's file is clearly marked in neat school-teacher script, right next to mine. I take both out and tuck mine under my sweater, securing it in the band of my jeans. I search through the desk drawers and find a map of Greater Sydney and a compass. The map looks old and I imagine a lot has changed. I take it and the compass.

When I return to the medic room, Jaxon is in the doorway with his arms folded, waiting for me. Esther is gone.

'What the hell happened?'

'Someone shot him.'

'No shit, Lucy.' He slows his speech down as if I can't understand him. 'What exactly happened? What did you see?'

'We were coming back on the north track, about half a kilometre from camp. Everything had been fine, but then there were gunshots and Tom was hit in the arm. I tied my scarf above the bullet wound and brought him back here.'

'I asked what you saw.'

'Nothing. There were gunshots and Tom was hit. We didn't see anyone.'

He stares me in the face and says nothing for a moment; I hold his gaze.

'Are you absolutely sure of that?'

'Yes.'

'I want you to listen very, very carefully. If you saw something – anything – I need to know. It doesn't matter what you thought it was. If you know something and you don't tell me right now, there will be consequences. If you tell anyone anything about what happened, without telling me first, you will not be able to stay here.'

'I didn't see anything. Please, I have to give this to Raahel.' I hold up the folder.

'You got that from the office?'

'Raahel told me to.'

'She gave you keys?'

'Yes.'

'Give them to me.' He holds out his palm.

'They're Raahel's keys.'

'Not if she's gonna give them to whoever she wants.'

'She needs to know his blood type. She's trying to save his life.'

He towers over me. 'Give me the keys, you little bitch.'

I want to tell him where he can put his keys. I want to kick and scream at him. I don't. But I don't give him the keys either. Raahel comes out of the medic room to find him looming over me with his face inches from mine.

'Lucy?'

I hand her the folder and pull the keys from my pocket to give to her.

Jaxon grabs my wrist but turns his attention to Raahel. 'You gave her the keys.'

'I have to treat Tom.'

He shakes his head, looks back at me and tightens his grip. 'You think you're a clever girl, don't you? You're actually just very, very stupid. If it were up to me, you'd be out of here. You better hope Tom survives – he's the only one who wants to keep you around.'

He releases my wrist and turns to Raahel. 'First warning.' He holds one finger up, as if she's a child. 'You have beautiful kids – they only stay if you follow the rules.'

THIRTY-SIX

I sit by the fire with Fin and he laces his fingers through mine, his left knee bouncing up and down with restless nerves. Max keeps asking me questions but I can't answer any of them because my mind has gone numb. The space blanket draped over my shoulders is somehow supposed to help with the shock caused by bullets flying past my head and hitting my friend beside me. My limbs feel disconnected from my body. This is what it is to fall to pieces.

Bit got hypothermia once. Not from the cold, but because her body went into shock as her organs started to shut down one by one, like lights going out in a house at night. For her the morning came. But that was before the winter, back when there was an abundance of food – she just had to pick it up and eat it. Now, where she is there is none.

The stacks of white boxes begin to sway like Jenga towers. The fluorescent light in my head flickers. I wonder where Declan Flemming is now?

All of those people turning to dust in the comfort of their own homes.

'Jaxon called me a little bitch,' I whisper to Fin.

Max stares at me. Maybe I shouldn't be saying this in front of him but I feel a need to pull the three of us back together, like we need to be ready for something. He needs to know whose side to be on.

'He threatened me and he threatened Raahel.'

Fin frowns. 'What? Why?'

'Because I wouldn't give him Raahel's keys after I got Tom's file from the office. She needed his medical records. Jaxon went mental and called me a little bitch. He grabbed my wrist. Hard.'

'He wouldn't do that,' Max says.

Fin glances over his shoulder.

'He shouted at Raahel and shoved her.'

Max looks at Fin. 'He wouldn't do that.'

'I'm not lying, Max.'

'But he's not like that!' Max's voice grows in pitch. Seamus lifts his head and Fin puts a hand on Max's shoulder. These past few weeks Max's friendship with Jaxon has kept his head above the swirling black water around us. I don't want to pull him under but if something really dangerous happens he needs to know who this person he idolises really is.

'Max, keep your voice down.' Fin leans in close to Max. 'You need to keep this here, between us three.'

'We've looked after each other since the beginning,' I whisper. 'We've trusted each other. We need to really think about whether we can trust Jaxon … I've been wondering if Noll would.'

Max looks up at me, his lower lip wobbling.

'We're safe here,' he says. 'You and Fin said so.'

I glance at Fin but neither of us can say the words Max wants to hear.

We wait in tense silence for any news of Tom. I want to go to the medic room to check on him but I don't want to be anywhere near Jaxon, so I do nothing. It's an hour before Jaxon comes into the rec hall and claps his hands for attention. He stands before us, eyes red-rimmed, and runs a shaking hand over his clipped hair.

'By now you all know Tom and Lucy went out on a hunt this morning. Tom …' Jaxon closes his eyes and takes a moment to compose himself as if he's close to breaking down. 'Tom has been shot. Raahel is doing an amazing job looking after him, but he has lost a bit of blood. We might be looking at a transfusion. I'm sure Raahel has already spoken to some of you about that. Lucy says she didn't see anyone or anything, but obviously we'll be investigating.'

Max looks at me. I think maybe he hears the accusation in Jaxon's words.

'Lockdown will stay in place until further notice,' Jaxon continues. 'I want to assure everyone that if we come under direct attack, we are prepared. I'll die before I see harm come to anyone here. We have to be vigilant and we all have to follow the rules that keep us safe.'

*

Later, Raahel walks over and crouches down next to me. 'I need you to check you over. Tom is in the medic room so we'll have to do it in the kitchen.' Her expression isn't right, it's too stoic. Fin flicks me a glance and I think he has noticed it too.

'Why can't we just go in the corner, behind the screen?'

Raahel shakes her head. 'No. It needs to be in the kitchen.'

I get up and follow Raahel out into the corridor.

'You need to cry and apologise.' She doesn't look at me as she speaks.

'What?'

'Think of whatever it is that will make you cry. You need to fall apart and apologise to Jaxon.'

'What for?'

'It doesn't matter.'

'No. He's a dick. I'm not apologising for anything.'

Raahel grabs me by the arm and stops walking. 'He doesn't like you. He doesn't like you standing up to him. He doesn't like you talking back. And now my children are on the line. If you want us to stay safe you have to be weak – you can't be a threat to him. Think of it, Lucy. Find the thing that will make you cry.'

'No,' I whisper.

'Close your eyes.'

I shake my head but Bit's face is already there: her sunken cheeks, her blue eyes and her cold hand on mine. I remember holding her spindly frame at night when we were running out of food, trying to keep her warm, waiting on her every breath. Declan Flemming's smug face and everything I imagined she must have felt trapped in his dad's stupid Mercedes. The bruises on her skin like petals of a dark flower. It wasn't your fault, my darling, beautiful sister. It wasn't your fault.

Jaxon is pacing the kitchen. When he turns around I can literally see his nostrils flare, like a bull. But when he sees my tears his expression changes – he looks pleased.

'There you are. I think we need to have a chat about what happened before, don't you? I'm willing to let it go. You were upset.' He stands less than a metre from me with his arms folded across his chest and waits.

Say sorry, Lucy. Say it.

'Fuck you,' I spit.

His height increases as the rage floods him. Raahel gasps when he rushes at me and shoves me against the wall. I still have space to move but I'm frozen.

'Say that again. Go on, you little bitch. Say it again.'

'Jaxon, stop it,' pleads Raahel. She's crying in fear but she walks towards him.

'Don't you fucking move,' he says to her.

I try to fight everything in my body that tells me to give in. I try and try. But I'm like a piece of paper – he's crumpled me up into nothing and I can feel every crease. 'I'm sorry, I'm sorry. Please. I'm sorry.'

His eyes are bulging and there's spittle in the corners of his mouth. He's so close that I can see the pores in his skin. He inhales slowly, then takes a step back. He reaches out to touch my cheek and I shrink away as he softly wipes a tear away with his thumb. He tilts his head to the side like he's trying to make a decision.

'I'm sorry.' I'm snivelling and I hate myself for being so weak.

'Shhh. It's okay. I understand. It hurt me when you ignored me when I asked for the keys. It's like you don't trust me and that really hurts because I work so hard for this place. For these people. For you.' He puts his thumb under my chin and tilts my face up. I'm malleable to him, like a puppet.

'I was scared when I heard what happened to you and Tom. But you did a good job. You got him back on that horse – you got him home.'

He turns to Raahel and smiles as if nothing has happened. 'Check her over. Make sure she wasn't injured out there. I'm gonna wait right out here. We'll go back into the rec hall when you're done.'

Jaxon steps outside the door without closing it behind him.

Raahel motions to a chair and I sit down.

'I don't need checking.' My voice quakes. 'I'm fine, nothing happened to me.' It's strange to be in a room with her after what's just happened and not be able to speak about it.

'I need to check your blood pressure; can you take off your jacket?'

It's as I'm shrugging off my jacket that I remember the gun Tom gave me – it's tucked in the holster at my side. Raahel sees it and straightaway pulls the jacket back over my shoulders. She silently indicates to me to only take one arm out of its sleeve so I can keep the gun hidden.

'That's it,' she says loudly. 'And your jumper and T-shirt, just put them on the bench and I'll check you over.' She mouths *keep them on.*

She leans forward and looks into my eyes with a little torch. 'Follow my finger,' she says and moves her finger back and forth in front of my face.

I feel like an actor on a stage; it's a performance, a game of pretend.

The rest of her examination passes with me sitting almost mute aside from yes or no. She tells me I'm okay, which we both know is ridiculous.

THIRTY-SEVEN

Jaxon calls all security personnel into the reception room. Shut out of the meeting, I'm helpless to do anything other than wait outside the medic room for updates about Tom from Raahel. Everything about the shooting and Jaxon's reaction is going around and around my head – something niggles at me and I can't work out what it is.

I need to tell Fin and Max what Jaxon did in the kitchen. But our altercation is a slippery thing – it makes me feel small and helpless just to acknowledge it happened. I was the helpless little girl against the big bad man. All I can do is stand outside the medic room and wait for the spinning compass of my instinct to stop and show me which way to go.

I will Tom to wake up. Maybe I didn't get him back in time, but he was so heavy to lift. If only he hadn't come off his horse. But at least I could get him back on; Jaxon was right about that.

The compass comes to a stop and the truth hits me in a hot rush of adrenaline and panic down my spine.

*

The security meeting finishes and I go back into the rec hall. Fin sits down with his sketchbook and props it against his knees. Seamus is lying beside him with his head on Max's lap. More people have gathered by the fire, so there's no way to talk to Fin and Max without everyone hearing. I sit next to Fin and he examines his drawing, biting his lip and frowning, rolling a pencil between his thumb and forefinger. It's the view looking north from the greenhouse: patchy grass laced with the intricate shadows of tree branches, the tall chainlink fence topped with barbed wire like strung stars, a figure and a dog slipping through the gate.

'Weren't you supposed to be on lookout?' I ask him.

'I was.'

'Drawing?'

The corner of his mouth curves up. 'Drawing is looking.'

'Who's that?'

'Don't know.'

Max looks at the drawing. 'That's Jaxon. He came and took Seamus.'

In Sydney, Fin did a drawing of his living room on a tilt with all the furniture sliding across the floor. He said he felt like the world had tilted and everything was sliding off. It's exactly how I feel now – we are all pieces of a chessboard that is being tilted up and up. We are all sliding and it's Jaxon's game.

I get up and find the Scrabble box in the cupboard.

Laying out the board I shake the letters onto the carpet and make my selection.

'You can't look at them first!' Max says.

'It's a different game, Max.'

He makes a dramatic show of rolling his eyes. 'Then it's a dumb game.'

I arrange the letters on the board and point to it.

WHEN HE DO THAT

'What's the score, Max?' Fin asks.

Max frowns.

'The letters Lucy used. What's the number?'

'Eleven? Ish?' Max says.

'Pass me the score sheet, Max. I want to check the numbers.'

I flick to a new page in the notebook and write: *J told me it was good I got T back on horse. Never told J that T fell off. He saw it. He was there.* I pass the notebook to Fin.

'Jaxon totally lied about the game this morning,' I say, tipping the letters off the board. I take the notebook back from Fin and write in it again: *What if J shot T?* I show it to Fin first, then Max.

Max shakes his head. Fin points to his drawing right as Rob walks by us. I tear the page from the notebook and flip the board. Max is a small child again. He draws his knees to his chin and wraps his arms around himself. I touch his shoulder and he jerks away.

'Look at me, Max.'

He turns his furious glare to me.

'We can't finish the game without you,' I tell him.

Around us people are settling down – the bedtime routine will begin soon. Fin – still pretending this is an innocent Scrabble game – arranges letters on the board and turns to me.

IS T AWAKE

I shake my head. I shuffle closer beside him and place my hand on the back of his neck, pulling him down towards me so our foreheads almost touch and my hair falls in front of my face like a curtain. He looks understandably confused.

'We need to get out of here,' I whisper. I kiss him and wrap my arms around his neck. We're two crazy kids in love, adorable and harmless. Nothing to see here.

'I don't know how,' he whispers back.

THIRTY-EIGHT

My immediate thought is that we are imprisoned by a monster, but the truth is more terrifying: Jaxon isn't a monster – he's a human and what he is doing to us is invisible. I want to say he's an abusive, controlling person with a hero complex and a terrible, terrible singing voice. I want them to know who he really is, but how would I even describe what Jaxon does? He stands too close? He doesn't use a nice voice? He's never hit me. He pushed me, but they could just say he was scared and stressed because Tom was shot. Besides, we know how people can respond. We've heard it all before: if you were so uncomfortable, dearie, why didn't you yell out? Or scream? Or run away? Besides, he's a good bloke. He writes songs about Esther. He loves Esther.

The way he makes me feel can't be described. It can't be proven. And what would all my accusations be other than snarky opinions about a good bloke who everyone knows is flawed, but still a good guy, right? Give him the benefit of the doubt, love. You might not like how he goes about things, but he gets the job done. He keeps us all fed and watered and safely tucked in at night.

*

The flames of the lamps are extinguished and the locks on the shutters double-checked. There is nothing I can do now except lie next to Fin and grip his hand.

In the morning, when everyone else is getting up and ready for another day of nothing, Fin rolls over and presses his forehead to mine. 'You need to get out of here,' he whispers. 'Go with Esther to Sydney. Try and find Mr Effrez; maybe he can help us. But if you decide you want to keep going and find your family, I understand.' He strokes my hair, a tear slides down his cheek. 'It's not safe here but Max isn't strong enough to leave. I have to stay.'

'Fin …'

He kisses me. 'You have to get out of here. You were right all along. I'm sorry.'

Jaxon keeps his vigil by the door to the medic room. The only person he allows in or out is Raahel, who tells us Tom is sedated and on a lot of pain medication. I don't get a chance to talk to her because Jaxon is always guarding the door and every time I try to approach Esther to tell her my theory and ask for her help, she walks away. Finally after breakfast I see her heading for the bathrooms with her toiletries bag. Straightaway I dash to the medic room, where Jaxon sits on a chair outside the door.

'Jaxon, I need to speak to Raahel.'

He raises a sceptical eyebrow.

'Please. It's a women's medical thing. I'm having a problem with my—'

An expression of extreme discomfort crosses his face and he holds up a hand for me to stop.

'It will only take a moment.'

He raps his knuckles against the door and Raahel comes out. She's surprised to see me.

'Raahel, I'm having … I need medical advice. Can you have a look at something for me? In the bathroom? I'm having my period and the blood doesn't look right.'

Jaxon's expression turns to disgust and he waves us away. 'We need to talk to Esther,' I tell Raahel when we are out of earshot.

When we enter the tiny bathroom Esther is washing her face with cold water from the bucket sitting in the sink. She finishes, pausing to look at us as she picks up her towel, and Raahel presses her back against the door to prevent anyone coming in. I'm glad Raahel is there because the look on Esther's face makes it clear she doesn't want to listen to anything I have to say.

'What's going on?' she asks.

'Jaxon is dangerous, Esther,' I say. 'You know it. We are trapped in this place with him and we have to do something.'

'No,' Esther says. 'No. He loves me. I love him.'

'But he won't let you look for your dad,' I say.

'It's dangerous! Tom was shot!' She looks at me. 'Are you insane? You were there!'

'I'm starting to think it's more dangerous here,' I say.

She pulls her toothbrush from her toiletries bag, ignoring me.

'Esther, I think it might have been Jaxon who shot Tom.'

Her toothbrush clatters to the floor. 'That's ridiculous.'

'Lucy?' Raahel looks panicked.

'He said it was good that I was able to get Tom back on Red. I never told him that Tom came off.'

'That doesn't mean anything,' says Esther. 'That doesn't mean he shot Tom.'

'If he would shoot Tom, we're not safe here anymore,' Raahel says.

'Tom is his friend!'

'Jaxon saw what happened,' I say. 'Fin saw him leaving the compound. Why would he pretend he hadn't?'

'I don't know. I just know he would never do that.'

'We've both heard how he talks to you, Esther,' Raahel says.

'He's done it to both of us too,' I say. 'Called me stupid, a bitch, shoved me against the wall.'

'You're jealous of me. Of how he looks at me.'

'I'm not jealous, Esther.'

'You are. He's told me what you've tried to do. You've flirted with him.'

'No, Esther.'

'He told me.' She laughs. 'He told me you're pathetic. You keep touching him.'

'He's manipulating you.'

'You wanted to train with me so you could show off in front of him.'

'Esther, I was wearing an oversized Spider-Man T-shirt and tracksuit pants.'

'You came on to him when you were in the greenhouse alone. He told me. You want me to go and find Dad so you can have Jaxon. He's not stupid. He knows what you're doing.'

'That's not true, Esther,' I say.

'Esther. He's threatened me and …' Raahel looks away wiping tears from her eyes.

'What?' Esther's tone changes; she's worried.

'He said that if I don't do everything he tells me to then Elia and Saramma can't stay here.'

Esther shakes her head, backing away. 'No. No. He wouldn't …'

'I hate what he's doing to you, Esther,' I say. 'I know your dad. It makes perfect sense that you'd be so fearless and determined and terrifying in a really good way. I hate that Jaxon's trampling all over that. He's threatened by you and your strength – he won't even let you have a gun to stay safe on hunts. He needs us all to believe we're in danger and he's the only one who can keep us safe,' I say. 'You know what's happening here isn't right. You saw Sarah and Polly. Jaxon says they lured him into a trap, but you saw that little girl, Esther. You saw her starving mother.'

'Yes, and you saw what happened when Jaxon went to help them. He was attacked.'

'According to him. No-one witnessed it.'

'Do you think he just, what, punched himself in the face?'

'I checked him afterwards,' Raahel says. 'His face was scratched and bruised but he had no other injuries, nothing at all on the rest of his body.'

'That's ridiculous.'

'I think he's willing to do just about anything to get what he wants,' I say.

'Which is?'

'Control? Power? Tom told Jaxon what track we were taking yesterday. Jaxon knew where we would be and what time we'd be there. If we were attacked by strangers, why wouldn't they take our food? Or the horses? Tom was hit and then nothing else happened. Maybe Jaxon didn't mean to hit Tom. The way he's acting now makes me think he didn't, but wanted to frighten us, to scare Tom.'

'Why?'

'Because Tom was starting to challenge him about how he was running this place. And about how he's treating you and stopping you from going to Sydney.'

'You don't know Jaxon,' she says.

'I do. I've seen guys like him before, Esther.'

Her eyes are welling with tears. I can feel Bit's cold, thin hands in mine. I can see the same look of disbelief in Esther's eyes as was in Bit's. I have to tell her.

'My sister's boyfriend. He was charming and funny and went on and on about how much he loved her. Everyone adored him. She wouldn't sleep with him. She was sixteen. He raped her.' I don't cry when I say the words. I raise my chin and look Esther and my pain in the eye. 'She was so ashamed that she didn't tell anyone except me. She thought it was her fault. I know exactly what Jaxon is. He loves being the hero, the good guy, the charmer, and he's used to getting everything he wants. If you say no to a guy like that he snaps.'

Esther closes her eyes like she's pretending she's not here. When she speaks I can barely hear her.

'If Dad loved me he would be here.' Her hands are trembling. 'But he doesn't think I'm worth the risk.'

'Is that what Jaxon has said to you?'

She starts to cry.

'It's not true. He was holding on to hope. It's strange he hasn't shown up here. He said he was going to come. He had fuel, he had food. There has to be a reason why he hasn't. It doesn't feel right.'

'Nothing feels right,' says Raahel. 'This lockdown, the changes to patrols. We have no idea what's going on outside the fence.'

'He says he's worried about outsiders coming in, but he's making a lot of effort to stop us going out.'

'Jaxon wants me to be safe,' Esther says.

'If this here is what safety is,' I say, 'I don't want it. I don't want to live in a place with someone like him in charge. I want to know what's happening outside of here, what's happening in Sydney and what's happened to my family. I'm taking Jack Frost. And a gun.'

'He'll never let you out of here like that,' says Esther.

'I'm not asking for permission and I already have a gun.'

'If he has shot Tom,' says Raahel, 'everyone here needs to know.'

'We have no proof. It's my word against his and I'm an outsider.'

Esther looks up at the ceiling and wipes tears from her cheeks with the back of her hand.

'Will you come with me, Esther? We can find out what's happened with your dad. Find out what's happening in Sydney.'

'And what about everyone here? What about you?' Esther looks at Raahel. 'And your girls? Fin and Max? Tom?'

'Jeff was friends with Elliot and Mary,' Raahel says. 'Everyone here has heard about him and everyone here loved Elliot and Mary. If Jeff joins us in speaking up against Jaxon we might be able to sway them.

'I can help you get out. Saramma can have a very unsettled night. I might have to put her in her pram in the middle of the night and take her into the kitchen. I'll pack her Peppa Pig backpack with food and water and leave it with the pram. By the exit.'

'What about Jaxon?' I ask.

'I can fix him a soothing cup of home brew to help him sleep. Maybe with an added sedative.'

Esther is hugging herself so tight her knuckles have turned white. 'The gun you guys had with you when you arrived is still in the safe. And I'm the one who changed the code. He never changed it afterwards.'

'So are you in?'
Something shifts in her eyes. She nods.

THIRTY-NINE

I can't see Esther from where I wait in the corridor, but I can hear her talking to Jaxon, who is still keeping vigil at the foot of Tom's bed.

'The horses need to be fed,' she tells him.

'I'll get a guard to go with you.'

'No, I don't want to go out there. I'm scared. Send Lucy. With any luck someone will kidnap her.'

Jaxon laughs. 'Fine. Tell her to go. Send someone with her.'

Esther rounds the corner of the hallway and gives me a nod.

Fin and I walk down the slope to the stables while I fill him in on the plan.

'You're sure you can trust Esther?' he asks me.

'I think so.'

'Is that enough?'

'It has to be. And she's Mr Effrez's daughter. I can't imagine she would lie to me or double-cross me.'

'Who'd have thought we'd end up in a world where we had legit reason to worry about being double-crossed, like it's a real thing.'

'Oh it's a real thing, my friend.'

'I'm beginning to see that.'

I tell him about Raahel's plan for our escape.

'You're taking Peppa?' he says. 'I won't worry about you then. Peppa can do anything.'

'My thoughts exactly. I have the gun Tom gave me and Esther will get our gun from the safe.' I've just called it our gun. It was Starvos's.

'Can you get us through the gate?'

'I'm not rostered on the border patrol anymore and I don't have keys, but if Jaxon's out cold I'll just tell whoever is on that Jaxon wanted us to swap.'

The horses put their noses over the stable doors when they hear our voices. Fin walks up to Jack Frost and rubs his face. 'You better look after her. Or I'll kill you.'

'Horses don't respond well to threats,' I say.

Fin looks to me and bites his lip. When he speaks there's a wobble in his voice. 'You'll be careful, won't you?'

'Yep.'

'If anyone comes for you, just shoot them – don't hesitate, don't think about it. Just shoot them.'

Fin on the ground gasping for breath. The sound of the bat cracking against Starvos's skull.

'And you'll need more clothes. You can't just walk out of the rec hall in the middle of the night fully dressed.'

'There's coats in the tack shed. Tom has a collection. And we'll put extra clothes in Raahel's pram. What will you say when he wakes in the morning and finds that Esther and I are gone?'

'I'll say you've gone hunting, that you snuck out because Tom and you didn't get enough meat yesterday. I'll say you left early because you didn't think Jaxon would let you.'

'He'll go absolutely ballistic.'

'Not much we can do about that. I've told Max that you might be getting out.'

'What did he say?'

'He's not thrilled, but he had a good idea for Seamus.'

The day drags. I'm confined, nervous and have nothing to do except wait. Esther, Raahel and I barely exchange a word or a glance all day. No-one can know what we are planning. On my way back from dinner I see Raahel heading to the medic room with a mug. Jaxon is still waiting at Tom's bedside.

'I brought you a drink,' I hear her say to him. 'I thought you could use it.'

'Thanks.'

'You've barely slept,' she says. 'I'm worried about you.'

A pause.

'This tastes weird.'

'It's moonshine, Jaxon. It's supposed to taste weird.'

'Can it poison me?'

'No, but it might help you sleep. That's a good thing. You can't keep operating like this without sleep. Now that Tom's out of action we need you. You're all we have to guide us through this.'

Before bed I find Max's backpack in a corner of the room. I slide my hand into the little zippered pocket on the side and find the relic from so long ago. The blank black screen shows my reflection in its cold, shiny surface. Without any expectation I press my thumb against the side of the phone and hold it down. It's been too long. Nothing will happen.

The screen lights up.

My sister's face squished beside mine as we smile into the camera lens. I can hear her laughing and feel the warm sun on my skin. Coconut scented suncream. Music echoing in the background.

I'll be able to show the photo to whoever I come across and ask if they have seen her. I slip it into the pocket of my pyjama pants.

It isn't difficult to stay awake for hours in the night when you have cause to ponder your possible impending destruction. If someone caught us out there in the dark, what would they do to us, I wonder. Jaxon's words make mischief in my tired head: *There's a lot of people out there who want what we've got … You don't wander around on your own … Hate to point out the obvious but you're a girl and you're small … A guy could overpower you … There are others out there and they're animals.* But the anger inside me is stronger than the fear and I'm sick of being on guard, not just since the winter but from the years before. From the years of being a girl. It's like one brick on top of another until, before you notice it's happened, there's a great wall between what you want to be and what you feel you have to be. I want to go walking outside at night.

Just try me, arseholes. I fucking dare you.

After two long hours mentally oscillating between fear and defiance I hear Seamus bark twice outside. I sit up. Act natural, Lucy. Nothing to see here, my friends, just a girl getting up to go to the bathroom. Normal. Maybe she has her period!

I feel the mattress beside me. Fin is gone.

The large room is lit only by the smouldering fire, so I have to tiptoe carefully around the soft mounds of blankets covering sleeping bodies. For some reason I think of a history class in year eight. Pompeii: a city of wealthy, sophisticated people who thought they had it all figured out until hell was unleashed in the sky above them. Men, women and children, forever preserved as a relic to the life taken away from them.

I creep into the corridor and beyond the toilets to the exit where the pram is parked. I take out the clothes and my boots, and go to the bathroom and change. Then I put the backpack on and push the exit door open. Fin is waiting for me outside with Seamus by his side. The dog sees me and wags his tail. Fin hands me a headlamp with a solar charge battery to attach to my helmet. He'd helped himself to three when he got dressed for his shift that night. I go around the side of the building and crouch in the dark, just in case anyone should come outside for some reason. My feet are completely numb from the cold by the time I hear the door open again. I stand and peer around the corner to see Fin hand Esther a headlamp. He looks across at me, jerks his head towards the stables and runs. Esther and I bolt after him in silence, Seamus galloping at our side.

Most horses sleep standing up. If the herd is attacked, they have to be ready to run. When I say his name Jack Frost wakes with a jolt, snorting and backing up into the wall of the stall, which only spooks him more. He's still unnerved by the shooting.

'It's all right, Frosty. Just me.'

He watches, nostrils flared, while he thinks it over, then lowers his head and walks over.

We saddle the horses quickly and walk the track along the inside of the fence to the gate. Fin undoes the padlock and pulls the gate open.

'I love you,' he whispers to me.

Don't, Fin. Please. I start to turn away but, what if this is my last chance? What if he never sees me again and he never knows? I put my lips by his ear. 'I love you too.'

And with that, we are two girls out on our own in the night.

Giddy-up.

FORTY

We have two route options. The first is to travel around the perimeter of the compound, join the road at the campsite entrance and ride the route we would take if we were travelling by car. This is the safest as far as avoiding potential attackers goes. However, Jaxon would also know that and presume it would be our preferred option. He may not have enough fuel to drive all the way to Sydney but he could catch up to us easily. The second option is to follow the narrower walking tracks on the map north before joining the back roads to Sydney. Travelling through the bush is slower and will make us more vulnerable – it's difficult to creep up to someone on a freeway. But who is more dangerous? Some faceless people in the bush? Or Jaxon?

We head along the walking track and our headlamps throw a bobbing white circle of light ahead of us. Seamus is our extra night vision and leads the way. The only sound is the rhythmic footfall of the horses. I'm not sure if the bush would have been so silent in the night-time before the winter. When we do hear the occasional rustle of movement in the darkness, Esther and I pick up the pace. I scan the bush all around us while Esther keeps her headlamp focused on the track. In the strange vortex of night, minutes start to feel like hours and hours minutes. Ahead of us Seamus stops dead and then spins around growling. The white beams from our headlamps slice through the dark, illuminating nothing but trees. Seamus give a single sharp bark, freezes and listens. I strain to hear any sound. A twig cracks and Seamus barks again.

'Possums,' says Esther, clearly unconvinced. 'Maybe we should trot.'

'No. The track's too rocky and uneven.' My throat is constricted, like there's a hand squeezing it. 'If one of the horses goes lame we're screwed.'

Seamus falls silent and looks up ahead. After a moment he whines.

'I think that means he's good to go on,' says Esther.

'We should have brought Max to translate.'

We ride on for what might be twenty minutes. Although the air feels frozen, I'm sweating under my clothes and my heart is pounding. Every time an owl hoots I jump. When one swoops down in front of us Jack Frost jolts sideways in fright and I almost fall off.

Soon the track snakes upwards, into unfamiliar territory, and we take regular stops to check the map.

As we reach the crest of another hill, a sharp sound pings the silence.

Esther pulls Cloudy up. 'What the?'

The ping sounds again and my pocket vibrates.

Esther stares at me. 'Did you bring a phone? Is that an alarm? Did you set an alarm? Why did you even bring a phone?'

'I think … I think it's a message.'

Esther's jaw drops open and I feel like I've slipped into an alternate universe. Or back in time. Or something equally impossible. I take the phone from my pocket and stare at the screen.

'I've got two bars of coverage.'

'You've got coverage?'

'Yes.'

'You've got coverage?'

'Yes, Esther, I've got coverage. The power is back on … somewhere.'

I press the little speech bubble and the message opens. It's from Bit, but is two months old. I read and I can't breathe anymore – it's like all the darkness around comes crushing against me.

1/2
Lucy, my darling, beautiful sister.
If you ever get this, know I love you.
Mum and Dad are still alive. I can't say they are okay.
I don't have much time left and I have so
much I never got to say to you. I'm sorry if
I ever asked too much of you. I know you were
hurting too.

2/2
I don't know if there's anything
after this world. I hope so because if there is
you will be there one day. But not too soon because
you've always been so strong and I'm
sure you will survive whatever this is.
Thank you for always,
always, being there for me. You are my hero.
I love you forever. Goodbye. Bit, Lop-eared Rabbit, Lop.
Penelope. xxx

She is dead. They are all dead. Of course they are. They are dead and I am here, in the night, spinning around on the surface of a planet that no longer contains my sister, my mother or my father.

'Lucy?'

My hands are trembling. I drop the phone. 'Sorry. I'm sorry.'

'It's okay. I'll get it.' Esther dismounts. 'What did it say?'

'Nothing much. It was from the day of the blasts.' I lie. 'You should try and call your dad.'

Esther's face is illuminated by the cold light from the phone. 'I don't know his number. How stupid is that. God. It ends in 325. I think. Oh my goodness, that is so stupid.' She starts to cry, staring at the phone as if it might help her remember. 'Call your parents.' She passes the phone to me. I open the contacts menu and my phone beeps again: low battery. When it dies I won't have the pictures of Bit. I scroll to my mum's number. Disconnected. My dad's. Disconnected.

'Esther, just try any number you can think of. Just keep trying – you'll remember.' I hand the phone back to her. 'Keep trying until the battery dies.'

She stares at the phone. They used to be such useful things, mobile phones. They ruled our lives. And now?

Esther closes her eyes, opens them again and begins punching numbers in. She puts the phone to her ear and in the dead quiet of the night I can hear it ringing on the other end. And then a crackling voice.

'Hello?'

FORTY-ONE

'Who is this?' Esther looks at me while she tries to process what she's hearing. 'Where? Tell me where. The battery's dying.'

I can hear the muffled voice on the phone. Esther frowns at me as she listens. She plugs her other ear with her finger. 'What? … Yes.' She covers the receiver and speaks to me. 'Get the map.'

I dismount and find the map in the backpack.

'Western turn-off?' Esther says into the phone. She shakes her head, pulls the phone away and looks at the black screen.

'Who was it?' I ask her.

'Libby someone – it was crackly; I couldn't hear much.' Esther's words tumble out in a rush. 'I don't know her, but she says she's with dad. He's alive. They're close by, at a farm. She was trying to explain exactly where but the phone died.' Esther takes the map from me. 'I think she said something about coming north and taking a turn off the freeway, Waiter Road or something?'

I look over the map. 'There's a Walker Road turn off the freeway?' I point to the spot.

'That could be it, we go west on Walker. It's mostly farms I think. The house is on a hill to the north of the road, about three kilometres from the turn-off.'

'Where is that from here? Where are we?'

Esther examines the map. She points to a squiggle among an expanse of green. I am a rookie with the map, no idea how to judge distances.

'It's not far. Five kilometres or so. We'll be able to move quicker if we take this track to the freeway and ride the rest on the road.'

It's too much to process at once. The perfect white boxes with all my thoughts about Bit are scattered. Fragments of images and conversations swirl and fall like flakes of ash, turning to dust when they settle. What did my parents do with her body? What has happened to theirs? What was it like for them, getting weaker and slower every day? Did they grow more and more tired and then fall asleep? Or was it painful? Did they panic? Maybe they didn't have the energy.

When we reach the freeway the pools of light from our headlamps show it to be less of a road and more a wide stretch with snake grass encroaching on either side and patches of leaves and twigs strewn across the expanse. Tall weeds rise from clumps of mulch and dirt here and there. We trot and canter north on the freeway until we get to a big green sign that reads: *Walker Road exit.* The exit lane slopes upward and we take it at a trot. At the top is a set of traffic lights; one lone amber light flashes, further proof of the unbelievable fact that power is back on.

'Give way to pedestrians,' Esther mutters.

As we take the turn onto Walker Road the sun begins to rise in the east and casts orange and pink light into the brilliant polluted sky. I'm hoping Esther is paying attention to the landmarks because my mind has turned to mush and, incapable of much coherent thought, all I can do is follow her. Five minutes later she points at a house on the side of the hill to the north.

We ride up the dirt driveway towards the house like it's gold at the end of a rainbow, hoping like hell it's real.

The house is one of those typical old farmhouses: tin roof and timber panelled walls, with a wide wraparound verandah perfect for sipping tea and gazing at the sunset. Dead rosebushes and emaciated hedges mark the garden. Faint light glows behind the leadlight window in the front door.

Esther and I pull the horses to a halt.

'Stay here,' Esther says. 'Cover me.'

I keep Cloudy and Seamus with me while Esther takes her gun and goes to the front door. She raps on the window and waits. Moments later the door opens to a woman's silhouette.

'I'm Esther. You're Libby? Where's my dad?'

The woman nods and looks at me warily over Esther's shoulder. 'Were you followed?'

'No. Where's my dad?'

'He's inside, but … he's not well. He was injured and—'

Esther pushes past Libby and enters the house. Libby hurries down the front steps to me. I open my mouth to ask about Mr Effrez but she cuts me off.

'Where's Max? Is he okay? Jeff is sure he saw Fin, but he hasn't spotted Max. Is he at the camp?'

'Yes.'

Libby starts crying. She is so emotional she can barely talk. 'I thought he might have died.' I now recognise Fin in her deep-set blue eyes and wavy dark hair.

'You're their mum.'

'Yes. And you're Lucy. I saw you walking with Fin in the bush once. I tried to get to you both, but a man came running down from the camp. I'm—'

The anger rushes at me so hard it could push me off the horse. 'You left us for dead in Sydney.'

'I didn't. I—'

'Don't lie. I was there. My mum put me in a car and sent me to Sydney – she risked never seeing me again in the hope that you might be able to help me.'

'I know, I—'

'Noll died because of you. If you'd helped us he wouldn't have been shot. In front of your son.'

Libby covers her mouth with her hands.

'He was killed right in front of Max.'

'Oh God.'

'I can't believe you—'

'Lucy, listen to me.'

'I don't want to lis—'

'LISTEN TO ME!' she shouts. 'Is your surname Tenningworth? 28 Banksia Avenue, Mount Riverview?'

'Yes, why?'

'Your mother is alive.'

I have the sensation of being outside of my own body, as if Libby has said the words to someone else and I'm just watching.

'What do you mean? She can't still be alive.'

'She is.' Libby looks beyond me, scanning the paddocks all around. 'Let's talk inside. Hurry. Around the back there's a yard with a fence where you can leave the horses.'

I lead the horses down the side of the house and put them in the small yard. On the back verandah several pairs of dusty boots are lined up beside a doormat declaring my welcome. Withered plants in terracotta pots sit alongside a small table and chairs by the back door. An embroidered cushion says *Poverty is owning a horse* and a wooden sign hung on the wall proclaims it to be wine o'clock somewhere in the world.

Libby unlocks the back door and lets me and Seamus in, bolting it shut behind us. The house is lit only by the early morning light and the glow of an electric heater in the corner of the living room. Seamus sniffs the carpet and the floral couches.

'Some substations have been repaired and once the power came on we began a recovery operation. We have access to fuel and transport again. The military is working through suburbs and towns looking for survivors, distributing food and medical supplies. Records are constantly being updated and I've been checking your area because … I wanted to find Fin's dad. I thought he might have made it home. I have access to the data; Mr Effrez gave me your surname, which is how I found your mother.'

'What about my dad and sister? Penelope, her name is Penelope.'

Libby reaches out as if she's going to touch me, but she hesitates and pulls away again. 'I'm so sorry …'

Bit.

'They didn't survive.'

I can't stop all the pictures closing in on me. She is behind my eyes, she is in my chest, she is standing next to me – she is everywhere and nowhere all at once. And my dad. My beautiful, gentle, worried dad.

My mother alone in her house – her daughter and her husband turning to dust.

But not both her daughters; we aren't both gone.

My hands are shaking.

'Lucy?'

I look up and lock eyes with Libby. 'I want to go home.'

Libby nods. 'I can help you.'

FORTY-TWO

Everything in me is drawn away to the door, to the road, the mountains, my home. When I mentally pull myself back into the room I remember Libby saying Mr Effrez has been injured.

'Where is he?' I ask her. 'What happened?'

'Come.'

She takes me to a bedroom at the end of the hallway. The door is open and another heater glows in the corner. Esther is kneeling on the carpet next to the bed. She holds her dad's hand to her forehead. Mr Effrez lies beneath the blankets, his head turned to Esther. His eyes are open just a little.

Esther looks up at me, tears trickling down her cheeks. 'Lucy's here, Dad. She's okay. Fin and Max are okay too.'

Mr Effrez's lips move a fraction and he makes a sound, but he can't speak. There's a strange scent in the room – antiseptic muddied with a sour fleshy smell.

'He has a bullet in his arm,' Libby says. 'The wound is infected, the skin is all black. He needs penicillin but …' She shrugs.

Esther wipes her cheeks. 'See if Libby's or Dad's charger

fits your phone,' she says. 'Take a screenshot so we can show everyone at Wattlewood that there is coverage and power back on.'

'Evidence.'

Esther nods. I don't tell her that my mother is alive or that I'll use Libby's phone to take the pictures because saying it out loud acknowledges that she will be going back there without me, that I might never go there again. I might never see Fin again, or at least not for a long time.

Libby and I leave Esther to be alone with her dad and go back into the lounge room. I stand by the heater and stare at the orange glowing tubes while I warm my hands to try and stop the shaking.

'I can offer you tea,' says Libby. 'The power's on, but we can't turn the lights on in case he comes looking for us.'

'In case who comes?'

'The man from Wattlewood. Big guy. He was there when we first tried to get in about a week ago. He had an assault rifle – military issue but he clearly wasn't military anymore. We asked if he knew you, Esther, Fin and Max. He said he'd never heard of you three and that Esther had never arrived. We told him the power was on in parts of Sydney. He was shocked and then he got really angry. He pointed a gun at us and told us to leave, said if we came back we'd be shot.'

The impact of her words nearly knocks me over. 'Jaxon,' I whisper.

'We weren't sure if he was telling the truth about you. Neither of us could see any reason why you wouldn't have made it to Wattlewood when you had enough fuel to get there. We hid and I came back later on my own. We figured I wouldn't be as easy to spot if I was alone. That's when I saw you and Fin, but there were guards everywhere. I knew if I yelled out they would hear me, so I was slowly getting closer and closer to you … And then a guy with a gun came running down.'

'It was Tom,' I say. 'He was worried about us.'

'Tom? Jeff's friend? Oh God. I didn't know. If only I'd known that's who it was. Jeff drove back two days later. He was determined to find out what had happened to you all.' Libby sighs. 'He thought he could talk his way in, or that maybe someone who knew him would be at the front gates this time. But no. It was Jaxon. He threatened Jeff again, and Jeff was leaving when Jaxon shot him in the arm.'

It's horrible enough that he shot Tom. But Mr Effrez? I have to sit down in an armchair. My tea spills on my hands; I don't feel a thing.

Libby continues, 'I can only think that he didn't kill him because he didn't want anyone to find Jeff's body. I've tried to do my best with what I have here; there's a lot of vet supplies, bandages and antiseptic, but the bullet wound is badly infected now.'

The horror of what Jaxon has done – his lies, his control – grips my entire body and I feel like I'm going to collapse. But I won't let him paralyse me anymore. I stand up, go back into the bedroom and sit beside Esther. Unmoving, she looks at her dad while I tell her all of what Libby has told me. Everything Jaxon has done. When I finish speaking she takes her gaze from her father and looks at me. She says nothing, just reaches over and takes my hand in hers. She holds it tightly and in that small but heavy moment neither of us is alone.

FORTY-THREE

In the kitchen Libby gives me Mr Effrez's phone and I take a screenshot showing the bars of mobile coverage, and photos of Mr Effrez and his wounds. I plug my own phone into the charger. Afterwards I sit holding the mug of tea Libby has made me. She tells me that my mum is still at our home. In my mind my house is kept beautifully wrapped and safe in a white box, like a doll's house, every detail perfect and unblemished. The reality will be different but all I can see is that perfect image, and all my skin wants is to feel my mother's touch.

'I'm sorry I let you down,' Libby whispers. 'I wanted to find out about your family before I came here – it's the least I could do for you after letting you down like that. And I'm sorry about Noll,' she whispers. 'I have huge regrets. I could have come with Fin and Max, but I played a big role in the recovery. That was my job.' She wipes her eyes. 'It still is, but I couldn't carry on any longer without them. Once the power came on and things felt more hopeful I used the government database to find Jeff. I was so relieved he was still there. He'd been waiting for Esther but I convinced him there was more chance of her being here than coming to Sydney now, so he came down here with me.'

'I'm going to have a shower, then I'll ride home,' I say. 'I have enough food and water. I have a map and a compass. I should be able to get there in twenty-four hours.'

'I understand you wanting to go on your own, but you have to be careful. It can still be dangerous out there.'

'I know. But I have to go to my mum. She's alone now.'

Libby nods. 'Are there medical supplies at the settlement?'

'Yes. There's a doctor and there might be penicillin left. Raahel, the doctor, has been treating Tom. I think Jaxon might have shot him too. Esther can take you back with her. Take Mr Effrez's phone with the photos to prove what Jaxon has done and lied about.'

Before heading to the shower, I go into one of the bedrooms to look for something clean to wear after I wash. The room is so neat and perfect it's disturbing, like a showroom version of a teenage girl's bedroom; fairy lights are strung above a brass bed frame, the duvet is smooth, the cushions are carefully arranged. A white chest of drawers is topped with a gilt mirror and an assortment of moisturisers, perfume and nail polish, each arranged according to size. A large blue rosette from a dressage competition is tied to one of the bed posts and a picture on the wall shows a smiling girl atop a big grey horse. The horse is adorned with a wreath of roses around its neck and the same rosette pinned to its bridle. I recognise the horse: Jack Frost in his past life. I wonder which one he prefers.

I pull open one of the drawers and find some clean T-shirts but not much else. Of course she wouldn't have left any warm clothes behind. The wardrobe is the same: school uniforms, some summer dresses – nothing of any use. I reach up to a high shelf and pull down a big plastic box. Inside are several pairs of white jodhpurs, the kind you would wear to compete in a dressage competition. I strip off my grotty jeans and pull a pair on. They're baggy, which is perfect because I can layer two pairs for warmth. I rummage around in the tub and my fingers find crinkly plastic. I have struck gold – TimTams. Even better, double coated. I leave the box on the floor and go through the rest of the wardrobe. My efforts yield another packet of TimTams (caramel), a block of Cadbury Top Deck chocolate, a Mars Bar and three large packets of M&Ms.

I'll never know what happened to her and her family – if they survived, if they're still alive now. I don't know why anyone would make a break for Sydney or Canberra or wherever else they went and leave behind some of the most calorific food substances known to humankind. Unless she didn't want to let anyone know she was hiding them in the first place.

I put all the chocolate on the bed and take a closer look at her picture on the wall. If she is still alive and she comes home, how will she pick up her life? What will she do? She sits on her horse with the wreath of roses around his neck but she doesn't smile, not really.

For the first time since the missiles I have a hot shower and it feels like I actually get properly clean. Afterwards I go out into the living room where Esther is sitting on one of the couches. Her face is blank and a cup of tea sits on the antique coffee table untouched. I dump the chocolate on the table and Libby looks up at me in surprise.

'That should keep you guys going for a while,' I say.

'Bloody hell,' says Esther.

'My thoughts exactly.' I go back to the kitchen to get my backpack. I can hear Esther and Libby talking in the living room.

'I don't think you and I can just show up there,' says Esther to Libby. 'This morning he would have noticed that Lucy and I have gone and he'll know something's up, no matter what Fin says to him.'

I begin emptying the contents of the backpack so I can make sure I have everything I need to ride to the mountains.

'He'll be out looking for us. If he finds us before we get back to the camp …' Esther trails off.

'You think he would kill us?' Libby asks her. The silence that follows shows this is exactly what Esther thinks.

'So maybe I just go back alone,' says Esther. 'I could say that Lucy kept going for home but I changed my mind and came back, or something like that. I go in and show everyone the pictures of Dad and tell them that the power is on and … I don't know … hope everyone overthrows him?'

I have two water bottles and some dried meat and flatbread. Hopefully it will be enough. I go back into the living room to get some chocolate. Libby has her head in her hands.

I want to go home.

I pick up the Mars Bar from the table and in that instant see the hospital room where I threw one at Bit's face. I see her tears. I remember the blood in the bathroom and the terrible shame that she should never have felt. The shame that belonged to someone else.

'Esther, Jaxon will snap as soon as you make any accusations,' I say. 'You don't have Tom, remember. Jaxon will definitely have a weapon on him. We can't … I mean, you can't just overpower him on your own. He's too big.'

I want to go home.

I want to go home.

'He won't just give it all up,' I say. 'He'll be so humiliated. He won't be the hero anymore. He wants the power and control so badly. He'll do something terrible and make sure you feel like it's your fault. That's what guys like him do when they can't keep what they think belongs to them.'

'But Dad needs penicillin. What are we supposed to do?'

'I have to get Fin and Max out,' says Libby.

I'm sweating even though it's not overly hot in the room, so I go out to the kitchen sink and splash my face with water. In the drawers I find a stack of neatly pressed tea towels, all folded to an identical size, and I dry my face. My coat hangs from a hook by the back door. My boots are beside the welcome mat. The backpack is ready to go. I'm tired but I can make it home to Mum.

I go back into the living room to say goodbye. Esther has wilted.

'Maybe you can go in and say nothing about the power or your dad,' I say. 'Organise a time for Fin to be out at the gates on watch at the same time Libby arrives. Maybe someone else can contain Jaxon somehow and Fin can be on watch and let them in. If Jaxon's able to be caught off guard with no weapon …'

I want to go home.

I want to go home.

I want to go home.

My mouth turns dry. I look at my backpack by the door. I only have to pick it up and walk away. I can take Jack Frost. I can go home and wake up in my own bed.

'Fin won't be on watch. Jaxon will know he helped us get out. No matter what Fin says.'

'Maybe you can convince one of the others. You can do it,' I say. 'You're really strong. You're the strongest woman I've ever met.'

Esther watches me, her lips just parted a fraction and her eyes searching my face. She knows it and so do I:

we're different now to who we were. All of us are. Even the girl from this house. If she's alive and comes home, nothing will be the same because the girl who lived here doesn't exist anymore. Like the Lucy who waited at the bus stop that morning doesn't exist anymore. I can go back home. I can wait at the bus stop, but Fin will never walk around the corner again. *He's one of the good ones, Bit.* I see the room, the bat, Fin on the ground.

I did it for him.

I go to the door and put on the backpack. I can't stay here with his mother's eyes watching me. The one who broke his heart when she abandoned him. But then, for the first time, I see his heart didn't break because she abandoned him. She didn't. His heart broke because she abandoned Noll and me.

I turn back to Esther and Libby. 'We play the scared, silly girls who went out on their own and got frightened. Jaxon will love that. We're humiliated; he's proven right. We tell the others what's happened so they can contain Jaxon. Libby, you bring Jeff to Wattlewood in your car and wait up the road from the gates. Then Fin can let you in.'

'They'll learn who Jaxon truly is,' Esther whispers.

'A bit of a dickhead, actually.'

Esther gives me a wry smile. She is as terrified as I am.

FORTY-FOUR

On the ride to the compound Esther and I move at a canter wherever we can and Seamus gallops along beside us, living his best life. In my head I go over Tom's instructions for firing the gun, which is in the pocket of my coat. I cannot think about Mum because now it feels like I have so much more to lose. The ride that took us an hour and a half through the bush the night before now only takes forty-five minutes.

As we near the compound my whole body clenches and my insides feel as though they have turned liquid. Jack Frost can feel it and tenses too. We approach a rocky part of the track and have to pull back to a walk.

'You must think I'm an idiot. How stupid am I to actually fall for a monster like him?' Esther says, her eyes focused on the track ahead.

'I don't think that.'

'Sure.'

'Esther ... I told you about my sister. What her boyfriend did didn't make her stupid. She was really, really smart. And also kind and trusting. Good things to be. He was the twisted, messed up guy who took advantage of that. Everything she did to herself afterwards was really just him hurting her over and over again. He wasn't a monster – he was a guy who had an opportunity and a choice. Just like Jaxon.'

Esther glances at me and I can see in her eyes that she is exactly the way she needs to be if we are going to pull this off – angry.

It's another day of blue sky, and the sun flickers golden through the gum leaves above us. It could be a beautiful ride were it not for the fear that prickles down my spine. But we have an advantage: we know how to operate under fear. Women do it all the time – we've rehearsed terrible scenarios in our minds whenever we've heard footsteps behind us on the street.

We ride towards a sharp bend in the track and Seamus bolts around it ahead of us. I'm totally unprepared for what follows because he doesn't bark in warning. When I round the corner Jack Frost jerks his head up and jumps sideways as a figure in a balaclava steps out onto the track. Seamus sits at his feet, tail wagging.

Jaxon.

'Well, well, well,' he says as he approaches. 'There they are.'

'Hi, Jaxon.' I'm surprised at my choice to greet him as if we were casually lining up by the kitchen buffet.

'Hi, Lucy. Esther.' Jaxon stands in the middle of the track in front of us. Two cockatoos swoop low in the sky, their loud screeches like pterodactyl screams. I flinch at the sound.

'Beautiful morning for a ride. Where have you two been?'

'We went hunting.' I know our story will be like a ball of twine – it will roll out of our hands and end up in knots if we don't have a firm answer to every question. I try not to rush my words. 'Food is low, like you said.'

'All on your own? With no permission?'

'We knew you would say it's not safe.'

Jaxon is motionless. His expression gives away nothing. 'And?'

'We couldn't find anything,' says Esther.

'Where'd you look?'

A beat. Two. Too slow, Lucy. He could have been looking all over for us.

'It's not a hard question,' he says.

'Sorry, I get confused with directions. We went really far east. We thought there might be kangaroos over that way.'

'Mate, I was so worried about you. You can't do that. You were out here on your own after Tom has been shot. Are you thick?'

He walks up close to Esther and puts his hand on her knee. 'I've worked so hard to protect you. I love you so much. And you go and listen to that silly little bitch.'

Esther swallows. 'I'm sorry.'

'Yeah, you should be … Give me your gun, Esther.' He

holds out his hand. With the other he draws a pistol with a silencer from underneath his coat. 'I mean, I've got a pistol, but I should take yours too.' He looks Esther right in the eye. 'Never know when I might see a rabbit.'

Esther stares at him, frozen.

'I didn't forget about the one in the office. I know you have it. Come on, babe, hand it over.'

I don't think I can move quick enough to take my gun out of my coat pocket and shoot him. I know Esther could.

Esther breathes in and out. I can see her chest rise and fall and feel each breath as though it were my own. She pulls the gun from her pocket.

'Funny gun to use for shooting roos,' Jaxon scoffs. He reaches up and takes it from her hand. 'Lead the way, girls.' He sweeps a hand across the path before us. 'I'll follow.'

FORTY-FIVE

Jaxon opens the back gate for us and we ride up to the stable block where Esther and I dismount and tether the horses to the fence rail.

He leans on the stable wall, holding the pistol casually at his side. 'How'd you get out?'

I undo the buckles on Jack Frost's bridle.

'Lover boy find some keys for you, Lucy?'

I look at Esther. Her face is white with fear. The ball of twine is unravelling, rolling away from both of us.

'Oh no. For someone who can't keep her mouth shut, you seem a bit lost for words, Lucy.'

My mind has gone blank. It was stupid to think I could do this without implicating Fin. He wouldn't have expected us to be back so soon, especially if we were riding all the way to Sydney. I pray that he has seen us and that he has a gun. 'I took the keys,' says Esther.

Jaxon contemplates her for a moment before walking over. He places his hand under her jaw and tilts her face up to his. 'You what?'

'I took the keys.'

'From where?'

'From Tom.'

'Liar. I have Tom's keys. And, just so you know, every gun in that place is locked up now. So no-one's going to run down and save you.' Jaxon turns his attention to me. 'Lover boy let you out the gate, didn't he? I'll deal with him when I'm done here.'

Esther scrunches her eyes shut. 'Fine! I'm sorry!' She points at me and starts crying. 'It was her and Fin. It was all their idea and I went along with it. I'm so stupid. Please, I'm sorry, Jaxon. I should have listened to you when you told me not to trust her.'

I can't breathe.

Jaxon shakes his head. 'I wish you hadn't done that, baby.'

'I'm sorry! I'm so, so, so sorry. Please, Jaxon, I was selfish and wrong. I love you so much.'

'Put the horses in the paddock. Lucy, you stand right there and don't move.'

Esther unsaddles the horses and puts their rugs on. She leads them over to the gate without looking at me and turns them loose in the paddock. Jaxon watches her and when she returns he goes up to her and stands very close, looking down at her. His face softens, and he pulls her closer and whispers something in her ear. When he kisses her forehead she flinches. 'You go on up to camp. I need to talk to Lucy.'

Esther's eyes flick to mine. 'Give me that coat,' she hisses. 'It's mine. I don't care if you freeze to death.'

I take off my coat and hold it out to her. Esther takes it from me and pauses.

'Bitch,' she spits. Then she turns and walks around the side of the stables towards the main building.

If Jaxon kills me I will be with Bit. I try to hold on to that thought. It's not so bad, Lucy.

'You thought you could turn Esther against me?' Jaxon scoffs. 'Are you kidding? I *own* her. She'll do anything I tell her to. What were you doing out there? I'm not an idiot – I know you weren't hunting. I asked your boyfriend but he said he doesn't know anything. He's a bad liar.'

'What else would we be doing?'

'Looking for Esther's dad.'

'If that were true why would we come back?'

His right heel jiggles up and down. He lifts his hand and points the gun at me. It's a feeling unlike anything else I've ever experienced. All my senses are tuned to the black object in front of me. I can't move; I can't think.

'What were you doing out there?' Jaxon growls.

'Hunting.'

'You think you're so clever, but you're really just a smart-arsed little bitch.'

Somehow within me my fear turns to rage and I resign myself to the knowledge that I will die. 'So shoot me, dick face. You're the one who's afraid of a little girl. Explain that when everyone sees you've shot me unarmed. What a man!'

He smiles and shakes his head. I see the half squeeze of his finger on the trigger as he prepares to fire. I shut my eyes. Maybe I will be like those people who watched the missiles flying through the sky and not feel a thing.

I hear footsteps, and then a voice.

'Put. It. Down.'

I open my eyes.

FORTY-SIX

Esther is standing behind Jaxon. She has the gun that was in my coat pocket and she's pointing it at the back of his head. Seamus, who has been observing everything, goes and sits at her feet.

Jaxon glances over his shoulder and sniggers – clearly he doesn't think she's capable of using it.

'Calm down, babe, you'll do something stupid.'

Esther responds by firing a shot, which hits the wall of the stable just to the left of Jaxon's head.

'Don't move,' she says.

But he's fast and he has almost turned around to face her, pistol raised, when she fires again, this time hitting his right hand. The gun and some of Jaxon's finger falls to the dirt.

He staggers to the side and Esther shoots the wall again.

I hear shouting from the main building and the evacuation whistle sounds. Seamus begins barking.

'Shit, Esther! Stop it!'

'Just so you know, if I wanted to shoot you in the head just then, I could have. I'm actually pretty bloody good at this.' She keeps the gun trained on him. 'Kick the gun to me and get on your knees.' He kicks the pistol to her feet. 'And the one you took from me. I know it's in your left pocket. You try anything and I will kill you.'

Jaxon takes it from his pocket. 'Can we talk about this?'

Esther fires another shot at the wall. 'Put it on the ground!'

He drops it and kicks it to her. Esther gives me a nod and I collect both guns.

Seamus barks and whines like he's not sure of his loyalties. Pick us, Seamus, please choose us.

'Get on your knees,' Esther says.

Jaxon does. He grips his right hand with his left, holding it up to try and slow the blood flow. It trickles and gathers at the cuff of his sleeve. It's a horrible thing to see pain inflicted on a person, to watch while they bleed. I thought it might be different if it was someone you hate, but it appears not. Perhaps that's a good thing.

'You shot my dad and you lied to me. You lied to us all. The power is on in Sydney and there's a recovery operation.'

'Es—'

'Shut up! My dad came here for me and you sent him away.' Tears begin to trickle down her cheeks.

I see Fin and Rob running down the hill. A third figure hobbles behind them: Tom.

'What the hell is she doing?' Rob yells at Jaxon.

Esther turns the gun on Rob. 'Shut it.'

Rob holds both palms up and Fin sprints to my side.

'The power is back on,' Esther says. 'He knew and never told us. He was going to kill Lucy. He also shot my dad.'

'Can I talk? Just for a minute?' Jaxon interrupts.

'No.'

'Let him speak!' Rob shouts at Esther.

'Rob, do not shout at me.'

'I'm sorry,' Jaxon pleads. 'Please. I can't believe I did that to Lucy. I panicked. Esther, I love you. Let me fix everything. You're the only thing I have in this world.'

Tom arrives at the stables and grips the wall to steady himself.

'Tom, please, mate. You need to hear me out.'

Rob points at Esther. 'She's lost it.'

'Lucy, show Rob the photos before I shoot him,' Esther says.

I hand one gun to Fin and the other to Tom so I can get the phone from my pocket. I find the photos of Mr Effrez's wound and show it to Rob, Tom and Fin. I swipe to the screenshot showing the network coverage.

Rob swears under his breath in shock.

'Is Jeff alive?' Tom asks.

Esther keeps the gun pointed at Jaxon, but her hand shakes. 'Just,' she whispers.

'The wound's septic,' I say, remembering the most urgent thing we have to do. 'Raahel needs to treat him.'

'Where is he?'

'Fin's mum should be bringing him to the front gates now.'

'My mum?' Fin stares at me in disbelief.

'She was with him. We found them in a farmhouse.'

'Fin, there's baling twine in the tack room,' Tom says. 'Grab it and tie Jaxon's wrists.'

'Tom!' Jaxon says. 'There's an explanation for all of this. Listen to me.'

'I knew as soon as I came to that you were up to something. Give me my keys.'

'Tom, please—'

'Shut up or, God help me, I'll shoot you myself.'

Jaxon struggles to unclip the keys from his belt with his left hand.

Tom grabs them and tosses them to me. 'Lucy, go let them in the front gates. Fin, I'm going to need you here to help with Jaxon.'

'I'll stay with Jaxon,' says Rob.

'All due respect, Rob, I don't trust you.'

'Tom, you can't believe everything these girls are saying?!' Rob says.

'Yes, I can.' Tom looks at me and Esther. 'Go. And hurry.'

My feet slip on the mud as I sprint up the hill, Esther beside me. But when we arrive at the front gate there is no car.

'Where is she?' asks Esther, panicked. 'She should be here by now.'

I unlock the padlock and we run down the driveway to the road. Still there is no sign of Libby.

‘Maybe there’s a problem with the car?’ I say.

‘We have to go there. We can take the horses.’

‘But how will we get him here?’

‘We can take Raahel with us. Cloudy can double.’

I stare at the empty road.

‘Lucy, come on!’

We turn around and begin running back to the compound. Esther’s faster and she’s way ahead of me when I hear the car.

‘Esther, they’re here!’

I run to the car and Libby winds down the window. She is alone.

The look on her face tells me what has happened.

FORTY-SEVEN

Esther runs to the car, looking frantically through the windows.

'Where is he?!' She is gasping and wild-eyed. 'WHERE IS HE?!'

'Esther, I'm sorry …' Libby says.

Esther falls to the ground. She screams and slams her fists into the dirt.

'He passed away not long after you left,' says Libby quietly. 'I think perhaps he had been waiting for you to come and then after he saw you, he could finally let go.'

I crouch down next to Esther and put my hand on her shoulder. 'I'm sorry, Esther. I wanted so badly for him to be okay.'

When she turns her face to mine I recognise the look in her eyes; I've seen it before: all the light within her is gone.

Libby and I help Esther get to her feet and into the car. Libby drives into the car park and I turn around in my seat to face Esther.

'Everyone needs to know what he's done. This is your time to be heard.'

I think she's going to say no. But she nods.

Inside, the rec hall is empty and I tell Libby that Max will be down in the bunker with everyone else, and that Fin is at the stables.

'Is Max safe down there?' Libby asks.

'Everyone's safe now,' Esther whispers.

I climb down the ladder with Libby and Esther following behind me. Voices from the bunker echo down the concrete passageway. When I open the door everyone looks at us in surprise. Raahel mouths to me *Did you find him?* I nod, but she can see something isn't right. Max, who is huddled in a corner next to Raahel, looks at his mother with uncertainty, like he's not sure if it's safe to believe she's really there. His eyes light up and I can see how he would have been years ago as a little kid waiting for his mum to pick him up from preschool.

'Maxi,' Libby says.

He gets up, but he doesn't run to her like a little kid. He walks to her. And wraps her in his arms.

'The power's back on in parts of Sydney,' I say. 'Jaxon knew and kept it to himself. He's been lying to us all. Tom and Fin have him down at the stables.'

Fin's mum holds up an identification card with her photograph on it. 'My name is Libby Streeton.' Her strong and assured voice shows she's used to speaking in public and I recognise her as one of the government spokespeople from the bushfires years ago.

'I work for the government department leading

emergency response. Several electricity substations are functioning again in Sydney and surrounding areas. Now that we have power, we also have communication and access to fuel supplies, so we have been able to distribute food and medical supplies to the survivors.'

'How many survivors?' someone asks.

'The early numbers suggest two thirds of New South Wales's population have perished. Jeff Effrez and myself arrived here about a week ago to inform the settlement of the developments in Sydney. Jaxon turned us away. Jeff came back and tried to get in but Jaxon shot him. Unfortunately he passed away less than an hour ago,' Libby says.

Shocked murmurs travel around the room. Raahel covers her mouth with her hands. Beside his mum, Max hangs his head, then he looks at me and his hands curl into trembling fists.

There's nothing I can do to make it better for him. He's lost another friend.

Raahel raises her voice, both her girls clinging to her while she speaks. 'We need to think about how to …' she pauses, searching for the right word, 'proceed with Jaxon.'

Some of the other residents speak up – everyone wants to hear Jaxon's explanation.

Beside me, Esther is hugging herself like she did in the bathroom. I touch her arm but she flinches and steps away.

*

Max and Libby walk down to the stables with me. When Libby spots Fin she rushes to him but he takes a step backwards, watching her with caution.

'Fin,' she says softly.

He holds the pistol down by his side and rubs the back of his neck with his other hand.

'Fin, can I hug you?'

'We can't do this now.' He turns to me. 'Is Effrez with Raahel?'

'Fin …' My voice wobbles. 'He didn't make it.'

'He died not long after Lucy and Esther left us,' Libby says.

Fin swears and begins pacing. He looks at me and points to the stable block with his gun. 'I want to kill him.'

'I know. I think a lot of people do. Maybe we could bring Jaxon up to the building and talk it through with everyone in there?'

'No, he's too big. We got him into one of the stables and locked him in. If we move him I reckon he'll try to get away; even though he's not armed, he's strong. I'll go up and get everyone, bring them down here. Tom should hear about Effrez from you.'

Fin gives his mother a glance and walks away up to the top building.

Tom is sitting on a milk crate at the stable door with the pistol lying across his lap. Rob is further away with his back turned to us and I can see Jaxon slumped against the wall in the corner of the stall. He doesn't look at me.

'Tom …'

'Lucy, I need to talk to you.'

'I—'

'This is bloody important,' he interrupts me. 'I've failed you and I've failed Esther. I've failed everyone.'

'No.'

'Don't bullshit me, mate. You came to me for help and I did bugger all. But you didn't need me in the end. You've done good,' he says.

I nod. 'Thank you.'

'And you know I don't say that lightly.'

'Oh, I know, don't worry.'

He gives me a crinkly smile.

'Tom …'

'Sorry, mate, I cut you off. What did you want to say?'

'Mr Effrez, Jeff, he … he died. We couldn't get him help fast enough.'

Tom sways a little, like he's underwater and the words are waves washing over him. His eyes stay on the trees in the distance. 'Where's Esther?'

'Up in the main building.'

'We're going to have to look after her.'

'Yep.'

Tom looks over his shoulder at the stable door. He takes the gun from his lap and passes it to me. 'You take that. I don't trust myself.'

FORTY-EIGHT

When everyone is gathered at the stables, Fin unlocks the door and he and Rob bring Jaxon out. They put him on his knees and Fin stands beside him with his gun ready to fire if Jaxon tries to stand up. Esther hovers at the back of the group. The wind whips her hair across her face and she pulls her coat tight, hugging herself.

Jaxon's hands, tied behind his back, are covered in blood.

'Raahel,' Jaxon pleads. 'Please, my hand – it hurts like hell.'

Raahel walks closer and looks down at his hand. 'I can't leave his hand like that. I have to treat it.'

Tom stays silent, thinking.

'He deserves to be treated,' says Rob.

'Fine,' says Tom.

'I need the first-aid kit.'

'There's bandages and antiseptic in the tack shed,' I say. 'Will that be enough for now?'

Raahel takes another look at Jaxon's bloody hand. 'Okay. But he's bleeding badly, he can't have his hand tied at his back – he needs to be able to hold it up in front of him.'

Tom glares at Jaxon. 'I'm doing this for you because I'm a decent human being. Not because you deserve mercy. You make a move or try anything and I'll shoot you.'

'Tom, I didn't—'

'Shut it.'

Raahel gets the kit and snips the ties from Jaxon's wrists. She sprays his hand with purple antiseptic and Jaxon winces. Then she wraps his hand and tells him to hold it up.

'Thank you, Raahel.' He gives her a charming smile and turns to the gathered residents. 'You have to listen to me. I didn't believe that woman was with the government, same with Jeff Effrez. I thought they were intruders. I thought they were trying to trick me, just like what happened with that woman and her daughter.'

'Bullshit,' I say. 'You staged that whole thing.'

Jaxon looks at the faces surrounding him. 'I didn't. It was a trap. I was attacked.'

'Where are they, Jaxon? What did you do to them?'

He ignores me and pleads again to everyone else. 'I've created a safe place for us all, a life. You know me – I've done so much for you. I'VE DONE SO MUCH FOR YOU!' He turns to Rob. 'Rob, tell me this place wasn't chaos before I turned up. You'd all be dead if I hadn't come here.'

'Jeff came here with Libby and told you the electricity was back on,' Tom says. 'You lied to us all. You killed Jeff.'

Rob shrugs. 'If he didn't know for sure who they were, he did the right thing in turning them away. We're full up. Can't take everyone. Just 'cause you don't like it doesn't make it untrue.'

'Jaxon was going to shoot Lucy,' says Esther, her voice so quiet it's barely audible.

'Says you.' Rob looks around at everyone. 'I came down here and Jaxon's there with his fingers shot off and *she's* got a gun to *his* head.'

'I believe Esther and Lucy,' says Tom.

'So we're supposed to?' Rob walks closer to Esther. 'I reckon you two girls and that kid' – he points to Fin – 'didn't want to be told what to do anymore. There are no long-term resources; it's places like this that will survive. Electricity's irrelevant to us. Jaxon didn't want to lose anyone from here. He had a long-term vision.'

Murmurs spread through the group.

'Rob's right. You want to go back to Sydney?' Jaxon shouts. 'I was there with the army when all this started. We were going house to house giving rations when I heard about this place. I couldn't be a part of what was happening in Sydney anymore, it was brutal. I thought maybe I could come to Wattlewood and turn it into something really, really good. It was a mess when I got here, and it was me who built it up again.' He jabs a finger at his chest. 'It was me who saved you.'

'But you wouldn't share it with anyone,' Raahel says.

'We couldn't! We weren't ready. You can't feed everyone,

Raahel. I know you think we should all be bleeding hearts but that doesn't work. Not if you want your kids safe and fed. I've made mistakes. But I've never meant to hurt anyone here.'

'Meant to?' asks Raahel. 'That means you have.'

'No! No, I didn't mean that.'

'You shot Tom,' I say. 'You knew exactly where we'd be and when. Fin saw you leave the compound.'

Tom looks shocked.

'Of course Fin would say that,' says Rob.

'Was it you?' Tom asks Jaxon.

Jaxon cowers on the ground, gripping his wounded hand. 'It was an accident, mate. I never meant to hit you. You were thinking dangerously. You had to understand we were under threat.'

Tom turns around and walks away from the group, shaking his head.

'All I ever wanted was for everyone to be safe. I have never deliberately hurt anyone here.' Jaxon looks up at Fin. 'I've worked so much for Max, you know that. We are under constant threat here; everything I did was for the good of this place.' Jaxon looks at Max. 'I'm sorry, Max. I didn't know she was your mum.'

Fin clenches his teeth. 'Don't speak to him.'

Jaxon looks frantically from face to face, searching for someone who will have pity on him. 'Please, I know I've lost it, okay? I've totally lost my head. I'm traumatised from Iraq. It messes with you.'

Libby hasn't said a word but now she walks closer to Jaxon.

'You're a veteran, Jaxon?'

'Yes. Iraq screwed me up. I know what people can do to each other. I've seen people at their worst.'

'I bet,' says Libby. 'We don't understand what war is like here.'

'Exactly. Nobody gets it. I'm sorry and I want to try again. I just need help.'

'When were you in Iraq?'

'2007, 2008, 2010.'

'That's odd. Australian troops were withdrawn from Iraq in 2009.'

For a brief moment something seems to come loose in Jaxon, like he can't hold himself anymore. Despair washes over his face before he straightens again, jaw clenched in defiance.

'No, I'm confused. It was 2008 and 2009.'

'That's a pretty big thing to lose track of, Jaxon,' Rob says.

'It's trauma,' Jaxon scrambles for control. 'I get confused.'

I think of Matt in his army uniform, barely older than us. And Bahri, the soldier in the snow next to his truck in Sydney – his boots now on Fin's feet. Jaxon is supposed to be a man but he's a pretender desperate to grasp on to some sort of glory. Matt just wanted to go home. Bahri just wanted to go home.

Rob walks over and crouches in front of Jaxon. 'Were you there?' He points a finger at him, inches from his face. 'You told me you were there too.'

Jaxon cowers. 'I … I was, Rob. Swear to God.'

'What unit were you in?'

Jaxon doesn't answer.

Rob spits into the dirt. 'You're an insult to everyone who's ever worn a uniform.'

I don't like Rob. I don't like how dismissive he's been of me or Esther. But he isn't who I thought he was. Maybe he never craved glory at all, not like Jaxon. Maybe, like Matt, he was truly just trying to do his job, not trying to enjoy it. The awful decisions Matt had to make as a soldier ultimately ended his life. He'd tried to save Noll by shooting another soldier and he chose not to go on afterwards. Jaxon has invented reasons to make terrible decisions, like it's a glorious thing to do. He wanted to be the hero without knowing that the hero is the last person anyone should want to be – because they have the hardest job and they have to live with it forever. My hate for Jaxon rises within me, a slithering black thing.

'We can't believe anything you tell us,' I say. 'I know you found Polly and Sarah; where are they?'

Jaxon stays silent.

'You wouldn't help a woman and her starving daughter!' I scream at him. 'You lied and manipulated all of us! You *knew* the power was on in Sydney; you *knew* they were giving out food!'

Jaxon switches quickly from hurt to fury. 'Who are *they*, Lucy? *They* are the same people who let everyone starve. You've seen what *they* do.'

He looks at the faces staring back at him, sensing a moment to sway them. 'Think about who you want to trust. If Lucy hadn't turned up here we would be getting along just fine. No problems. We don't even really know her. This is someone' – he points at me – 'who hit a guy and killed him for his food.'

Everyone turns and looks at me.

'No. He was going to kill Fin. That's why I did it.'

'And maybe there was no, what did you say his name was? Noll? Maybe you just made him up as a sob story. Either way the same people who wouldn't help you are still running the show, even if that bitch is down here now.' He points at Libby.

There's a streak of red and white – the red and white of Max's Swannies beanie as he hurtles across the ground toward Jaxon, all limbs pumping. Head down he smashes into Jaxon's side. The strength of surprise topples Jaxon and Max is on top of him in an instant, fists laying into him.

'I hate you! I hate you!' Max screams, but Jaxon grabs him by the arms and throws him off. Max's head thuds onto the ground as Jaxon gets to his feet and runs. Fin roars in fury and sprints after him. I chase after Fin because I know what's in his head – I feel it too and I've felt it before.

Jaxon runs through the trees towards the back gate near the stables. I see that it's open – he never closed it after he brought Esther and me through.

Fin screams, 'I'll kill you!' He trains the rifle and fires a shot that grazes Jaxon's side. He cries out and falls. Jaxon scrambles back up and hauls himself forward but Fin sprints up behind him and strikes the back of his head with the rifle. I've never seen such brutality in Fin.

When I catch up Fin looks at me – there is so much darkness in his eyes they are unrecognisable.

Jaxon rolls onto his back. He sees me and laughs through his pain. 'Here she is! Can't do it without your little bitch holding your hand, Fin?'

Fin kicks him in his side.

Mr Starvos kicks Fin in the stomach. Again. Again.

Jaxon curls his arms over his head to protect himself as Fin kicks at his face.

'Fin, stop!' I shout.

I wrap my fingers around the handle of the cricket bat.

Fin puts the tip of the rifle against Jaxon's temple.

Starvos pulls the gun out from his belt.

'No!'

'I have to.'

'You don't. We can think of something else … we can …'

Fin shakes his head. 'Effrez is dead. Noll's dead, Matt's dead, Alan's dead.'

The gun clicks as Mr Starvos cocks it.

'Why does he get to live when they don't?'

'Because you'll feel it every day if you kill him. You'll wonder about his family. You'll wonder about his parents, about his mother. You'll wonder if she's still alive and waiting for him. You'll picture him as a little child. You'll wonder what his favourite memory was, what made him laugh. You'll go through it every day, over and over, to try and figure out if there's anything else you could have done. You don't have to kill him. Don't do it, Fin.'

Fin pushes the gun into Jaxon's temple. Jaxon scrunches his eyes closed. 'He was going to kill you.'

'But he didn't. Fin, it's done, it's finished.'

'Not while he's alive it's not.'

I'm scrambling through the white room of my mind; everything is scattered chaos until my thoughts land perfectly still.

'Noll.'

'What?'

'If Noll was here with us …' I start to cry. 'He was full of grace, Fin.'

He breathes deeply, in and out, in and out. 'So what do we do with him? Release him into the wild?'

'No. I don't know. But you don't have to shoot him. You can be one of the lucky ones who gets through this without hurting anyone.'

Curled on the ground, Jaxon looks small and scared.

'Fin,' I say.

Fin turns to look at me and Jaxon reaches out, grabs

Fin by the ankle and yanks with enough force to pull Fin onto the ground, then he gets to his feet and starts running again, although it's less of a run and more of a stagger. Fin is up fast and quickly gets Jaxon in his line of fire. I push Fin back with my left hand and grab the rifle with my right.

'Lucy!' he screams at me. Jaxon runs through the gate and Fin gives up his grip on the gun. 'What did you just do?'

I watch as Jaxon disappears into the gums.

'I just saved your life. Again.'

FORTY-NINE

When we approach the stables without Jaxon, Esther leaves the others and runs to us.

'Where is he?'

'He left the gate open when he brought us through. Fin had him but … he got away.'

Her eyes lock onto mine. She knows that if Fin had a gun and Jaxon didn't, the answer isn't so simple.

'He's gone, Esther,' I say.

Her gaze shifts to the wilderness behind the boundary fence and she takes a few steps towards it. Then she sits down and hugs her knees to her chest.

Fin squeezes my shoulder and keeps walking to the stables but I walk over to Esther.

'Do you want me to stay with you? Or do you want to be alone?' I ask her.

'I think you were lying,' Esther says.

'What?'

'The message you got on your phone out there.' She turns around and looks up at me. 'You were lying – it wasn't nothing.'

I sit down beside her. 'It was from my sister. She was

saying goodbye because she knew she was going to die soon.'

The trees seem bigger and taller today, their foliage denser, darker. The wind has picked up – it's the kind that slices exposed skin and sounds like a roar from within the trees.

'Does it feel like the Jaxon you loved died?' I ask her.

'I think he died a long time ago,' Esther says. 'And now my dad. None of this feels real. Is this real?'

'Yes. It is. I'm sorry.'

'The way I feel now,' Esther says through tears. 'The way I feel about my dad and knowing what Jaxon did – it's worse than anything else. Worse than the fear after the blasts, worse than the cold and the hunger and the dark. Jaxon came here and I stopped being afraid because he was never afraid. He could fix every problem, had a solution to everything, was never intimidated or helpless. He was a good distraction. He found everything about me fascinating. Or he said he did. Maybe I was just useful to him. I served a purpose.'

'How about you cry for a bit, and I'll cry for a bit and then we can go back to everyone,' I say.

So we do. We're salt and snot and pain that thuds against our ribs. We gasp for air and shudder. Then we wipe our faces, stand up and walk back to the others.

In the rec hall some people are silent with shock, others are teary, some are wide-eyed with anger at Jaxon. And then there's a few others who look relieved, as if they never really trusted him either.

'What if he comes back?' Raahel asks.

'There's nothing for him to come back to,' says Tom. 'We all know he's a fraud.'

'I don't think he's interested in anything else other than what people think of him,' I say.

'But what if you're wrong? He could try and take the camp back from us,' says Susan.

'He's injured, and he doesn't have food, water or a weapon,' says Tom. 'I don't think he'll last long out there.'

So he'll die in the wilderness like an animal. I don't find particular comfort in this, but I don't find comfort in any of the other scenarios I can imagine either. I know now that, for me, death – no matter whose – will never feel right.

'What would we have done with him if he hadn't run away?' Fin asks.

Tom shakes his head. 'I don't know. But I do know I've failed you all as much as he has, especially Esther, Lucy and Raahel. Probably all the women here. He was abusive. I never confronted him – I tried to but I couldn't find the courage to do it properly.'

I could say to him that he has done nothing wrong and has nothing to apologise for, but he wouldn't believe me and neither would I. Tom saw who Jaxon was and said nothing for the sake of peace. I don't think we all have that luxury. So I smile at him and nod that it's okay. He's forgiven.

'And we benefited from his crimes,' says Tom. 'We used those weapons to our advantage. They must have been stolen. I think we all knew that …' Tom trails off and I see Max look down at his lap, as if he's remembering the conversations we had with Noll about stealing Mr Starvos's food.

A vote is held and it's decided that the camp should remain under semi-lockdown for a few more days in case Jaxon does attempt to come back. It feels like a strange cloud of exhaustion falls across us all. The kitchen staff decide that a hot meal will help, so I find myself by the fire with a bowl of soup in my lap and Fin silent and restless beside me. His mum and Max – bruised but otherwise fine – are on the other side of the room. Fin's barely looked at her. Libby walks over and kneels awkwardly on the carpet next to him.

'Will you let me talk to you?' she asks him.

'How could you let us go like that?' he asks her. 'You couldn't find *any* way of helping all of us?'

'Fin, I was torn apart that day. But I had a really difficult job to do. I was fighting for things to be done the right way, as ethically as possible. It was one impossible decision after another, but I was able to make a difference.'

'We had to leave because you wouldn't help us, and Noll was shot, right in front of Max. Our other friend

Matt was a soldier; he was so messed up from what he'd seen and been ordered to do that he killed himself.'

Across the room Max is curled up on his bed with Seamus beside him, staring into the middle distance.

Libby closes her eyes for a moment. 'Exactly. That's exactly why I had to stay. I had to try and stop more people dying. I'm sorry, Fin. Lucy, I'm sorry.'

The three of us sit in silence until Fin shuffles over and puts his arm around her. I imagine what it would feel like to hold on to my mother again. Fin's face crumples.

'Shhh.' His mother rubs his back, like he's a child. 'Shhh. It's okay. It's okay.'

He straightens up and turns his face away from her, wiping his eyes with the sleeve of his coat. 'Have you found out what happened to Dad?'

'Yes.'

'And?'

She takes his hand.

'Tell me, Mum.'

'His car was at a road closure up north. It looked like he'd been heading back towards Sydney from up there. His body was found on the highway close to Sydney during the recovery effort. He'd been dead quite some time. Months maybe. My theory is he left the car at the road closure and was trying to get home to you and Max.'

Fin squeezes her hand and stands up. 'I'm going outside,' he says. 'I need to be on my own for a bit.'

FIFTY

It's barely even twilight but I'm so tired I have to lie down and try to sleep. Everything whirls around in my head and I can't grab on to any of it. Trying to get comfortable, I turn my pillow over and that's when I find the folder I took from the office when I went to get Tom's file for Raahel. My name is written neatly on the front, like it could be from school or a medical centre. I open it up and read the page of notes Jaxon has written, beginning with the facts of our arrival: the date, a list of things that were in our car, an abbreviated transcript of everything I said during our 'interview' and some medical notes written by Raahel. The heading on the next page is:

Lucy General Notes:

- *-Intelligent*
- *-not overly trusting*
- *-hostile on arrival*
- *-gutsy, not easily intimidated (could be problematic but potentially useful)*
- *-physically fit (although currently has injured ankle)*
- *-loyal, unlikely to tolerate mistreatment of Fin or Max;*

likely to become loyal to the camp
-Funny and likeable; will probably assimilate well into community

Update: Highly capable and brave rider. Kind. Very valuable asset to camp.

The last line is written in different handwriting, perhaps Tom's. I close the folder and gaze at my name on the cover. It wasn't Jaxon's private record; Tom and a few others would have had access to it, so Jaxon couldn't have recorded any opinions he wouldn't want the others to read. It's interesting that he wrote I was funny and likeable. Did he like me until he decided I was a threat to him? Was he capable of friendship, or was he always calculating? We won't ever know, just like we won't ever know what our lives would have been like if the winter had never happened.

I put the file back under my pillow and think about all the questions I will never have answers for. I think about my mother and the questions she's lived with – about me and how I've survived. And the one she's carried for even longer: the question about why Bit unravelled at sixteen. I think it's time to break the promise I made to Bit – I've held on to it for too long. My mother needs to know the truth.

I haven't told Fin any news about my family. Sleep will be impossible for now.

*

He sits on a log near the woodblock, arms slung over his knees, and gazes at the ground between his feet. The sun has been swallowed by the strange puce-coloured clouds we are so used to now. I pull my woollen beanie down over my ears and sit next to him. The light is fading fast and soon the two of us will be sitting in darkness. After a while Fin mumbles something I don't quite catch.

'Pardon?'

'I said thank you. I don't think it would have been good for me to kill Jaxon.'

'It wouldn't.'

'You've never really talked about Starvos. I'm sorry, I didn't know it played on you like that. I don't think you had a choice, for what it's worth. He would have killed me. But I suppose that means you did have a choice – you chose to stop him.'

'I play it over all the time and each time new things snag at me,' I say. 'Did he wake up and try to crawl to get help and then die? Did his wife come and find him dead? Did he have kids waiting for him to come home, like you and Max were waiting for your dad? The worst one is why did I find it so easy to do, because I did find it easy, Fin. I didn't stand there agonising – it was a gut reaction. And I wonder if it was because of you or because of my sister that it was so easy.'

'Why would it be easy because of your sister? You never talk about her. So many times I've wanted to ask but I didn't. I think I was worried I wouldn't know what to say.'

'Do you remember how I told you she was sick with an eating disorder for a long time?'

'Yeah?'

I reach over and grab Fin's hand. I grip it tightly and I tell him what happened to Bit. He listens as I tell him everything about that day – about Declan Flemming's charming smile, the blood on Bit's skirt. I tell him about the years in and out of hospital, the way I plugged the holes at home and the emotional independence I had to forge before I was ready. I tell him about the shame of my resentment towards her and the pain of leaving her behind.

He doesn't say anything; he just listens while I get it all out.

'I've never wanted to hurt anyone the way I wanted to hurt Declan,' I tell Fin. 'And that night when I walked into the room while Starvos was kicking you … I couldn't let another beautiful person be destroyed. And I couldn't have the world lose a gentle guy. There aren't enough of you. Maybe that's why it was easy.'

'If the power is back on maybe your family is alive. If Mum could find Effrez she might be able to find them.'

'She has. My mum is still alive. Not my dad though.'

'Lucy, why didn't you tell me?'

'There was kind of a lot going on.'

'I'm sorry. I'm so sorry. What about Bit?'

I reach into my pocket and pull out my phone. I open Bit's final message and hand it to him.

'Oh, Luce. Oh no.' He pulls me in, wraps his arms around me and kisses my hair. 'I'm so sorry.'

I allow myself to stay there with my ear pressed to his chest: a place I've always felt safe.

It's dark now and we haven't moved. I can just make out the profile of his face.

'When are you going?' Fin asks me.

'What?'

'When will you go home?'

'I never said—'

'But you will because you are unstoppable. And I wouldn't dream of trying to stop you this time even if you were.'

'Were what?'

'Stoppable. Which you are not … I can come with you when you go.'

'No, I can go alone.'

He turns his face to mine. 'Mum is here with Max. I can come.'

The tears on my cheeks turn cold in the wind. 'You should stay. Help the others – Raahel and Tom. You should be here for this place, for these people. I hear there's been a change in management.'

He ignores my joke. 'Lucy, what if I was just there for you, just looking out for you? Let yourself be looked after this time, just for a little while.' He leans his forehead against mine.

'You can't ride a horse,' I whisper.

'I'm a fast learner.'

MAX

If you are reading this it's because I've been assassinated.

Ha. Just kidding. I'm fine.

Lucy said I cried when I saw Mum, but I didn't. I was just heaps happy. But also a bit angry. It's complicated, and I guess I'm a complicated guy living in a complicated world full of mutant flesh-eating koalas. (Ha. Not true.)

After Jaxon left, Esther and Tom went for a massive walk and found that woman Sarah and her little girl. There were some other people with them and they all live here now. (It's really good and stuff but Polly is kind of annoying. She made friends with Elia and now they follow me around everywhere.) Sarah says Jaxon found them and told them he'd kill them if they didn't stay away from Wattlewood.

I'm seriously pissed off at Jaxon. I can't believe he lied to everyone. I thought he was a really cool guy but he was actually a dickhead. But it's weird because I still kind of miss him though – I feel like there were two Jaxons and I miss the old one.

The best thing is that Tom got some fuel for one of the utes and he's teaching me to drive it on the fire trails.

And he's not annoying about it the way Fin is when he's giving instructions about stuff. Tom also taught me how to shoot rabbits, which is fun. I don't like killing the ones that are trapped in cages, but. They look too cute. For some reason it's easier to kill them when they're far away.

I didn't want Fin and Lucy to go. I was so worried because Fin looked like an idiot on the horse – he couldn't even get it to run. The last thing I said to him was like, 'You are so going to fall off and die.' We didn't hear anything from them for ages until finally Mum could call them. They were in the Blue Mountains and had found Lucy's mum, so that's good. She was really hungry and a bit sick but they gave her some food and that. Fin says she's good now. They're going to bring her to Wattlewood when they can get a car.

I wish Dad was still alive. He would like it here. Noll would too, but in a weird way I feel like Noll isn't totally gone. There's still parts of him in Lucy, Fin and me. Good parts – parts we need.

ACKNOWLEDGEMENTS

This book is dedicated to every woman or girl who has ever been abused, gaslit, intimidated and controlled by a current or former partner.

Thanks to Nathan Zorn, Elijah, Ayrton, George, Kristy Bushnell, God, Grace, Clair Hume and the team at UQP, Chris R, Kelly Zorn, Carla, Loz, Marcella, Kate Cole, Razzla, Damo, and Katie Tunks Leach. Also Sarah, Polly and Seamus for their donation to the RFS.

Thanks to Kaye, Margaret and Irene for the DNA which makes me a little bit fearless.

I am forever grateful to Anglican Deaconess Ministries for the financial and pastoral support I received during the process of writing *When We Are Invisible*. Thank you for being such an epic champion for Christian women in all our fields of work.

Finally, I must thank all the readers who loved *The Sky So Heavy* and hounded me for a sequel; *When We Are Invisible* would not exist without you.